"…a lovely read, vividly descriptive and richly lyrical, almost a prose poem in book form…the author has a gift for making a scene come to life with simple, almost musical phrases, immediate, clear and sensual…essentially a philosophical debate about identity, society, the self, and relationships, in which the reader is invited to participate, told in a vigorous emotional style that can veer from calmly meditative to fiercely confrontational and back in the span of a paragraph. CONFESSIONS OF A CLOAK ARTIST is for readers who enjoy the journey as much as the destination, and who revel in exploring both interior and external worlds."

—*IndieReader*

Confessions of a Cloak Artist

Copyright © 2017 by Jeff R. McGowan

This is a work of fiction. Names, characters, businesses, places, events, and incidents are either the products of the author's imagination or used in a fictitious manner. Any resemblance to actual persons, living or dead, or actual events is purely coincidental.

ISBN 978-0-9990033-0-5

Published by:
Knockout Press
San Francisco, CA

CONFESSIONS OF A CLOAK ARTIST

A NOVEL

JEFF R. McGOWAN

"Because Indo-European language dictates that we express all our thoughts in past, present, and future tense, we have the notion that time is an abstract backdrop moving in one direction, like the hands of a clock, from past to future. None of the hundreds of Aboriginal languages contain a word for time, nor do the Aborigines have a concept of time. As with creation, the Aborigines conceive the passage of time and history not as a movement from past to future but as a passage from a subjective state to an objective expression. The first step in entering into the Aboriginal world is to abandon the conventional abstraction of time and replace it with the movement of consciousness from dream to reality as a model that describes the universal activity of creation."

—Robert Lawlor
Voices of the First Day:
Awakening in the Aboriginal Dreamtime

"And so may a slow
wind work these words
of love around you,
an invisible cloak
to mind your life."

—John O'Donohue
Anam Cara

For Ross...
May you wallow in wonder, love, and adventure.

CHAPTER ONE

Traveling 1991

"The mists had all solemnly risen...
and the world lay spread before me."
—Charles Dickens *Great Expectations*

W E'RE AT A HOSTEL on the Pest side of the Danube. Back to dorm beds. Backpackers congregating, sharing information, reveling in freedom. A group's about to go out, but I'm exhausted, crawling into a lower bunk and feigning sleep. And this is when I first hear her and first glimpse her; this marks the moment my freedom ends.

She's across the room, four bunk beds away, but I've seen her and heard her, and now everything is impulses and dreams. I'm seeing swaying black hair and long legs, cut-off jean shorts and blue Chuck Taylors, beautiful olive skin, and a glimpse of deep green eyes, just like my dad's stunning ex-girlfriend, Ana Paoula, but that's another story, that's later, even though it's before. I'm hearing that sweet laugh and voice, and her name—"Sabrina, are you coming?" I'm reaching for shoes, sneaking into the bathroom, rushing out to join the always-welcoming travelers. But they're gone. All's silent and calm. I'm outside. Nothing. I'm looking both ways, running to one corner. Still nothing.

Back inside, I'm standing by her bunk; her pack's against the wall. On the bed, there's a green bandana, a book on how to excel in college, a copy of Dan Millman's, *The Peaceful Warrior.* I've seen others reading it, and now I want to read it, almost pick it up right there.

I can't sleep. Waiting. Darkness. Curfew. They're back, all hushed and silent. I'm smiling. She wasn't a dream after all.

In the morning, I'm first up, sitting in the silence of the lobby with my coffee and books and assumed freedom. It's the only way in and out, and no one'll be up for a while. I'm realizing Kayne's been out all night, resenting the worry, although I'm more concerned for what he'll do than what might fall on him. As if summoned, he appears, and as expected he's already on his way to getting us dragged again.

He's waving Hungarian bills in my face, saying he's doubled our depleted funds. Some "friends" are coming as we speak, and boy do they have ideas.

"What do you mean 'our money?'" I ask.

"I doubled your money. I didn't want to wake you."

"You did what?"

"Don't worry Skinny, we're all good."

These days Kayne only calls me "Skinny." He never calls me "Jim."

"The exchange rates will kill us," I say.

"Skinny, I got it covered, got some friends comin' right now, got a deal going."

"I can't go anywhere right now."

"Why not?"

"Just can't."

"Skinny, this place is ripe!" His round, half-Japanese face is flushed red. "All these kids, dreamin' about America. This communist shell lifted. Jeans, Skinny! They want jeans! Real jeans, the real deal, not the fake shit. I'm already on it. My friends are coming!"

"What the hell are you talking about Kayne?"

But he's already going on about quadrupling our money, about Indonesian bungalows, and fishing and surfing, about me reading tantra or quantum physics or whatever the hell I want all day and all night. And Kayne knows I'm hooked, knows I wanna study the whole damn world, knows I'm feeling crazy and lost, searching for answers, something to grasp.

"Just don't fuck it up," I say, waving him away from my silence and my peace.

But fuck it up he does; it isn't twenty minutes, and there he stands, defeated.

I'm relaxed, the hostel's awakening; I'm poised for Sabrina. "What, Kayne? What happened?"

"It's not good, Skinny, not good."

"Kayne, what happened?"

"It's gone."

"What's gone?"

"Our money."

"What do you mean it's gone?"

"Two guys went off to get the jeans, the other stayed with me, then he ran off."

"Which way?" I'm outside, my head swiveling. "What do they look like?"

I'm running. Kayne's dragging. "It's no use Skinny, I've already tried."

But I'm running. Don't even know what they look like. But we have nothing—nothing! And what can we do? Go to the police? To the American Embassy? Fuck! I can't even look at him. And now I'm all pissed off, in no state to meet Sabrina. I'm walking. The streets are humid and dirty and coming alive. But we're sunk. We're broke. We'll have to go home, get a desk job, live a spiteful existence. I'll have to call Mom; I'll have to call Irvine. Told Dad I wouldn't call asking for money, but he never specifically mentioned Mom. She might send money if she can, but then again, she might not. They've already helped enough. "This is *your* trip," she'll say.

Back inside, Kayne's already off, says he's gonna fix things. The young Swedish girl at the front desk asks if I'm ok. I tell her what happened, and she frowns and sighs as if it's her own money. "So many scams," she says. "One guy was charged a thousand bucks in a bar for a drink he'd bought a woman. He'd tried to leave, but five guys surrounded him and threatened to cut his balls off. And the police did nothing. I'm so sorry. Yes, you can call the States from the post office. About a ten-minute walk. Just opened. Here, here's a phone card. Sometimes people leave them."

I ask for paper. I'm writing: *Sabrina. My name is Jim. I know this sounds crazy, but I'd really hate to leave here without meeting you. But I have to leave right now. It's 8:00 a.m. I should be back in an hour. Hope to see you then.*

I fold it and write *Sabrina* and hand it to the Swedish girl.

The post office is dull and gray, an old communist place full of crazy Cyrillic signs. They look like commands. There are two phone booths, and both are occupied by elderly women dressed in gray.

Twenty minutes. Forty minutes. I'm about to explode.

Finally, an open booth.

The phone's ringing. Actually, it's beeping.

"Hello."

"Hi, Mom."

"Hi, Honey."

The line's cracking. There's a pause and static between words. "I'll make this quick, Mom. Our money's been stolen. I need you to wire me something, Western Union. That's all I have time to tell you." I want to get this over with.

"Are you okay?"

"Fine, Mom, don't worry."

"How much did you lose?"

"All of it."

"All of it?"

"I know, I know."

Then it comes. My stepfather. The phone's fumbled. "Listen, Shithead. There's a thing called a job. You should—"

"Okay, Honey," Mom says, back on the line. "No problem, you'll be fine, we know you will. Thanks for calling. Be safe, now. Love you."

The line's dead. I'm feeling the weight of destitution. She'll send it. She'll find a way.

The streets are now steaming. As I approach the hostel, I can see a group getting into a white van, and I'm starting to walk faster, and then I'm running, and the van's pulling away and turning a corner, and I'm standing there, slumped over, sweat dripping onto concrete.

Inside, I'm standing by the swiveling fan, wiping my face with a damp shirt. The Swedish girl's handing me a note.

> *Jim. I can't say that I know who you are, but I thought your note was sweet nonetheless. I'm curious, and would've stuck around longer, but we'd already booked a flight to Istanbul. I'm on my way to Uganda, but I don't have to be there for a month, so we're gonna check out some of Turkey first. Mila told me what happened to you. I'm so sorry. Perhaps we'll meet after all.*

I'm wondering why she's going to Uganda. I can't stop thinking about her, and I'm already pondering Turkey before remembering we don't even have money for today's food and lodging. And anyway, our next flight's out of Rome. Again, that weight of destitution. Perhaps we could hitchhike or beg for train fare? The Swedish girl's drawing a map to the Western Union, explaining, says it doesn't open until noon, and there are no guarantees.

I'm looking at Sabrina's note. Uganda, it says. Uganda.

CHAPTER TWO

Australia 1993

"Every bum is a writer."
—Charles Bukowski

T'S NOW TWO weeks since we came back to Australia. Linden got us one last visa extension, shit went down, and off we went. That was three and a half months ago.

We've only been gone some three months, but it feels like forever. And this is why we must be careful, for it hasn't been forever. Time transcends itself, stamps impressions, and leaves forgotten or suppressed signposts. Months on a sailboat dragged by currents. Long days lounging on silent beaches, in villages inhabited by masters of timelessness and hedonist varieties. No ports of entry—nothin'—like we never left. But we did leave, and our visas expire in ten weeks. Time's real. Things have happened. So it's disconcerting to discover ourselves existing in this dream-state, this existential vacuum.

A second Australia tour.

An improbable and stupid thing—us being back after everything that happened. But back we are, and now it's as if we just appeared and have to find our way out again. I can only conclude that larger powers are indeed behind our destinies; I can only surrender, for the variables that fell into place defy explanation. This surrender, however, is never complete, and I wonder if I'll ever accept it. Without understanding, acceptance is like a far-off star that may or may not still exist. But here we are. Back to the place we'd so desperately fled. Back. Unbelievable. And still wanted by the law. The flat's the same. Shirley, our landlord and surrogate grandmother, has taken us back in, but we have new roommates—a beautiful German girl named Hanah and a hilarious Swede named Peter.

Our jobs are also new, unconnected to Linden Armstrong, the man who'd earlier sent our lives into a tailspin. They don't pay what Linden did, but we're saving money to get out again, at least out of Surfers Paradise because our anomynity is gone, our strolls no longer relaxing. I'm flinching and ducking like a madman at the sight of every cop or familiar face. But this is still a place we can work and surf and act like we haven't a care in the world; it's still our best chance to get back on our feet in a flicker and easily shoot off to inexpensive lands. So that's what we're doing. Sometimes you just do. And besides, I'm enjoying my moments with Hanah and the writing is flowing, something I've learned to interrupt at one's own peril.

Some call Surfers Paradise a little Waikiki, the bars and restaurants packed with sunburnt tourists in shorts and sandals and colorful shirts. Tacky high-rises and the smell of Coppertone mix with perfumes, ocean breeze, and hot sands. And jobs are a dime a dozen. Again, that's why we've so stupidly returned. We're already connected, and we've no time to waste. Kayne's a barback, and now, since last week, also a bouncer at The Beach Club. Last week, a group of U.S. Marines started helping themselves to the inner thighs of waitress Julie. The big Abo-Samoan bouncer was knocked out by a roundhouse kick and a flurry of drunk Marines, but Kayne gorilla-charged them, knocked down the whole lot, and withstood the five-Marine onslaught for four and a half minutes. The police arrived, broke it up, and Kayne—welted face and all—slunk out back and into the sympathies of the female staff. I recognized one of the cops, but he didn't see us. With Kayne it's one fuckin' thing after another. But now he's a bouncer getting paid twice what he was before. "Too visible," I said at first, "Cops are always coming around that place." So he got himself a mask, a donkey mask, and he puts it on whenever the cops appear. And I'm not making this up.

My job renders no such excitement. Charlie's Cafe. Eight p.m. to four a.m., every night but Friday. I lug the rack of dishes from the seating area to the kitchen, load the dirty ones, and do it all again. Back and forth. All night. No fights. No cops. Some hot girls and free sandwiches, but that's about it. The restaurant pays me double time after midnight, and with this and the recent increase in Kayne's tips, we should soon have enough to somehow get out and hit the road again. I'm thinking Indo magic and up into Thailand; I'm dreaming of months lost in the Himalayas. And it keeps me busy, keeps me tired, makes it easier to forget my still-longing and aching heart.

People say that certain things are just meant to happen. I guess it makes them feel control over something that is beyond control, as if by not having control they actually have more control. It gives them control over their feelings, allows them to forgive and forget, and to accept. I don't know what to think.

Hanah, our hot German roommate, brought it up last night. The sun had just set, and we were hanging out on the porch. Once the sun goes down, we usually leave the roof and hit the porch. We still only have two pieces of furniture, both rented—a dining table set with four chairs, and a couch—and the couch is often dragged from the living room to the patio. Back and forth. Like my job. Peter, our Swedish roommate, and Kayne are off to work, and I'll soon be off to work myself. But not yet, and these are precious moments with the house so quiet and still.

We grab a comforter, a few pillows, open two Victoria Bitters, light a candle, turn on the radio, and watch the metamorphosis of the sky. We often do this. Most everything is the same—the couch, the beers, us—but the sky is never the same, nor is the conversation. Last night the sky was cloudless and orange and red, streaked with yellow and purple, then it got dark, opaque, then some fluffy little clouds appeared as if from space above, and lay still—light yet heavy. If there are clouds, we usually describe the shapes or faces, the things, the letters or words we see. Sometimes we see the same things. But more often we don't. "Oh yeah, I guess I could see that," we might say. But we don't see it. There are times I find this amazing, like last night when I saw a shark with two eyes, a mouth, a pointy noise, and a tail. There were even streaks for gills, and for a moment, a dorsel fin. But Hanah just couldn't see it. She saw two eyes and a nose, but not a shark. It was right there, so clear, but she just couldn't see it. So I guess it's not surprising that there's so much else that we all see differently, so many different opinions. And opinions are even more abstract, less tangible; they can't be seen in physical form.

Hanah has stopped talking about clouds. She's resting her dark-blonde curls on my shoulder. Sometimes her breasts touch my arm or shoulder and I have to start thinking about the waves or some ugly woman or one of those kangaroos from the sanctuary that greedily scratches my arm and stares with those big, black eyes like a dog.

I'm longing to kiss her. It would do me good. But she's still treating me like a wounded duck. She knows I'm heartbroken, still a mess. She knows. So she just stares with those big, compassionate eyes. To me, they are eyes of pity. When I first met her, they reminded me of Sabrina, even heightened the heartbreak I thought was dissipating. But now they scream pity.

"Logic only goes so far," she says in her darling accent, staring into the night. "Some things are just meant to be. I really believe that. So what can you do?"

I'm not sure if she's still referring to my longing for Sabrina. Sure, it's been a while now. The dense pain is gone, but it was still yesterday, and I'm still reluctant to accept such platitudes. "I don't know," I say. "Maybe some things are just meant to be. But with others, there's gotta be places where we screw up, where we do things, make mistakes, that alters our destiny. I can't help but wonder if I made a wrong move, made mistakes, overthought things."

"Maybe those mistakes were just part of what was meant to be," she says. "So in the end it was still just meant to be."

"Yeah, maybe."

I've learned a lot about Hanah from our many evenings sitting on the couch sipping our beers. We usually talk about clouds for a while, then move onto something else, often something personal, about our lives growing up, our travels, our relationships.

"Tell me about life in Irvine," she always says. "Please, Sire. Take this farm girl to California." She smiles all innocent and cute, squeezes those great breasts together, and says in her best country voice, "Take this farm girl on an adventure," or, "Take this farm girl to another country." Or she'll talk about her Germany, the rolling Bavarian hills and the pinewood fence that surrounds her family's farm, the brown windmill, the thick forest that so enchants. It is, she says, full of myth and mystery, wild creatures and barbarian ghosts. The sheep and horses and German Shepherds. The smell of morning dew and pine. The birds. She says my voice is comforting, that she loves our philosophical wanderings, but she mostly just wants to listen to my stories. I enjoy doing both.

Both allow me to deal with myself, to process some of those experiences, those books and theories, those thoughts that come and go like the clouds. Some stick around for a while, some fly right by. But all come and go. So I watch them, let them run their course, like the clouds. Other times they're conveyed, set free, injected into the dreamworld. Or sometimes I just get lost in a story. All is filtered through an aching heart, but stories have a way of lifting one above themselves, of presenting opportunities for perspective. I, of course, am looking for answers, searching for explanations. Not so long ago I was walking on clouds, swimming in sublime seas, wallowing in the kind of yearning that creates monuments to love. Even lost in self-stories and projections, you couldn't wipe the smile off my face. I must have been so annoying. And now it's all gone. Like it never happened. But it did. So I keep telling Hanah stories.

First I write them down. Then I read them aloud. On the porch, the stars flickering, the breeze ruffling Hanah's hair and white cotton dress. And she keeps plying, pushing for stories: how we got here; our adventures; how we got in trouble; what happened with me and Sabrina; what it was like growing up in Southern California. Perhaps something will come of it? Perhaps the confusion will dissipate? She wants to know about life in Irvine—the California dream. "Please Sire, please," she says, that accent echoing off the walls of the porch, the quiet of the night. "Take this farm girl traveling. Tell me a love story; tell me your love story. And tell me your growing-up stories. I love them. Write them all. I want to hear them all."

I've been writing for several months now, ever since we first arrived in Australia, and I've tried different versions—past tense, present tense, both—but Hanah prefers the immediacy of present tense, says she falls right into them, whatever that means. So I'm adapting. That's what I do: I write and I revise. I adapt.

She closes her eyes. Her face softens. The Aborigines, I've told her, believe that life is all a dream, that the line between past and present, real and unreal, is like the line between molecules and ourselves; they're all around us, as real as our hands, but we forget, and have a hard time believing. Such abstractions are difficult to process, to hold onto, and thus we lose sight of them. We forget. But I think I get what the Aborigines mean. My grandfather's been dead for five years, and yet I can still see him in memories and dreams. I can smell his aftershave, hear his voice, see his wrinkled skin pulsing, see the moles with the tiny little hairs. I feel close to him. Am I dreaming? Or is this real, this past that feels so present? So I write and read my stories in present tense, just as Hanah requests. I am reliving the moments, for better or worse. Perhaps I can crack myself open? Perhaps I'll get somewhere?

Again, Hanah says, "Tell me about love."

"I know nothing of love."

"I think you do," she says.

"I don't. All I do is think about it, fantasize. I'm all bottled up, may be forever."

She's tilting her head. "What do you mean by that? You're all bottled up?"

"I don't know," I say. "I don't know what I mean. I'm just confused."

"Well, aren't we all?"

"Not like me."

"Tell me what you've learned," she says, "what your travels have taught you. You mention Africa and Israel and all these places, but you never elaborate. And tell me what happened with Linden, why you left so quick on your first trip here. You still haven't told me. You jump at the sound of sirens, and I'm still wondering why."

"You want to know a lot," I say.

"I'm a curious girl," she says, shuffling herself upright. "Let's go to Irvine," she says. "Tell me about an early love. Then we can get back to Sabrina. And to adventure."

I'm smiling.

"What?" she asks.

"Irvine," I say, shaking my head. "When we first got there."

"What about it?"

"You'll see."

"And is there love involved?"

"You'll see."

The VB's cold. The stars are strong. The sky's clear. The smell of apple candle, Hanah's lotion, chimney smoke from down the street. "I've written a new version," I say. "From the beginning of our journey in 1991, as you asked for. And one in Irvine as well, California, when we first moved there. You ready?"

Hanah's head is touching mine, her cheek on my shoulder. "Ready," she says. "Ready."

CHAPTER THREE

Irvine, California 1981

"Never let your schooling interfere
with your education."
—Mark Twain

'M ELEVEN YEARS old when my parents divorce, and my
mom, younger brother, and I move from Seattle to Orange
County, a place called Irvine. On the plane I'm pissed,
all huffy and puffy, and some moron leans over and starts
talking about what a nice place it is and how much we're
gonna like it, says there are orange groves for miles and
parks at every turn, says there are quiet suburbs and good
schools with new gyms and baseball fields, and that there
are skateparks and BMX tracks and lots of malls with movie
theaters and ice cream stands. Mom's lappin' it up, nodding
and saying, "Uh huh, uh huh," and the moron's all proud of

himself. He's leaning in and whispering, "And there are lots of pretty girls." He's winking and smiling, and right then an overweight and pimple-faced kid rises from the seat in front of us and lowers a disgusted gaze. The kid's looking at the moron before turning to me. "I call it the Orange Curtain," the kid says, "Others call it the Fourth Reich." He's falling back into his seat and sighing. I don't know what any of that means, but I can taste his disgust.

We've rented a house in a community called "The Terrace." The houses are the same color—tan with brown trim. The sidewalks are clean and gray, the lawns and gardens manicured. There are banyan trees every twenty feet, and a curtain of tall eucalyptus in the distance. It's all so contrived. "Where's the wilderness?" I ask. "Is there any damn dirt around here?" Even the birds look trained.

Mom's turning and giving me that look, and she's turning away and her head's tilting and swaying as she exhales loudly through her nose. We're driving in silence, stuck in this smell of rental car. Radar, our fat cat, is in a cage at my feet. His big, yellow eyes are looking up. Skip, my brother, is looking around all excited. He's picking his nose and looking at his finger, and he doesn't even notice me staring at him. "What about the minibike?" he asks, leaning forward and touching Mom's shoulder. "What about the minibike?"

"That depends on your grades," Mom says.

"I thought it was dependent on us moving here," I say.

"And your grades," Mom says.

"That's not what you said before."

We're pulling up to a house with an Atlas Van Lines moving truck in front. Three men are unloading boxes into the garage. Mom's jumping out and barking orders. She's upset that the boxes are stacked like sardines in the garage. She's distracted. I'm nodding to Skip, and we're sneaking our bikes out. Time to explore this contrived and superficial land.

We're riding along, looking for potential minibike terrain, when we come upon a kid sitting on his bike and blocking the path. He's short and stout with curly, dark hair and a freckle-filled face, and he's looking at us, arms crossed, as if we just kicked his dog. He's wearing a black Led Zeppelin shirt, black jeans, black shoes, and a large, silver chain necklace.

Skip says, "Hi," but he's like a tiny bird chirping from the grass below, and the kid's staring at me.

He's looking back to Skip. "Is that a girl's bike?" he says.

"Is *that* a girl's bike?" Skip says.

But I'm shushing him and staring the kid down. "We're gettin a minibike," I say, "lookin for places to ride. Know of any?"

"I ride motorcycles," the kid says, "not minibikes."

"A minibike's not as loud," I say. "And we can actually ride it around here."

"Good luck with that," the kid says, dropping his bike and walking across manicured grass toward a house with a sliding glass door. "Wanna see something?" he says.

Inside it smells musty. There's a fancy guitar in the corner, an amp, and a stereo. There are posters on the walls of

Ferraris and Kawasaki motorcycles and half-naked women. There's an Icee machine and a small, circus-style popcorn maker. There are also two fist-sized holes in the wall.

"Is this your room?" I ask.

"Who else's would it be?" The kid says.

"Cool," Skip says. "Where are your parents?"

"Gone. You want a beer or somethin'?"

Skip's looking at me.

"Sure," I say. "So what's with the holes?"

"My mom's dumb-ass boyfriend got all pissed off one day, broke one of his dumb-ass fingers."

The kid's gone, and there's the fridge opening and the sound of bottles clanking. He's back, and he's got sliced-up limes in one hand.

"What are those for?" Skip asks.

"For the Coronas," the kid says. "Don't you know anything?"

The kid's squeezing limes into the beers.

"You'd better share," he says. "Wouldn't want you to kill yourselves."

I'm slugging, then Skip, and we're both smiling.

The kid's gone again. I'm looking around. There's a backpack inscribed with BENJAMIN NEEDLEMAN, a pack of cigarettes, and a bunch of *Star Wars* figures.

He's back, this time with *Playboy* and *Penthouse* magazines, and a pink, banana-sized plastic thing.

"What's that?" Skip asks.

"Don't you know anything?" the kid says. "Where you from, anyway?"

"We're from Seattle," Skip says.

"They don't have dildos in Seattle?"

"But what is it?" Skip says.

The pink gadget's buzzing.

"What's it do?" Skip asks.

The kid's still shaking his head. "It makes the girls moan, stupid."

"How do you know?" Skip asks.

"'Cause I just know, you moron. And my mom's always moaning."

Skip's looking at me. "Does Mom moan with these?"

"I don't think so," I say, but I'm wondering, and the thought reminds me that we have to get home for dinner.

Dinner's waiting. The meatloaf's steaming. A bowl of mayonnaise for artichokes. Corn from a can. I sit down and reach for the meatloaf.

Mom's glaring. "Maybe you could wait for your brother and me?"

Skip's all cleaned up. He even put on a new shirt, knowing it would please Mom and piss me off. He's smirking all chipper, and it's all I can do not to smack him.

"Mom," Skip says. "Do you moan with ...?"

My milk's spilling.

"Oh, Jim," Mom's saying, cleaning it up. "What's that, Honey?"

I'm staring.

"Oh, nothin," Skip says.

"I have something to show you guys," Mom says, dropping a booklet on the table. "Mr. Walker from down the street came over today and gave me these community rules. There are some things you're not gonna like."

"Oh, here we go," I say.

"Come on, now," she says, "there are always rules."

"Just tell us."

"You're not supposed to play in the street, or on the grass around most the houses."

"Then where are we supposed to play?" I ask. "The freeway?"

"The big greenbelt areas are okay," she says.

"That's it?" I ask.

"I agree," she says. "It seems a bit much. But rules are rules. And there are plenty of parks around."

"So we can't throw the football on our own street?"

"I'm sorry, Honey."

"Who's this Mr. Walker anyway?" I ask.

"He's that old guy on the corner," Skip says, "with the cane and the thick glasses. He was watching us as we went by today."

"How the hell do you know that?" I ask.

Mom's glaring. "Watch your language, young man."

"His name's on the mailbox," Skip says.

"So we'll just take his glasses," I say. "What he doesn't see won't bother him."

"C'mon now, Jim," Mom says.

"This place sucks," I say.

"I like it," Skip says. "We met a friend today. His name's Ben. He lives alone. We—"

"Alone?" Mom's saying, "How old is he?"

"He's our age. And he doesn't live alone. His mom was just gone for a while."

"You shouldn't be in somebody's house without their parents around."

"We didn't know," I say. "We just met him, and he invited us inside."

"Just be careful. That's how trouble brews."

"It's no big deal Mom. We were just hangin' out. You want us to meet people, don't you?"

"Just be careful, especially when you first meet someone. Oh, and while we're on it, the rules say no minibikes in The Terrace."

"It's a damn minibike!" I say. "We're not like drivin' a bus or something!"

"What have I said about talking with food in your mouth?"

"Whatever," I say.

After a while, Mom says, "About the minibike. I don't appreciate your attitude, but I do acknowledge that it isn't fair to tell you 'yes' and then turn around and say 'no'. And I know this divorce and this move have been hard on you two. We can't break the rules, but we still might be able to work something out. Maybe we can get one and ride it elsewhere. I'll look into it."

Skip's squealing like a little girl.

"I don't even care," I say. "This place sucks."

Worse than having to live in "The Terrace" is having to endure the forty-five-minute bus ride to UPP Elementary School. Mom says it's the best school in the district, so that's where we're going. Her bowling partner's a bigwig principal who's pulled a bunch of strings to make it happen. It might as well be in Siberia. The one and only consolation is that it'll only be for one year. Another of Mom's endless carrots. If we stay out of trouble and get good grades, we can attend the local middle school next year.

On the bus the kids are looking at us like we have huge, pussing sores on our faces, and it takes me a while to figure out what's going on. In Seattle, the cool pants were bell-bottoms, tight around the ass and upper legs with a cone-shaped flare at the ankles. So that's what I'm wearing, adding thick shorts and Long John's to make it look like I have an ass at all, and to thicken my stilt-like legs. In my mind we're steppin' up our game—new Levi's, sweet, palm-laden shirt, big puka around my neck—and Skip's wearing his new denim vest with thick, fluffy, white lining. I love that vest. But all we're getting are looks of utter disgust and revulsion. Somebody's saying, "Look, it's Buffalo Bill and Disco Dan," and I'm wanting to punch the smirk off somebody's face, but I'm kinda scared and I know Mom'll kill me, and all hopes of a minibike will go down the drain. So I'm counting to ten like Grandma always taught.

Finally, off the bus. Forty-five damn minutes. Our heads are turning every which way, kids are dispersing, and now we're alone, the driver's baggy eyes bearing down. Her hair's frizzy and disheveled. Her ass is rolling off the seat. "Well, whaddaya waitin' for?" she says in a gravelly voice. "Go on. Shoo."

The hallways are lined with drawings from different classes and posters about rules and positive thinking. Kids are scattering like ants, and by the time we find Skip's class the bell has rung and I'm left alone in the silence of the halls. I have to find Room 17, which is two buildings over and might as well be in another state. I'm walking slowly, bracing myself for a First-Day-Late-Walk-In.

Room 17. I'm standing outside, breathing. I'm cracking the door and all heads are turning. There's giggling, and I'm avoiding eyes and staring at the teacher who's thin and chiseled with dark whiskers and shiny, slicked-back hair. He walks over, places his hand on my shoulder. His sweater is gray and his bow tie is black. He turns me toward the blackboard, whispering, "Please excuse their rudeness. They simply laugh at things they haven't seen. Love the pants."

"Sorry," I say, handing him my registration papers. "I got lost."

"Yes. It's understandable," he says, looking the papers over and nodding. "Jim, Jim Murphy. And you're new to the area. Well, welcome. My name's Mr. Herrigan. Take this and take this, and write your name on both sides of that. You can sit over there in the back corner, seat 19." He's turning and introducing me. "This is Jim. He's new to the area, so let's make Jim feel welcome." The kids, however, say nothing. Most are staring apathetically, and one kid, I notice, is squinting and glaring and looking me up and down, and I'm meeting his glare for a split second before turning around to sit in seat 19. Mr. Herrigan's raising both hands. "Question," he says, "Which two regions of America fought during the Civil War?" And a kid's raising his hand and answering "North and South." And Mr. Herrigan, hands now down, is asking, "Which side was more industrial, and which side was more large plantations?" And another kid's answering, and Mr.

Herrigan's raising both arms again, an apparent signal for the entire class to answer in unison. "And which side depended on slavery for its existence?" To which most all except, I notice, the kid who'd been glaring at me, answers, "The South."

It's then that I see her, a beacon of light. I'm sitting down and I'm staring, and she must feel my eyes because she's turning and I'm suddenly looking square into her blue-eyed soul. She's looking away and I'm becoming bug-eyed and still and conscious, and all's now slow. I want to wait, but I'm turning back, twisting to see her nametag. The cursive's perfect and multi-colored. KRISSY PORTERMAN. Her blue eyes are gone, now facing forward, and the curly blonde hair is swaying and settling on her purple sweater's shoulder pads. Mr. Herrigan starts going over rules and expectations, and I'm watching Krissy Porterman taking notes, wondering what she could be writing about when everything he's saying is right in front of us.

I start to take notes myself.

> *Krissy. I bet your little butt looks great in those jeans. From here they look like Jordache. I'm sure they are. If they're not, I'll buy you some. An angel like you should only wear Jordache. I'll take you to the mall on my new minibike. Did I tell you I was getting a minibike? Oh, well, you know, it's no big deal.*

"And Jim," Mr. Herrigan says, "could you please read the next rule."

I'm trying to figure out what number we're on. "Uhh ..."

"Number six, please."

"I will use positive language," I say, thinking, '*What a bunch of shit*, and then it's back to watching Krissy Porterman.

My mind's seeing nothing but Krissy Porterman's sweet face, the little freckles around her nose, the blonde tufts at the base of her neck. Even the minibike is a distant star. Dreams have invaded all waking moments: us walking hand-in-hand across the schoolyard; us eating lunch together; us kissing under the eucalyptus tree outside my house. They're all-consuming; nothing else exists.

At school I'm layin' low, keeping to myself, watching her, sly and astute. On the fourth day, the sun's strong, the air's crisp, the birds are singing, and I'm walking to the bus stop, rolling my head and breathing in the warm freshness, knowing that this is the day that I'll step up and ask Krissy Porterman to the mall. I'm wearing my favorite OP shirt, light blue with a big rainbow, clouds, and a picture of a surfer on a wave. Mom says it brings out my eyes. I'm wearing my new white, slip-on Vans. My hair's feathered like Sean Cassidy's. This is the day. This is it. I'm feeling the intensity of an upcoming battle, an oral report. And it continues, this intensity, throughout Mr. Herrigan's vocabulary and his slide show on the anatomy of a frog until, finally, the clock strikes three.

Kids scattering. Kids congregating. Kids laughing and kids walking alone. It's now overcast and cold, and my skinny legs are bumpy and hard. I should've put on a jacket, but I wanted her to see my shirt and my eyes.

She's huddled among a group of girls who're giggling and whispering.

The word flies out as if on its own, before thoughts can stop it. "Krissy."

It's out; it can't be taken back.

She's turning and looking; they're all looking. They're giggling. She's breaking from the flock. She's moving toward me.

"Hi," I say.

"Hi," she says.

"I was wondering if ..." My voice is shaking. I'm stopping and gulping and exhaling words. "... if you wanna go to the mall with me on Saturday?"

She's silent. She's smiling. She's laughing. They're all now laughing.

I'm sitting. I'm alone. Feeling tears. Skip's standing above.

"What's wrong?" he asks.

"Nothing," I say.

We're walking. Skip's handing me a Dr. Pepper.

On the bus, the faces and streets are blurry. Voices are murmuring. The hard, plastic seat's vibrating. Someone behind says, "Can't wait for Skate Night."

I'm turning. The kids look up. "Did you say, 'Skate Night?'"

"The school Skate Night, Friday night," one kids says, looking at the other. "What planet have you been living on?"

"Where?"

"Laguna Hills Skate Palace. Where else?"

The plan's already brewing, the Big Bang, the Universe from nothingness. It has power. It has spark; it may create life itself.

CHAPTER FOUR

Bali, Indonesia 2014

"I have had women, I have fought
with men; and I could never turn back
any more than a record can spin in
reverse. And all that was leading me
where? To this very moment..."

—Jean-Paul Sartre, *Nausea*

WHEN YOU HAVEN'T smiled much, your facial muscles forget
and skin gets sculpted by scowl creases. Atrophy and
recycled cells building facial topography. And neurons
are their own world; thoughts are waters and winds carving
canyons and glaciers and elegant and not so elegant valleys.
Once etched they are long to change. A mirror framed in
Balinese teak won't change a thing. Fervent green rice fields
and distant ocean birds won't change a thing. All external,

outside. Adventure is stepping out, but it's also stepping in. To read and rewrite these twenty-year-old stories is to remember hope. A world of order, of reason. Meaning was external, yet existed somewhere someway. I thought I could control the waters, be the God of my own mind, stand above and dictate creation.

But here I am, a walking self-help manifesto, a cloak artist.

As I think, so I am. And I choose love; let others have their hate; let them have it. Vision, Purpose, Awareness, and Discipline. I am nothing and I am everything. Just do what you can; let be what you can't. Nature, Dharma, the Tao, Buddha, Jesus, Brahmin, the Great Spirit, God, Allah, the mystic's Absolute—All The Same—Oneness, Non-duality. All is Harmony; tap it; settle into Source. Love is stronger than hate—stronger. Suffering is a gift. Enemies teach patience. So take responsibility. Ground yourself in Love and Character and Integrity—they are shields. Stop barking; you're not in the Universe, you are the Universe. So Work, Give, and Love; command all desire and anger and lust; let vastness and voidness and wonder—let God—swallow them whole.

And Never Forget: all are suffering. We all want Peace; we all want Health and Security; we all want Love. Everyone naturally wants Happiness; no one knowingly harms oneself. Thus...they know not what they do. And thus...their actions should be Forgiven. Reprimanded, legislated, and controlled, but Forgiven. For only then, are we Free.

Do you hate fire for burning? Water for flooding? A tree for shedding its leaves? Nuisances to say the least, but you don't hate them. Do what you can, accept, and move forward with compassion. Prepare your fire retardant and flood gaps. Have your rake and water pump, your blower gassed and ready.

The Jim Murphy I was is the Jim Murphy I still am, and I see myself in every act and word. And yet I am not the same; I can never be the same. My cloaks are far too tattered. And yet I must persist; I now have a son; it's not just me anymore. My soon to be ex-wife's already done with me, but it's not too late for me and my son. He's only three, too young to understand what he's witnessing. But the crossroads loom, the roads defining our future. If I'm indeed my own pilot, now is the time to seize control. Something must be surmised from all of this. Something must happen. So many questions: Can I still become a positive, loving person? Can I transcend this nausea, this digust? Can I cultivate enough positive attitude and intention to offset experience, the empirical evidence before me? Can I suspend neverending judgments? Can I go beyond this endless search to understand the world, myself, existence? Or will I forever be stuck among words, exponential and seemingly infinite interactions: myself and other; interpretations; biological variances; nuances upon nuances?

I see two paths, two sides of myself—an angry self, and a content and integrated self—although both are murky, sheathed in fog. Will I find a way through this anger, this cynicism, and become my vision, a positive, loving person, a person who empathizes and feels for others' pain, who understands why they're acting like self-absorbed assholes, who helps? Or will I continue building disgust, sneering on a dime, upchucking guffaws at every slight and example of human confusion? Can I recarve myself before it's too late? Am I indeed my own master? Or am I simply another slave?

So here I am, back in Bali. I must find a way, if not for myself, for my son. His name's James, named after my father and his father and kings from times past. If cells recycle every seven years, perhaps I too can reinvent myself. And time, the mystics and physicists say, is an invention, that it isn't real. Perhaps there's no going back, no mending the holes in my cloaks. But I must try. Perhaps I can distinguish weak threads, replace them, apply patches. They are ugly, these patches, but they are functional, and functional is all-important. It's oh-so cold out, and I may not survive without functional cloaks. The weather'll kill me. The elements will beat me down. I must do something. I don't want James to see me this way. He deserves a real father. He'll inherit my scars; our souls will merge, and I don't want to handicap him. So here I am, writing. Twenty-three some years ago I began writing stories about traveling, about my broken and yearning heart, about Australia and Hanah, and about growing up in 1980's Orange County. I was trying to make sense of things, just as I am now. My skin was three cycles of seven years younger, and there was more time ahead than behind. But I was the same person. Those heavy eyes house the same ponderous creature. And writing has always been my processor, the muck sorter. It's a bit like life itself, a slow torture at times, punctuated by moments—even periods— of joy, of bliss, of love and wonder. The best of us can sustain such states, and the best of writers can write through the muck. But for most of us, humans and writers alike, it's a slow torture. And yet, it's all we have. We can give up, as so many do. We can numb ourselves and/or prance around in all our embroidered cloaks, but it won't end the torture; Sartre's Nausea cannot be glossed over. So I'm going back to stories written long ago, back to a more innocent time. Writing is creation, and creation is life. And I need life. Perhaps creation can save me? I shall undress and stand naked before the world. It's something to do. And sometimes one just must keep doing. And then, if creation and destruction and entropy do their job, stuff happens.

CHAPTER FIVE

Traveling 1991

"With this he quieted his mind, and went
on his way, taking whatever road his
horse chose, in the belief that in this
lay the essence of adventure."

—Miguel De Cervantes, *Don Quixote*

THE ORIGINAL ROUND-THE-WORLD plane ticket—that stack of
hard papers which, when held, could be fanned out like
playing cards, and which, in itself, held future wonders,
stories, and endless possibilities—did not include Istanbul.
Kayne and I had washed 400 cars and parked another thousand at a palm-laden resort, and our parents were forced, as
agreed on (albeit gladly), to match our stack of earned cash.
Middle-class privilege. The travel agency had a big world map
with lit-up destinations, and Kayne and I had spent hours

choosing our hubs. Once decided, they couldn't be changed. The flight dates could be changed with a fee, but not the destinations, and all flights had to be used within one year.

Back then a year was a lifetime, but now, as we're beginning to see, we'll be shooting off here and there, pulled and pushed and thrown, and we'll be crawling back to our hubs in good shape and in bad shape. Paris, Rome, Cairo, Nairobi, Brisbane, New Delhi, Kathmandu, Bangkok, Auckland, Nadi-Fiji, Honolulu, and back to L.A. These are the original destinations. The plan was to travel until our money got low, then shoot to Australia for work, then travel through Asia. A plan. A structure. A future. And now these hubs are shackles, confining and stifling.

The mind must not always be sure what to do or think or feel in exotic places because there's often a period in which time feels slower, where the eyes see things for which there's no mental construct, and consciousness enters a phase of mild confusion. Drag us here and drag us there. Who or why raised no hairs with all our faith and wonder. All I did was tell Kayne about the girl I'd seen, how I'd lost her, and how she was off to Istanbul, and next thing I know Kayne's waiving around two tickets to Turkey, laughing and rolling his head and, just like that, we're back in this spontaneous and magical place of freedom. He must've felt guilty, and I didn't even bother asking where he'd gotten the money. A Soviet plane, the Danube, the big Black Sea, and here we are, strolling the cradle of civilization, the intersection of East and West. Men are begging us to join them for apple tea and to look at their wonderful carpets, and there's the smoky smell of lamb and peppers emanating from a dirty chrome stand worked by a Cyrus-the-Great look-alike. And Mom and Irvine even came through. Took five hours and three trips to the Western Union, but there it was, a receipt for $500, a gift from the heavens. And a note:

> *Here's enough to get you back on your feet. Use it wisely. Go where you can work. I can't do this again. I Love You. Mom.*

Saved by Irvine; saved by the world I've come to resent.

The cab drivers are circling. They're shouting in Arabic and broken English, touching my arm and my pack, but I'm ignoring them. My pack is lined with chicken wire. All zippers are padlocked. They could still knife me and take everything, but the day is bright, and Allah is watching. I'm a new man, an experienced man, a vigilant and distrustful man. "Trust in God," the Arabs say, "but tie your camel." So I've tied my camel, and I'm enjoying this surreal confusion, attempting to trust in God.

I walk to an old man with a large, silver teapot, buy a disposable clay cup of tea, and sit on a bench, a gray mosque in the hazy distance, one of Justinian's treasures. Loud and distorted chanting blares from invisible speakers, and men are rushing off to pray. The smog's thicker than the clouds, and all is noise and movement. But I'm in this slow bubble, like scuba, calm and unaffected, the kids now standing back and watching with crinkled foreheads. It smells like everything the breeze has scooped up: salt, trash, exhaust, those lamb kebobs, an old man's pipe, dried sweat and wet sweat.

Another new place. Just like that. Tea in hand, I'm opening the book. Constantinople, Byzantium, the Ottoman Turks, janissaries and sultans with multiple wives. It almost makes the stench and the stained concrete charming.

Kayne's calling me. A cab is waiting, and it's now I realize we're here for a reason with no plan at all.

For three days I'm searching every hostel and tourist site in Istanbul. I have no picture, no full name, no real information. Her name's Sabrina. She has long, dark hair and green eyes. She would've arrived in the last couple of days. She's with three guys. She's beautiful.

I'm getting all kinds of questions. "You're looking for a girl you don't even know? Why would you do that? What color is her burka? Do you have a picture? What the hell is wrong with you?"

"I don't know, I don't know," I keep saying to each and all, plunging forward, thoughtless and content in my all-consuming will. I must've reread her note a hundred times. Yes, it definitely says Istanbul. But it also says Uganda. Yes, it definitely says she wants to meet me. Delusion wrapped in desire and creative fiction. I must be insane, thinking about going off to Uganda. But what else can I do? I've no choice. I have to find her. I have to know if this feeling, this whole story, is real.

The next thing that happens is very strange, one might even call it synchronistic, I don't know. All I know is I was succumbing to depression, to exertion and despair. I'll never find another woman like her; she is the archetype, and I've painted myself into a mental corner. I can barely see straight.

My resolve is weakening. Kayne has plied me with two dark coffees and dragged me into a musty building, an inconspicuous door on an insignificant street. He pays our entry fees, we're handed informational pamphlets, and I'm beginning to read while still in the light, for I can see darkness through the open door, smell the mold and dust awaiting. The pamphlet says that the Basilica Cistern, was built in the sixth century by Emperor Justinian, an extension of an earlier project by Constantine. I remember Constantine because Mr. Herrigan, my sixth grade teacher, always made a big deal about how Constantine had had a dream about crosses, like Jesus and the crucifixion crosses, and how he'd then painted them on the shields of his soldiers who'd gone on to kick ass and eventually spread Christianity throughout the Roman Empire. Mr. Herrigan always made these stories so dramatic, so romantic. I think that's why I remember them.

This Basilica Cistern was some kind of water filtration system, built with pillars pillaged from older buildings. As we descend the stairs, these pillars rise; they're spread out evenly, and many are adorned with sculptures and Ionic and Corinthian engravings. Several have large Medusa faces as a foundation. There's a deck and swampy water below. It's hot and musty. It's the high arches, columns, and majesty of Rome, except it's underground and dark.

I'm whispering, questioning, the words echoing and trailing off into silence, and I am standing there in awe, looking up and down and around, and then there's a whisper from behind.

"Yes, sir, this was once filled with water, and there's much more to the story as well." And I'm turning to see a handsome and slim Turkish man, a guide to a German family who's also watching him and who's now also watching me. Kayne's turning too, making bug-eyed faces, and we're all standing together nodding and smiling and continuing to look around. "Some seven thousand slaves helped build this," the Turkish man's whispering, "and it's said that many who died are still entombed in the concrete below. It's also said that this cistern was used to hide women and children during the threat of invasion, not just from the Huns, but also the Mongols and others."

Kayne's whispering, "Whoaa," in his own exaggerated, comical way, and we just keep walking in awe of this incredible feat of engineering and the colors of the light shining off the smooth, green water, and after a while I'm beginning to enjoy the musty air and the moving dust and the sound of the occasional movement of water when the deck's stepped on. One can imagine, almost feel, the women and children hunched quietly, listening to the horrors above, wondering and praying. The Turkish man's asking where we're from, and he's asking where we're going, and I'm telling him we're not sure and that we're looking for a friend, and he's whispering, "Oh, I see," and he's staring politely, his eyes blinking, slowly, his head nodding, his thin body still and poised and respectfully waiting for more information.

"Actually," I say, the words dripping surrender and defeat, "we're looking for a girl. I saw her in Hungary and am obsessed with finding her. At this point though, I don't think it's going to happen. I've no idea where she could be, no idea at all." The German tourists have walked on, pointing and shaking their heads and talking German, and Kayne's behind them, absorbed in it all. The Turkish man's watching them, and now he's looking back to me.

"Why are you so obsessed with this woman, if you don't mind me asking?"

Despair's made me raw. Defeat is humbling. There's nothing to hide. "Love at first sight," I'm whispering, looking down, as if talking to myself. "I guess that's what it is. Stupid, I know, but I can't stop. She's the woman I've always pictured—the perfect woman. I can't think of anything else. And I haven't even talked to her. How stupid is that? But I have to find out. I just have to. She wrote me a note. She was coming here to Istanbul and heading to Uganda, but I've no sense of time, and I know nothing."

The slim and handsome Turkish man's smiling and nodding and, again, his head's tilting curiously, and now it's rotating in tiny circles. He's smiling. "Is her name Sabrina?"

Redemption. Intuition's core. If I'm silent, God will speak. Sometimes I call this Big Mind. It's my own little term. Huge, All-Encompassing Mind. A mind that sees and feels all at once. Chaotic, perhaps, but whole. Big Mind. I feel it here and there, sometimes think I can settle in and trust it. I rarely, however, know when it begins and when it ends. But here I must have faith. I must not waiver. That I now have a sign is auspicious.

Kayne's back, standing to the side, listening.

The thin and handsome Turkish man's an angel, a messenger, and I'm now watching him with my own curious eyes, even reaching out to touch him and smile and stand upright. Yes, he's real; this is all real. He was their guide for two days. Sabrina, John, Leo, and Danny. Nice people. Yes, he says, she's going to Uganda. They're all going to Uganda, joining an organization that helps build schools in remote villages.

But first they're going to Greece. They have a month. They were talking about Kenya, but he's not sure why.

The Big Mind moment is over, and I'm feeling raw. Big Mind moments are typically brief, for the little mind's conditioning is strong, a lifetime's energy. I'm asking the thin and handsome Turkish man if Sabrina was "with" one of the guys. He's whispering he didn't get that impression. I'm breathing and looking around. The huge ancient pillars, the shadows and the glistening water. Back in Big Mind, for a moment. I'm forever vacillating.

"Where in Greece?" I'm asking. "Where, exactly?"

"The islands," the Turkish man's whispering, "they're going to Izmir, catching a ferry from Kusadasi to Samos. They mentioned Santorini and Ios. That's all I heard."

Kayne's all excited. "All right Skinny! The Greeks Isles!"

We're saying our good-byes, watching all walk away.

We're booking a shuttle to Izmir and are informed of the sacrilege of bypassing Cappodoccia, these tremendous limestone formations, this stretch of medieval cities carved in rock, and I'm quickly outvoted in not wanting to wait another day, in not wanting to endure a long night's bus ride across vast lands, and just like that, we'll be heading east, away from my desires. Sometimes Kayne just makes decisions. I never know when it's coming, but when it happens, it just happens. The compromise is that we'll only lose a day, will leave tomorrow evening, and be back in Izmir by morning. A ridiculous excursion, but a mighty one we're told, and we're now settling into excitement. And Sabrina's real. A path to her is forming. Perhaps true love and destiny exist after all?

CHAPTER SIX

Australia 1993

"Alas, of all the enemies, habit is
perhaps the most cunning, and
it is cunning enough never to let
itself be seen, for he who sees the
habit is saved from the habit."

—Søren Kierkegaard, *Works of Love*

EVERYONE ASSUMES THAT all our travels have rendered us insights into life and human existence. They want to hear what we've learned, what marrow of understanding we might've sucked from the abyss of confusion. Actually, not everyone. Older people don't seem to care. Maybe they've already been there, or they don't want to ponder lost time? Maybe they long ago lost their freedom to travel, to wander, and can't bear reminders? Whatever the case, they just don't care as much. It's the young and idealistic travelers who want to hear.

Hanah thinks there's something to be learned from my stories. And worse, she wants to hear about my entire damn childhood. She thinks that everything's somehow connected, that one's own understanding of the world and supposed universal truths will eventually cross paths. As for me, I don't know what I've learned from growing up in Irvine; I certainly know nothing of universal truths, and the travels have only served to solidify confusion and distrust. So what's the point? I once read that Socrates always said, "I don't know," that, perhaps, he too felt stuck in uncertainty, unable to accept any one interpretation. "I don't know" was all he had left, that and more questions. I can't, however, shake the feeling that there's something to know, something to be learned, something that will help me sort out the confusion in my head. I want to believe in answers, and I guess this keeps me thinking and keeps me telling Hanah all she wants to hear. And here I am, still writing it all down.

Peter, our other roommate, is standing on the porch, eyes closed, sniffing the air. "Shirley's making cookies," he says in his thick Swedish accent. He's gone, emerging below, trotting across the lawn, picking two white lilies and disappearing, the screen door creaking and shutting. He's back, handing us fresh cookies, and squeezing onto the couch between me and Hanah. He's smitten with Hanah, but she's not smitten with him, so she uses me as a shield. He knows she's not interested, and she knows he's harmless, but his flirtations continue as if it's just easier for him to behave consistently. And his infusions into our conversations, although often breaking sensual spells, are almost always relevant and entertaining—and he'll soon be off to work—so I usually don't mind.

"I remember the exact moment I decided to come to Australia," he says. "I was sitting on some rocks in Stockholm, sipping peach tea, and when I thought about going to Australia, I just knew it was the right decision.Then, as if to clarify, a distinct breeze right then rippled across the sea, straight toward me. I could see where it began some hundred yards out, and it came straight at me, not an inch off kilter. I'd adjusted my scarf and put on my gloves. It smelled of sweet smoke from a nearby restaurant. The seagulls were circling and squawking. I felt such peace. It was an essential moment, and I knew I was supposed to go to Australia."

He'd been staring into the dusky grey sky, but now he's turning, and seeing my raised brows, he stops cold. "What?" he says.

"Oh, come on," I say. "Don't you see the convenience in that? Don't we just see and feel what we want to?'"

"Of course," Peter says. "But there's something to it, that moment when thoughts settle and one is overcome by a feeling, a knowing."

"Sure," I say, "But how can we ever really know?"

"Maybe we can't," Peter says. "But in that moment, I felt I did, and I decided to act on it. Maybe it's not logical. But I choose to believe. I choose to follow that feeling of essence when it comes."

At that, as if to drive home the point, he up and changes and leaves to work without another word.

Dusk's unfolding. First, the clouds are dark and plump, then large and disorderly droplets are falling and splattering and creating little rivers along curbs, and then, all is sprinkles and mist and greyness. The Chopin seems part of the orange candlelight. The comforter's draped. I catch myself almost kissing Hanah's head, which rests on my shoulder, almost chest. She's still wearing her blue work uniform, and she smells of perfume diluted by the day's sweat. Now she's up, off to shower. Steam's floating down the hall. The cat's gone. The puddles lie silent.

She's back, wearing the white dress that drives me crazy. "So," she says, sitting and lifting her knees, the white cotton sliding. She's now lime shampoo and coconut lotion. "What's on your mind tonight?"

This is usually how it begins. An open-ended question. Even when I know it's coming, or not in the mood, Hanah has a way of getting me to talk. I usually just start talking, trying not to think.

"Not much," I say. "Thinking about Peter's comments. I'm not sure what to think about the concept of 'essence,' can't help but wonder if it's all romantic hogwash."

"Hogwash?"

"Nonsense," I say.

"How can there not be some underlying essence?" she asks.

"There's just too much confusion. We humans think. And thoughts rarely represent reality."

"So stop thinking."

"That's the goal," I say, "but I question the possibility of that. Just thinking about not thinking's still thinking."

"Yes," Hanah says, "I see what you mean. This is why I love talking to you."

I'm not sure why Hanah places so much gravity on my words and thoughts, for I've done nothing to earn this distinction. Others do the same. Perhaps it's because, again, we're traveling so freely and because I'm always reading something heady and meaningful. They assume I know something. Of course, I know nothing.

"I want to believe in essence," I say. "But I always seem to get in the way."

"I?" Hanah asks.

"Yes," I say, "the thing, whatever it is, that's thinking about essence."

"I see."

"Why haven't we kissed?" I ask, wanting to suck the words back, remembering the moment I first spoke to Krissy Porterman, as if it were yesterday.

She's reaching for my face, turning me toward her doe-eyed gaze. "A kiss I've so wanted," she says. "But we're just wandering, and Sabrina's still with you."

"What do you mean, still with me?"

"She's still in your heart. You're still in pain."

"I'm just confused. May always be. Lost in stories."

"Aren't we all," she says. "And you'll be leaving in a few weeks, yes?"

"Yes."

"You know," she says, "you often stare off for long moments, even minutes when you're not talking. Then you awaken, like you've turned a channel on the tellie."

"I've always stared off," I say. "My mom calls it selective hearing. She says all men have it in one form or another."

She's holding my hand. "Tell me more about Sabrina."

"What do you want to know?"

"What exactly happened. You talk about everything but that."

"There's not much to tell."

"Try."

"It's just another story. I'll write about it."

"Good. I'm glad you're writing about it. But there's gotta be some particulars that stick in your mind, something that happened, that went wrong."

The large palm leaves are swaying and ruffling; more rain is approaching.

"You gonna see her again?" Hanah asks.

"I don't know."

"Have you talked or written?"

"No."

"Why not?"

"I don't have her contact information. And besides, I don't even know her. She was simply who I wanted her to be."

"What do you mean?"

"You'll see."

"So I have to wait for the story?"

"It's all story," I say, staring at the flickering candle, the rain approaching in wide and slanting curtains. It's tapping the roof, the palms, and now the deck.

"Please," Hanah says, "it's time for a story." She's hugging my arm, shifting her warm knees toward me. "Take me traveling. Tell me about love."

"Yes," I say, reaching for the pages, "it's time for a story."

CHAPTER SEVEN

Irvine 1981

"Boldness has genius, power,
and magic in it."

—Johann Wolfgang von Goethe

EVEN WORSE THAN riding the damn singing bus (and almost worse than my angel, Krissy, laughing in my face), is walking across the yard the next day (Thursday, the day before Skate Night), to see Krissy Porterman and Brian Daniels hand in hand. He's all smug, as if oblivious to the adoring eyes, and I'm looking around to see if anyone else notices this disgusting display, this act, looking for grimaces or shaking heads or someone spitting. But all are just admiring.

Everyone knows about Krissy laughing in my face. If they didn't actually see it, they heard about it, and this is even more dangerous with the viciousness of middle school imaginations and the inevitability of altered stories. And they get back to me. No one's out to protect my feelings, there's no such thing in sixth grade. One story has me throwing up all over myself. Another has Krissy spitting in my face. Another has me crying. I did, of course, briefly cry, but no one saw it, so I'm poo-pooing all as ridiculousness unworthy of response.

On this day, not one person talks to me. Skip's not around. During break, I'm leaning against the handball wall, watching little birds flutter and play, and I swear they're keeping me company 'cause they keep landing beside me and looking up and shaking their little heads. They're flying back to the top of the wall and over to the corner of the school and then back again. "I'm not gonna cry," I say to one, and I swear he looks at me as if to say, "I know you're not," and I'm thinking about being a bird or taking off into the wild, but I know I can't fly, and in the wild I might get eaten, so that isn't such a good idea.

The yard's filling up with screaming kids, now full of corndogs and sugar, the daily fruit and vegetables left rotting in baskets and tin containers on shiny, wheeled carts. The kids are scaring off the birds, and no one's still coming near me, so I'm left alone again, even worse because now everyone's staring and laughing and pointing in my direction. Kids or not, how can they be so incapable of empathy? Have they never themselves been shunned? Even I, a sixth grader, know it's only weakness and insecurity, but this's no consolation. I, myself, feel sorry for people, sorry for the homeless guy everyone ignores, sorry for teachers who don't have the gumption to handle little brats who need a big kick in the ass. Why so much pettiness, so much cruelty and weakness? Will it always be this way?

When school ends I'm feeling something pushing me forward, in this case to the bus and through the contrived and superficial streets of The Terrace and into a ten-mile bike ride to Laguna Hills Skate Palace. It's like I just appeared, standing in front now, thinking about preparations. For all I know California might have bigger floors or skate clockwise. I'll need to scope out equipment, dress code, and the rink itself. In Seattle, we'd skated all the time, even around the streets, but weekly at the rink for speed skates. I'm no good at going backward or fancy shit, but in the speed skate, the thing that really matters, I'm a thoroughbred racehorse.

I'm locking my bike and going inside. It's cool, air-conditioned, smells of cotton candy and popcorn, hot dogs and those big, salted pretzels. The Doobie Brothers are blaring through huge speakers hung above, shaking the floor. Reminds me of the old rink in Seattle. I miss Seattle. I had friends in Seattle, knew my way around, knew how things worked, and although I still had stilt-like legs and an assless ass, I wasn't an outcast. Wasn't Donny Osmond either, but wasn't an outcast. And the woods, I miss the woods. This place might as well be desert wasteland.

I'm thinking aloud, whispering to myself. "Skate Shop, rentals, bearings. Oh, and the DJ. What should I expect?"

The place is pretty impressive, even better, I must say, than the rink in Seattle. The floor looks smooth and fast. The arcade's huge. There's an entire wall of "Asteroids" and "Defender."

I'm inspecting the latest clothing, having already deemed all lame, when this thin and pimply kid appears.

"Can I help you?" he says. "Haven't seen you around. You new in town?"

"Just moved here a coupla weeks ago," I say, "up in Irvine."

He's wiping his nose with the side of his hand. "Cool. Irvine's cool. I live right down the street, by the Chevy dealership."

"Cool."

"You skate?" he asks.

"Yeh," I say, "first time here, though."

His name's Allan.

"So you know this place pretty well, Allan?" I ask.

"Been coming here since I was five," he says, "back when it was called The Skating Rink. It's all I really do know, that and math. I'm really good at math. Won the Capistrano School prize last year."

"Nice," I say. "Cool. You may be able to help me, Allan. I've got a situation."

"Yeah?" He's leaning closer.

I'm telling him about beautiful Krissy and Brian Jerk-off Daniels, how she laughed in my face, how the whole school's turned on me, and how "Skate Night" might be my only hope. "She's not like them, though," I say, "she's just caught up in the crowd."

I'm asking the girl behind the counter for a piece of paper and a pen. She has pink hair, black fingernail polish, and a black leather vest with chains. I'm writing the list, and handing it to him.

A seriousness is coming over him, like the entire world's in danger. "They treat me like that too," he says, looking the list over. "Right, got it. You're gonna use rentals?"

"I just prefer rentals," I say.

"Well," he says, "if you insist. Yeah, we can get you good bearings. Snack bar's no problem. I can even get you tokens. Make-out areas?"

His seriousness fades, softens. He's probably never made out in his life. Then again, neither have I. Of course no one in their right mind reveals such a thing. Maybe this is why I'm feeling sorry for him.

I think he senses this, 'cause he says, "There's a freeway overpass just outside that people use. But if you can pull that off, we'll get you into the manager's office. It has a sofa and soft red carpet, 'The Penthouse' we call it. Manager's always out bustin' kids for something, and he's rarely there." He's looking around. "As for music, let's talk to Leonard. He's a little weird, but he's okay."

The Sound Garden is perched above the rink in the back corner. Inside's a guy with long purple hair. The hair looks like a wig. There are blinking and multicolored lights. We're standing below. The DJ's wearing big headphones that make his face look small. He's sliding open the long, narrow window.

"What's up kid?" he says.

"Hey, Leonard," Allen says. "You working that school skate night tomorrow?"

"Of course, kid. You think they'd trust that idiot, Henry, or whatever the hell his name is? Was just doing a mix for tomorrow."

"This is Jim," Allan says.

"Hey, man," he says.

"Hey."

"Jim here needs our help," Allan says. "Got a girl problem, ya know?"

"Yeah, well, don't we all."

Allan's handing him the list, telling him about Krissy laughing in my face and how Brian Daniels, her supposed new boyfriend, is one of those uppity pricks he hates.

The DJ's looking over the list. He's grimacing. "First they want me to go to Nicaragua," he says, "and now you want me to play the Eagles? You know the rules, kid. No damn Eagles on my watch!"

I want to say, 'What the hell are you talking about? Nicaragua?' But all I say is, "I hear ya. I'm probably dreamin' to think about a slow skate anyway. What's really important is the AC/DC. Can you play 'Back in Black' during the speed skate?"

"Of course, kid. What else would I play?"

"Cool."

We're walking away. "What was all that Nicaragua stuff about?" I ask.

"I don't know," Allen says. "He was in the Marines. He's always saying stuff like that."

We're in the rentals room. Allen's putting fresh bearings into the wheels of some well-worn skates. I'm trying them on, taking them for a spin. Ten good laps. Four with speed. They're perfect.

I'm saying good-bye, thanking him. "No problem," he says. "This is gonna be great!"

CHAPTER EIGHT

Indonesia 2014

"In order to swim one takes off all one's clothes—in order to aspire to truth one must undress in a far more inward sense, divest oneself of all one's inward clothes, of thoughts, conceptions, selfishness, etc., before one is sufficiently naked."
—Søren Kierkegaard

ESSENTIALLY, I'M SPENDING most days managing unhappiness. And time, albeit a subjective creation, is always looming. Here, in Bali, I've all the time in the world, and it still looms. Take the other day when I was still on the Bukit Peninsula, above Bingin and Dreamland. I slept well, and thank God, for without sleep all else is fruitless. Indeed, as you'll see, parts of my routine are intended to induce exertion, mental peace, and smooth digestion, so as to promote slumber. I'm waking to a cool ocean breeze, to the sounds of waves and sea birds, rolling out of bed, and stepping outside to summon coffee, having already arranged for it the night before. An early misstep in the morning routine can throw off entire days. Two sips later, I'm shooing away four flies, and then covering the cup with napkins. I'm plumping up three pillows, lighting incense, and preparing to sit for a thirty-three minute meditation, part of which is concentration exercises, part the catharsis of recognizing feelings that delude—anger, desire, and any number of confusions. Another part is a cloak, this one a Buddhist contemplation on impermanence, the fact that all's in flux, changing, that all's thus voidness, emptiness, that nothing exists outside of something else, and thus, everything's connected, subject to cause and effect. I'm a man of facts, and these, it seems, are facts. It's the voidness of mystics; they call it God. All I need are facts—is that too much to ask? It's one of many such exercises, not limited by creed, culture, or subjectivity, although that—subjectivity—is a constant thorn, if nothing else because of language. This particular cloak—Cloak #1—and this exercise in general tends to temper extraneous and pesky thoughts; it provides an expanded and wondrous perspective that soothes and creates space when conventional thoughts are confining. And that, of course, is the purpose of cloaks: to conceal, to cover and protect.

Next, once the mind's pounded and plied, it's time to read. Eleven minutes per book, the first to bolster spirit, the second and third for knowledge, and the fourth a novel to inspire the next thirty-plus minutes of writing, sometimes pointless scribbling, the whims of a flying pen, sometimes the excitement of an unfolding story or novel, right now this explanation of my futile attempts to deal with myself and this reality which'll never bend itself around me, a general review and re-shaping of stories written when I was younger and fresher and less beaten, and the usual pounding of sentences with far too much flesh. And musings on what I "think," for what I "think," of course, is of utmost importance.

Next comes an hour of exercise, today some yoga in the gazebo atop a cliff. There are clay pots of purple and pink and white orchids and thin green bamboo shoots. The ocean below is green glass. I can see the reef, practically see the fish. It's perfect. But again, time's always looming. The sun'll soon angle through bamboo slats, and it'll be too hot to exercise. There's a fan in my tiny room, but not enough space.

Then, I'm done, standing, stretching arms to the sky, shaking my head—slowly—and sniffing a waft of oleander. The proprietor's young and pretty daughter is silently setting a table, leaving and then returning with fresh fruit, yogurt, and granola. She's pouring fresh coffee, bowing, and is gone. It's 9:00 a.m. This is the routine, the discipline. At home I'll wake at 4 a.m. to ensure enough time. But time's always looming, like a fog blanket that never lifts. Never enough time for all the books and all the countries. More's expected, and more's assumed to bolster. But more's not always more; sometimes more ends in confusion. And yet, I can't stop. So I keep going.

All is perfection, and yet, as most always, the day weighs heavy, and I'm forced to get busy, to move and to keep moving. I go surfing, sit with monkeys atop a cliff, eating thick noodles and peanut sauce while watching a pink sun and a purple and gray sky, all the while sipping Bintangs and nibbling on weightless cookies. The world's at war; the suffering's palpable. And I'm among perfection. There's nothing to bother me. Only birds, a breeze and a shimmering sea. And yet, I'm disgusted—with myself, the world, and this failed experiment that is me.

So it's time to return to my stories, to craft them once and for all, as if to verify they actually happened, to remind myself of lessons long buried under life's travails.

Sometimes I'm splayed emotional, a teary-eyed mess at every heartwarming story. Then I become stone, a rational crack-shot, deconstructing every motive to its selfish nucleus. Needless to say, I'm often confused. So utterly full of shit at this point that I don't know how to forgive myself. Or empty myself. Who would've thought knowledge could be such a weight?

It's been twenty-some years since this eager and naive eighteen-year-old first stepped out and into the world, this vastness of knowledge accumulated by souls from every degree, the world a great labyrinth of ideas, institutions, and perspectives, the greatest of puzzles. It was open and fresh, like the horizon on a magical day or the star-swept blackness and wonder of infinity. Hope and questions and adventure colluding to propel, a huge cannon firing me across the planet, across seas, and into new worlds where answers lie dripping with curiosities and future questions.

Twenty-five years of systematic study.

Assumption: If one studies—continuously—intellectual progress will follow.

Assumption: If one studies—continuously—perspectives can be absorbed, and the whole will reveal itself all splayed out and glowing.

Assumption: If one studies—continuously—the absorbed perspectives and the hard-won whole will reveal that which the soul most seeks: harmony and synthesis—some structure to it all.

Assumption: There's a way to think and learn my way out of confusion.

Twenty-some years of study and intention in a flash.

And where am I now? What have I learned?

I'm a cloak artist.

The walls of books, the passports plump with stamps and added pages, the countless moments and days spent in reflection. Integrity, perseverence, health—the congruity of body and mind and soul—the cultivation of compassion, of wonder, of the magic that is art and learning. God. Love. Knowledge. Creation. Structure. Purpose. So many cloaks to cover my suffering. To conceal. These are my stalwarts, the baseline; this is where I return when disgust becomes normal, when thoughts paint the soul in black lacquer. But focus and good intention and so-called knowledge are not, it seems, enough. Nor are contrived mystical conveniences, stories to placate the soul. If only I could surrender to faith alone, how gladly I would lie in that grass. I have my ways, so many ways. Meditation. Study. Religious scriptures. The mystics. Exercise. Love. I try to love. Alcohol. Nature. Art.

Books. I vacillate between purifying myself and the blessed numbness that is alcohol and over-indulgence, and I've become an excellent house-cleaner, errand-runner, gardener, internet shopper, handyman, cook, and arborist—anything to pass time. And I've done well; time's passed. My hair's graying, my skin's collapsing on itself, my legs are battered and bruised, my body is pockmarked with sunspots and old bug bites too long in healing. Most worrisome, however, is the heaviness in my eyes. There's no hiding it, no alleviation.

This morning I woke to the cackle of insects and a cool morning mist seeping through an ornamented window. A courtyard of Hindu temples is steaming, and streaks of mist are floating above and beyond lime-green rice paddies. Birds are whistling, a dog's barking in the distance, and mixed in with the smell of flowers and ferns is burning rice and incense. It's the reason I travel, this kind of scene, these exotic sounds and smells. They crack my routine open; they shock lethargic senses. At home, in San Francisco, I might not notice the beauty of the windswept trees or the elegance of the architecture. I might not go out alone to a random bar or coffee shop, and I might not wander the city with no plans at all. But here I'm eager and alone, pure independence, and such healthy and secure independence is magnetic; it attracts, draws people in. To travel alone is to become adventure. Egotistically, I'm Marco Polo, Tom Sawyer hopping barges, Kerouac jumping trains, Humboldt roaming mountainsides. Romantic nonsense, I know, but I can't help myself. It goes on and on. Fremont heading West, Washington surveying Ohio, Bolivar wandering the Andes. On and on. All begins with vision, the quest for knowledge and experience, for more. Muir sleeping under stars. Mountain men and sea-farers. Lewis and Clark. Jedediah Smith. Alexander's army of elephants. Magellan. Ingrained is freedom and wonder, and I long to recapture such fleeting spirits; I long to see, on every mirror, those all-curious eyes. But that's not what I see. That romanticism—crushed by mental gavels. And travel, like everything else, is just another cloak; it conceals the ugly realities within. I've become what I detest—a dullard, a cynic, an angry and boring man—a man who looks down on the world. The real baseline—pure and utter disgust. And knowledge is napalm. Knowledge leads to complexity, and complexity leads to assumptions and a pack of lies. What I really think is beyond sugarcoating; only honesty can alleviate. And what do I think? You don't want to know. You're curious, and you think you want to know. But if you're like me, a cloak artist—and most every last one of us is—you don't want to know. And if you're told, you'll probably just call me a bunch of names; you'll label me with inherently insufficient words and throw me into the nearest dumpster. It's just easier that way. Life's hard enough.

I've been asked: why so disgruntled? Why? You have health, a beautiful wife, and a beautiful little boy. Your first child, in perfect health—what a blessing! You have family, a good family, not all fucked up like so many others. In an age of insecurity, your job's secure. You get to teach history, to show students the world; you get to help, to give. So you've been divorced a couple of times. Everyone makes mistakes. It's hard. You're not the only one. And to travel every sum-mer—my God, you've traveled the whole damn world! Isn't that what you wanted? Isn't that what you set out to do? To see it for yourself? To gain perspective? To learn? To experience galloping adventures? You have comforts and conveniences and anything you need. You know how most of the world lives. You know how lucky you are. So how can you be disgruntled? How? What a little man you are. To which I've no answer, nothing but a nod of resignation. I don't bother saying that my second wife hasn't loved me for years, that we're getting divorced, that I'm unfit for the sterility of domestication, and that I'll soon be relegated to visiting my three-year-old three days a week. I could, of course, say plenty; I could go on and on with excuses and explanations. But no one wants a grump. So any disgust that jumps beyond my own skin is followed by fifty smiles.

To read and rewrite these old stories is to remember a time before cloaks. They existed, sure, but they were like kiddie clothes, smaller, throwaway versions. I was still gathering silk and threads and materials.

To read and rewrite these stories is to remember how it all started. So logical. So reasonable. My own little Enlightenment. Newton and Locke whispering sweet nothings on my shoulder. Rousseau massaging my soul. A world of order. A world beyond. Here's the knowledge, splayed out in all its wonder and glory. Here's the literature, testaments to transcendence. One can transcend; I too can meet God in mountains and in banalities. I'm not alone; I'm one of them. Ego rearing at every turn, shadows in mirrors upon mirrors. Methodologies. Theologies. Silence is one. And I can train myself. I can read and understand and wallow in knowledge, and then I can read about and on the silence and on the God of so many names, and I'll slowly grow and dissolve. I'll evolve. I'll overcome myself. And travels will build a pyramid, a self-monument to humanity, to potential.

In books I found hope stacked to ceilings.

In travels I found peoples as varied as the stars. Perspectives. Postmodern petri dishes. Everything, this entire onslaught of experience, is cement, paving roads toward understanding. Evolving worldviews. Spiritual experiments. A process. A structure.

So why hasn't anything happened?

Only confusion.

Even the most beautifully embroidered cloaks are subject to nature, to change, exposed to the elements, to ceaseless wear and tear. At some point one must bring in a seamstress to shore up holes, perhaps even add new lining and threads and fluffed up collars. Reality is dark matter, consciousness like icebergs—so much unseen. Some people keep their cloaks fresh; they dry-clean them weekly. Some keep them front and center, for all to see. Others wrap them in plastic and store them away. I'm the latter.

Assumption: I'm in control.

Assumption: There's an answer.

For twenty-some years now I've lived by routine, created a life supporting the structure that is me. How could I not support that which makes me happy? How could I compromise with my purpose? Travel, study, learn, teach, write, watch yourself, and grow. Don't worry about the world—change yourself. Forward movement. Self-knowledge. To not follow my whims would be to go against nature itself, to dam the rivers of bliss. Such selfishness is virtue. To know oneself is to be holy. And the world needs holy; the world needs awakening.

Keep your eyes on the prize. Don't become another pawn, a puppet, a workaholic sheep.

But at some point one awakens, and they're not the same person, but they are the same person. For time does exist, but then again it doesn't. Not that I know exactly when this happened. Nor do I have or expect an answer. So here I am, expecting nothing, but wanting everything.

CHAPTER NINE

Traveling 1991

"A man is like an ill-mannered billy goat,
mi hijita, he wants much more than his
stomach can hold, so he must be ignored
half the time. Do you understand?"

—Victor Villasenor, *Rain Of Gold*

O N THE FERRY from Kusadasi to Samos we meet a clean-cut, dark-haired, tall American named Jimmy. He's from San Diego, and all he talks about is women. Women he's had, women he wants, and women he's gonna get. He's been modeling in Italy all summer—a Slavic-American Adonis—and is spending a few weeks traveling before going home. Like us, he'd stopped in Ephesus, Turkey, to wander among Ionian glory, and, like me, his eyes glimmered as he spoke of sauntering through the weathered ruins, the stone

roads and columns and old rooms where people had lived
millenniums ago, had washed and loved and philosophized
in swaying tunics. We'd both explored the huge amphithe-
ater where Greek tragedies had once milked empathy from
huge crowds, and where Romans later roared like lions as
gladiators bled dry. Like me, he emphasized getting lost and
forgetting himself and forgetting about the hot Austrian
babe he was supposed to meet and who never showed. For
me, this wandering amongst ruins was the only moment of
mental equanimity since the Basilica in Istanbul when the
slim and handsome Turkish man had seemingly vindicated
my perhaps irrational urge to search for a woman I'd only
glimpsed for moments in shadowed light. But now it's clear:
I'm obsessed, and peace is nowhere.

Dreams. Sabrina and I are sitting on a Greek shoreline, the
warm, small wind-waves lapping our toes. We're sipping
Marathon beers, our shoulders touching, the sun descending
beneath a cantaloupe and magenta sky, and her dark, thin hair's
feeling silky and cool as she lays her head on my shoulder. She's
telling me about her tall Dutch mother from whom she aquired
her height and green eyes, and her shorter Venezuelan father
who passed down his olive skin and academic mind. He teaches
anthropology at UCSB, and just wrote a book on the impact
of Margaret Mead's New Guinea research on the feminist
movement. She, herself, is not a true feminist; she thinks men
should be men and women should be women, but freedom to
exist freely should be fundamental. She's never surfed, but she
wants me to teach her. We're talking about places we could

go together, and we're talking about Simone de Beauvoir and Liebniz, and she's telling me she wants to study philosophy at the Sorbonne. She's telling me about her younger brother who's being self-destructive, and I'm telling her about Erich Fromm's theories on self-destructiveness and destructiveness in general, and she's very impressed and appreciative of my earnestness and insight, and I'm staring at her long, tanned legs and thinking that I'm indeed earnest, but I also so want to kiss her entire body, marry her, travel the world with her, be a wonderful couple, and be blissfully happy. We're sharing personal histories with an intimacy usually reserved for family or old friends, and we're feeling we've known each other forever; we can't believe how close we feel. We're riding buses together (I'm not sure what happened to Kayne and I'm not sure exactly where we're going), and we're rarely not embraced in loving touch, so much so that we're annoying to others who assume we're naive and new to love, like starry-eyed teens. But we're not; we're the real thing; we're a true and deep and spiritual love, the archetype of all true lovers throughout endless time. People stare when we walk by, not because Sabrina's hot as all damn hell, but because we're the real deal, and they're wondering and hoping it's possible. It's rarer than white peacocks or auroras or albino alligators. Exceptions. All of God's handicrafts are special, but even He has favorites, projects given extra attention and detail. This is why I must find her. Such opportunities, if not seized, leave holes in our collective hearts and holes in the ethereal web of life itself, and I will not, cannot, endanger such entireties of existence; I must follow the law. I feel as if I'm living in two places at once, the present moment at any given time and within these dreams—albeit dreams brought on, I'm

entirely sure, by a true and fated love, inspired dreams that are
benignly dictatorial—and that I have no choice but to follow.

Jimmy's shirtless. He's lean and muscled and tan. He's tall,
with wide, developed shoulders, laterals that remind me of
Blake's Red Dragon painting, and eight clearly defined abdom-
inals that breathe independently as he speaks. He's wearing
a green headband and mirrored aviator sunglasses. He's a
walking Polo ad. He must get laid a ton. And he's over the
top; minus the good looks, he reminds me of Ben Needleman
when he'd get all worked up about girls.

"God, she was a hot bitch!" he says. "Thick-rimmed
glasses and the tightest bod, said she was a research scientist, talked about photons and plasma and shit like that. God,
she was hot!"

"A scientist?" I say. "That is hot."

"What?"

We're yelling over the rumbling engines.

"Nothing," I say, waving away the words.

He's looking around, as if searching for someone he's lost.
The long, vibrating sundeck is packed with travelers leaning
against backpacks. Some are drinking beers and taking shots
of Ouzo. It's midday; the party's already started, and it's looking
like it may never stop. We're on our way to Paros, then Naxos,
then on to Ios, but others will shoot off to Mykonos or Santorini
or wherever else. Those taking shots are likely going to Ios, and
I'm momentarily looking around myself, not like Jimmy, but in
a slow and methodical way, stopping on each group and couple
to see if I can ascertain their destinations. Mykonos is known

as a party island and a favorite for gays, Santorini for all-around romance and its quintissential steep and sloping hills adorned with whitewashed buildings and mini Greek Othodox-like blue domes. One couple we met in Istanbul said they spent all day on that hill, first sipping coffee and enjoying the morning sun, then enjoying lunch, the circling seabirds, and the shimmering sea, and then riding a donkey down the hill to lie on the beach before returning atop to another patio for beers, the sunrise, and lamb kebobs. If I don't physically visit Santorini with Sabrina, I'm sure I will in dreams and stories, and I'm surprised I've yet to imagine it. It smells of saltwater, diesel fumes and Coppertone, and I'm turning my sights to distant islands dry as Mars, thinking about sheer cliffs and aqua waters and ancient civilizations, when I see, out of the corner of my eye, Jimmy's head flop and his mouth gasp. He's now dead-set staring at two blonde and sun-worn young girls sitting along a railing, reading thick paperbacks. He's walking toward them.

Kayne's somehow sleeping next to the engine room, the only place devoid of people. How he can sleep with such mind-rattling noise is beyond me, but I knew he'd find a way when I'd seen the glaze in his eyes. He'd met Jimmy, ascertained that he was a party vortex and that we were all going to Ios, invited him to share a room with us, and left me to make small talk. I like Jimmy. He's entertaining. But I'm all about searching for Sabrina, and I can already see that he's a distraction. The parties are already forming.

We're docking at Paros, and, as expected, people are dispersing. Some seem to be staying in Paros, and some are heading for a ferry to Mykonos, but most are walking straight for an already-rumbling ferry to Naxos. This is the Santorini and Ios and wherever else crowd. With some groups, it's easy to distinguish who's heading where. The older people and most couples are Santorini- and elsewhere-bound, and most of the young people are going to Ios. But others I'm not so sure about, and I'm curious to see their end destinations. I'm exhausted.

Whatever happens later, I'll need some rest. I'll need enough energy upon arriving to search for Sabrina. I've already discovered that the main part of the town on Ios is small, and it should be easy to cover in an afternoon. We're only two days behind them. They could still be there. I may even meet her tonight. We could be off to Santorini tomorrow.

I'm heading straight for the Naxos ferry, stopping at the base of the swaying plank. I'm waving to Kayne, who's standing among others near the previous ferry. I know he'll get Jimmy, even though I somewhat wish he wouldn't. Regardless, Jimmy's Ios-bound, and he'll be on our ferry. The cafeteria below deck's already vibrating and loud and will soon be rolling side to side, but I'm exhausted and glad to be alone; I'll read myself to half-sleep, perhaps even get half-rested for the afternoon search and the evening's festivities.

At the dock in Ios are a dozen some people with trucks waiting to take new arrivals home. It's the usual deal. They're circling, showing pictures of accommodations, trying to strike a balance between the calmness of one with a superior product and the aggressiveness necessary to be seen and heard in the first place. Although Jimmy's previously been to Ios, I'm doing the dragging, so I take the lead and pick a cottage with a balcony and a nice-looking shower with colorful tiles. Jimmy and Kayne follow. We jump into a truck bed with hand railings, and are, just like that, whisked away from the frenetic dock and up a hill toward a blue sky streaming with whispy clouds. Minutes later, we're turning onto a cobblestone driveway, and, to our surprise, the place is as good as the picture. It's freshly stuccoed and painted white with Mediterranean-blue trim. It hugs a brown-and-tan hillside littered with bird droppings and loose rocks that blend with the dirt, and it overlooks the sparkling sea. I throw my pack on one of four beds and step onto the porch facing the great expanse of water punctuated by distant islands. The railing's marble, and the tiles at my feet are maroon and slick, as if polished.

"This place freakin' rocks," Jimmy says.

Kayne's coming out of the bathroom. "Yeah, nice job, Skinny. Check this out."

The bathroom has a large shower made from smooth slate inlaid with handpainted tiles of Greek domes, picturesque scenes, and iconic Greek places like the Parthenon and the Acropolis. There's a tile dedicated to Plato, another to Aristotle, and another to Socrates. The Plato tile has an allegorical cave and a transcendent sky from which Plato is glancing upward. Aristotle's shows the old, bearded man hovering over a young Alexander the Great, surrounded by stacks of Aristotle's scientific books and stacks of other books with blurred titles. I'm curious as to what books they're intended to be. Perhaps that was the artist's intention. The tile of Socrates shows him standing under an ornate archway, surrounded by philosophizing citizens, like in Raphael's School of Athens, and it shows him sitting, hands raised, cupping a silver chalice of poison. The man chose to die than live in a small-minded world.

I'm feeling energized by the excitement of a new place, this great house we've stumbled onto, and the excitement of searching for Sabrina. If I do find her, I'll unabashedly tell Jimmy and Kayne to split, and Sabrina and I will sip sangria on this patio and talk all night under moonlight.

Jimmy notices me lacing up my walking shoes.

"Where you off to in such a hurry?" he asks.

"I'm searching for a girl," I tell him. "It's kind of a long story."

"A girl?" Jimmy says. "This place is full of girls. She's probably at the beach."

"Maybe," I say. "But I want to check out the hostels real quick while I can."

"There's places like this one all over the island," Jimmy says. "Last time I stayed in one down the road. It's not like everyone's staying in town. You should've asked around down at the dock, bro. She could be at one of those places. Either way, like I said, she'll most likely be down at the beach, like everyone else. But why the hell you looking for one girl anyway?"

He's right, but I'm determined to check out town and the hostels. From there I'll taxi around before heading to the beach. It's a small island. If she's here, I might find her.

"Beach time!" Jimmy yells, shaking his head wildly.

"Yeah Jimeehh!" Kayne says, shaking his own head until his cheeks are practically slapping his ears.

"Brace yourself there, Romeo," Jimmy says, looking at me. "It's gonna be a long night. He's sliding on those mirrored aviators and tying a fresh, blue bandana around his head. "You can always tell the Americans," he says. "They wear big sunglasses and walk around trying to look like they're not looking at all the titty. The Europeans just look. They love it, and they know it. They don't try and hide it. I, however, enjoy the extra advantage. I can stare all day; I'm American through and through."

He's sliding the aviators down his nose and winking. "Seriously though, Jim, you should start looking at the beach. Everybody's there in the afternoon. It's where the party begins, then it's off to various bars for sunset, then dinner, then the all-nighters. Start at the beach. After that you can check the hostels, then the bars, and if all else fails, you'll probably see her at one of the all-nighters. If she's here, you'll see her, but in the meantime let's have some fun."

He's right. If she's here, I'll find her. And I should loosen up anyway. It's not good to be exuding this desperation. You'd think I'd learn. But no, I get all worked up, all caught up in expectations, stories, and dreams that don't pan out. Of course, Sabrina will be different—I can feel it. Nevertheless, Jimmy's right. I should relax, have a good time. She will, after all, be in Uganda. I don't know when, or where, but I'll find her. He's right. Just relax. Enjoy yourself.

"You're right, Jimmy," I say, sitting and unlacing my shoes. "Let's just have a good time."

"That's the spirit," Jimmy says.

Memory here's swaying and shaking, like water sloshing in a glass. I can see the water sloshing, and I can see it all happening, but it's moving so fast, and I'm not sure what's dream and what's real. I do remember the ride down the lonely, dry road to the sea. The sea's mainly a sparkling turquoise, but it's also blue and green and marine, and even brown in spots where slick-looking rocks meet land and sea. There's a curved palapa-dotted white beach stretching along a coffee-colored cliff. Half the beach is packed towel to towel, and people are splashing along the aqua shoreline. A raucous crowd's pouring entire bottles of liquor into watermelon halves and passing out wide, colorful straws, and I'm wanting to step through the towels toward the open, white beach beyond, toward what looks like a small cave in a quiet spot where water meets beach and cliff, and where there appears to be a precipice and shade. But I'm now on my knees, sipping terrible-tasting liquid from mushy water-melon, and there's a tanned blonde beside me with a bulging mound of pubic hairs. I'm trying not to look, but her pelvic bone's practically touching my nose, and I'm turning away and standing and walking back to Jimmy, who's handing me a beer. I'm having animated conversations with intelligent faces and accents, but I can't picture them. There are large speakers and a small stage set up under a blue shade tent similar to one I camp with at home if the sun's streaming through massive redwood groves or if I'm camping all open and exposed atop a grassy cliff in Big Sur where the marine and pastel colored ocean swirls below. And I'm dancing alone, but also dancing among a crowd of women with no faces, women who are as sweat-slicked as I, and who are skin-sliding and grinding with commensurate fervor and force.

Again, we're in a packed truck bed. The wind's cool, and my hand's slicking back sweaty hair, sliding down the back and side of my neck, twisting upward along my stubbly right jawbone and cheek. This I'm doing over and over, and I'm leaning my head back, eyes closed, enjoying the cool breeze flowing, as if standing two feet from a fan. The sky's darkening into grays and streaking colors interspersed with stratocumulus clouds.

We're walking and laughing our way down the maze of narrow, whitewashed alleys that wind through town. There are shops and eateries and open and closed boarded shutters in shaded blues, and my feet are stumbling across large, erratically rectangled stone tiles with thick white grout. Jimmy's handing me a gyro, and Kayne's passing a plate with cheeses and fava beans, hummus, pita bread, falafels, and dolmades. We're sitting in a shaded alley. There are large, wooden signs with erratic Greek lettering. We're walking again, entering a bar that stinks of stale beer and rotting wood. Women are dancing in bikinis and short skirts along a thirty-foot long bar and on rectangular picnic tables with iron nobs. Jimmy soon has a tray of tequila shots and a pitcher of beer and is ceremoniously explaining and showing three some girls a ritual involving twisting his hips, circling the shot glass above his head, slamming the shot, and guzzling half a pint of fizzing beer. We're all partaking, and others around are partaking, and we're dancing and soon slicked in sweat again. Kayne's doing head spins, then the worm, and when he stands he looks slathered in grease. The entire bar's watching him and laughing. A woman with curly dark hair and sparkling green eyes is dancing before me with an empty bottle on her head. Her body's gyrating slowly, and her head's swaying but staying flat. She's staring into me. She puts the bottle aside and pulls me into her. She's unbuttoning my shirt, and grinding. Her sweaty breasts are sliding across my slickened chest and across the key at the end of my necklace. We're kissing. We're outside. It's quiet. We're in the back of a truck again. It's cold, but it feels good. There's a moonbeam across the sea. We're at the house, stripping and stumbling over one another. We're on the balcony, naked under ivory moonlight. Her green eyes are occasionally meeting mine, and I'm staring into yellow flecks and deep, dilated pupils. We're on the bed, lying still, breathing heavily. Sweat's dripping from my hair and streaking down my right upper cheek, it's dripping down my pectorals, into my armpits, and onto the white cotton sheets. There's an ocean breeze ruffling sheer white drapes. My head's spinning. I think I'm falling asleep.

Next thing Jimmy's standing over me. I don't at first recognize him.

"Hey there, Stallion," he says, draping a sheet over my naked body. "Where's the girl?"

"What?"

"The girl. Where'd she go?"

He turns on a lamp. It's bright. I'm squinting.

"What?" I ask.

"The girl," he says, "where's the girl?"

I'm rising, planting my feet on the floor. The room's spinning. I'm reaching for the key, but the necklace is cut and the key is gone. My head and eyes are moving toward the closet. The safe's open, cavernous and empty.

CHAPTER TEN

Australia 1993/94

"The first thing you learn in life is you're a fool. The last thing you learn is you're the same fool. Sometimes I think I understand everything. Then I regain consciousness."

—Ray Bradbury

AT HOME THE morning's still singing its song. The birds, the smell of wet grass drenched in sunlight. I make coffee and take my place on the couch, under the window and the birds. I lean left, flick a match into flame, light the vanilla candle, and revel in its smoky vanilla smell. My stack of books, my own little monument, adorns the small coffee table, the one Shirley gave us. I'm reading. My head's bobbing. I need to sleep, but my routine's become all-important, and I'm reluctant to surrender. What just happened, though, and what happened last week, is stirring ominous thoughts—present, past, and future—like lumps of clay rolled together. That thought: *How lucky I've been.* All the stupid things I've done in my life. Those late nights in high school, driving all tipsy and stoned. I could've been pulled over and thrown in jail, abused, abused some more, turned hard and cynical, kicked out of school, labeled "bad" and "corrupted." I could've damn killed someone. I've been around people who brewed trouble like their morning coffee. Some people get in trouble for stupid things. Others don't. The difference between staying out of trouble and not is often an abstract line. *How lucky I've been.* Is it because I'm white with smart, respectable parents? Is it because I'm from Irvine? Or is it something that I've done, some way I've interacted with the world? That abstract line between success and failure, innocence and guilt. Perhaps it'll all catch up with me. I'm thinking, again, of our first year in Australia and those worries that've gotten lost in the routine, the work, the pleasure of the mornings, the stories told under clouds. But I've been getting dragged again. We should get out while we can. I should go home while I can. A storm's brewing. Those dark clouds stretched across the luminous and translucent seas. But they're there, those looming clouds, and I'm unsure what's just neurosis and what're ominous signs, messages from beyond, inscribed in blood and gold. Life here's too comfortable. Perhaps I've become too trusting, lost my edge. Too much head rolling and half-closed eyes as I weave Shirley's bike into the early morning ocean breeze. My head's still bobbing. I hardly slept last night.

The other day I got off work at four a.m. and went surfing with one of the cooks, Laughlin, a man with one of the strangest faces I've ever seen. It's a bony face, his eyes too big, his mouth too small, his nose flat, his hair too thin, and his skin blotched with white and brown spots. He's been bugging me for weeks to join him. He's driving like a madman, the beat-up, blue El Camino rattling along, squealing and sliding around corners. He's screaming over the blaring engine.

"We gotta get it early, the blue jellies will swarm us like a son-of-a-bitch! They'll come in with the tide, mate, we gotta beat the tide!"

The sun's beginning to shine through a quickly dissolving fog. There's a long pipeline that stretches out like a round pier between two jetties. Sea birds circle and stand along the ocean's edge, the wind-blown beach and the smooth and tan sloping dunes. We're running along the top, the plateau of a steep dune, the sand chilling our feet. We're jumping off a miniature cliff, and running towards the ocean.

It's then that we see it. It's definitely not a log or a bunch of seaweed, and I remember hearing about people drowning over the weekend. Half of Australia had converged on Surfers Paradise for the New Year's celebration. It was a drunken but peaceful affair. Women threw kisses like confetti. Even the cops were kissing girls, and the place was littered with red roses. The ocean though was black and churning and uninviting, and it'd swallowed four people. I'm remembering that the currents run north.

"Shit Laughlin," I say, "It's one of those bodies."

"No waaay," he says. "Let's take a look."

I'm stopping, curious of course, but stopping, for there's a figure standing at the top of a dune. The cops, I can only assume, won't be far behind.

Laughlin's standing over the lifeless shell that looks like a huge and tattered and unrecognizable stuffed animal, the lapping waves rocking flesh and bone. This once living and breathing and crying person, reduced to a lump of dead, inert flesh. I'm wondering who they'd been, whether they'd had dreams and experienced love, and I'm staring. The face is green and blue and white, swollen, and the body lies bloated and awkwardly twisted. Small chunks of flesh are missing, as if bitten off.

A voice from the dunes. "Don't even think about touching that. That's right, back away. No, farther than that. And stay there. I wanna talk to you."

We're walking along the shoreline. The sand's cold beneath our feet. The fog's lifting, and there's now a warm and whistling offshore breeze. Stay calm. He just wants to ask routine questions. He could care less about you. Just two guys going surfing. That's all. Just surfing. Let Laughlin talk.

The cop's trudging through the sand toward us.

"Did you touch it?" he asks.

"No, sir," Laughlin says, shaking his head. "Just looking. Never seen one, you know?"

I'm nodding, averting my eyes, but trying not to be too obvious. The cop might've seen my picture.

"How long you been here?"

"Not but a minute, sir," Laughlin says. "Pretty messed up, I reckon."

"All right guys," the cop says, "go surfing."

The morning after the dead body, I mention my trepidations to Kayne, tell him I've been thinking about going home soon, about what to do with my life, that I've a feeling we'd better get out while we can. I tell him I'm leaving, with or without him. But he just says, "You gone thinkin' too much again? What're we gonna do at home?"

Not in the mood to talk, I just leave it alone. He knows, however, that I'm ready for college, thinking big, and he knows we'll have to leave soon. If we're gonna go south with time to saunter, we'll have to start moving before our visas expire in three weeks. As if reading my mind, he says, "Reckon it's time for a party, Skinny."

The other night a gang of bikers came into the Beach Road, said they'd heard Kayne was a crazy motherfucker and that they like crazy motherfuckers. Kayne says he likes them because they're smelly and most of them have a pig-belly like him, but he's just trying to rile me up. He's now saying he's gonna have them over for dinner and a few hundred tinnies, and that they're gonna bring their "house" girls. He's really laying it on thick, and with stuff like this I can never tell if he's serious or not.

"Just a few friends, Skinny," he says.

"We both know what that means," I say, "And that's all we need. Your high school parties almost got me thrown in jail."

"Just a few friends, no problem."

All I can do is plan our escape and pray he's not serious.

Hanah and I are lying on the roof, our arms and legs spread wide, the subtle feel of tiny roof rocks under our blanket. There are no clouds tonight, but stars are unusually splattered across a crystal clear sky. It isn't a complete and utter awe-inspiring splatter, but we can make out the Milky Way, and it's still wondrous and worthy of extended observation. Like with clouds, we each point out shapes and forms, and it's amazing how, if one looks long enough, forms change and imagination continually discovers new sights. The stars, unlike the clouds, aren't moving before our eyes, but our minds, if allowed time and space, see new shapes. Like with clouds, we point out our visions to one another, explain, and sometimes even tell small stories connecting one shape to another—an animal family or a tribe or colleagues in an office. It's as if imagination is literally fueled by more staring into this magical space, this sky where tiny glimpses into wondrousness taps infinite creativity. It doesn't always happen. Often I'm thinking about too many things. But when we lie around long enough, when we stop talking and stare and breathe long enough, our imaginations soar, and our visions and explanations feel fresh and real. Lately, I've been reading books on science, its history and the continually evolving field of quantum physics, and I can't help but wonder if these books are fueling my thoughts. Our fingers are touching, and I want to hold her hand. But I'm inching it away 'cause I can't think straight.

Hanah says, "So at this point in the story, you haven't even met Sabrina?"

"No," I say, "Hadn't even talked to her."

"Then why the urgency to find her?" Hanah asks. "Why change all your plans?"

"I don't know," I say. "I just had to meet her. I had a feeling, you know. And we didn't have any real plans, that was the point."

"But didn't you have a flight out of Athens?"

"Yes," I say, "but we had time, and we weren't thinking much about it."

"So what is that?" Hanah asks. "How do you fall in love with someone you haven't even talked to?"

"I don't know," I say, "It's just a fantasy, I guess."

"I'm just wondering," Hanah says, staring off. After some silence, she says, "You did get to see a bunch of places you might not have otherwise. And you did experience love, yes?"

"Yes," I say, "we did. And I guess I experienced love. I'm just not sure anymore."

"And following your instincts has brought you back here," she says, "which feels right to me."

"Yes," I say, "that's true. And it feels right to me too, despite the risks."

"You've really helped me, Jim." Hanah says, "I still don't know what I'm going to do in the next few months, and I don't know what I'm going to do with my life, but meeting you guys, reading your stories and talking to you has reminded me that traveling freely is worthwhile in itself and can help me figure things out. Before I met you, I was feeling like I was wasting time. But now I see what an opportunity this is."

"It is," I say, "isn't it? We're very lucky."

"I'm even learning to surf," Hanah says.

"That's awesome," I say. "It's the best."

Her hand's clasping mine, and she's squeezing and holding it as we watch more long and wispy clouds float across the sky. I'm thinking about her naked body, and I'm getting all worked up, so I release her hand and try to remember what we were talking about.

"What're you going to do when we leave?" I ask. I know she's been thinking of leaving herself. She likes Peter, and Peter's harmless, but I can tell it'll be awkward when we leave, and I know she's wondering if Peter will get all weird. I also know she doesn't want to deal with finding new roommates. I can't blame her. I wouldn't want to deal with it either. Us leaving might pressure her into making decisions, and I can tell she's struggling with this. I'm thinking about how I can help her, but I really have no answers.

"I don't know," she says. "I really don't know."

I'm nodding. As expected.

"Tell me about the two science books you've been reading," Hanah says. "I was looking through them the other day. And tell me how they found you. I always love that."

"There are actually three," I say. "The first one, *The Turning Point*, by Fritjof Capra, was lying on a dorm bed in Poland, with a note that read, *If you're interested in the history of science, read this book*. I felt as if the note was written just for me. The second book, *Dancing Wu Li Masters*, by Gary Zukav, was given to me by an Argentinian guy I met at a hostel in Nairobi. We were on our way to Uganda, and we were only there for one morning, but this Argentinian guy, Leandro, was reading this book, and we started talking, and we talked and talked, and he was as into this stuff as I am. We both happened to be finishing our books, so I gave him mine and he gave me his. He invited me to Buenos Aires, and I invited him to California. You know how it goes. I have a feeling I'll see him in the future. The third book, the one I'm finishing now, is called *Wholeness and the Implicate Order* by this guy, David Bohm, a physicist from Princeton who was colleagues with Albert Einstein. This book was a gift from my dad's ex-girlfriend who I was just sailing with."

"The hot one with the crazy husband?"

"Yes," I say, "more stories."

"Can't wait."

"She'd asked my dad if there was anything she could get me, and he'd told her to get this book. I'd written my dad a letter and mentioned how much I was enjoying the history of quantum physics and such, and I'd told him what I was reading. He mentioned it to a colleague of his who raved about this David Bohm book. So my dad had Ana Paoula get it for me. And it couldn't have come at a better time because I was ready for a new history book, and it was wonderful to have during our sailing adventures. The point of all this is that these books keep amazingly finding me. And it's not just these books, it's all my books, the philosophy, the history, the novels, you name it. And they all lead to so many other books. Sometimes, when another book is referred to, I get this deep feeling that I should read it. And now I've got a list as long as my forearm."

"So what is that?" Hanah asks. "Is it intuition?"

"I don't know," I say, "but that's part of why I find all of this so fascinating. I'm experiencing all these things, this kind of synchronicity of events. When I'm able to just go with the flow, to not overthink stuff, things seem to happen that feel like they were meant to happen. We meet the right people, go the right places, and all feels right. Everything that happens isn't necessarily good, but if I'm calm, if my thoughts aren't going wild, if I'm not partying too much and all, I do feel as if I'm on the right path—as crazy and illogical as that path may be. And all my studies, all of these books, are part of this process. They're amazingly finding me, and they're all about this crazy process I'm talking about. Some, like these history of science books, are teaching me about how quantum physics is changing our understanding of the universe and our place in it."

"And what does quantum physics have to do with it? Please, I love when you explain things."

"Kayne says I explain too much."

"Well I love it. Please ..."

"Okay," I say. "If you insist. The quantum physics stuff is just verifying all these other things I'm learning and thinking about, even, like I said, experiencing. I mean, how do all these coincidences just happen? Why do some things just feel right? I'm planning on going to Thailand and to India, you know, so I've been reading about Buddhism and about Hinduism, and this quantum physics stuff's related to it all. These Buddhist and Hindu texts describe a universe and a world that's fundamentally connected, a giant web. Nothing exists outside of anything else. We're essentially part of the stars and the rocks and each other. According to these philosophies, how we perceive and how we act in this world makes all the difference, and because all's connected, we really do sow what we reap.

Whether we realize it or not, we're all continually creating ourselves and the world, and vice versa. Most people are just bumbling along, and that's where they are. That's what they do. We all do what we do. But if we can become conscious of the process, we can gain control over our lives. We are both creation and creator. If all's intricately interconnected, then everything we do affects everything else, and everything that happens is essentially a reflection of everything that we do, everything we are. It's hard to see, and quite frankly, I don't know what it all means, what it means about myself, but I do see it, and I do see the interconnection of all of these ideas. Metaphysics and psychology, biology—you name it, every ology there is—they're all analyzing the world through their own lens, and each is a valuable piece of the whole. What I'm seeing, and what I'm reading about in different ways, is how all of this is integrated, how it all fits together, and how, if this is true, the synchronicity of events that I'm experiencing actually makes sense. You and I meeting, you making me write down these stories, us talking and helping each other out, us sitting here right now talking about all this stuff, everything that's happened to us—it all fits together if viewed holistically. But we humans—myself included, of course, because I can see it in my own mind, in my own thinking—are rarely able to perceive the whole; our minds unconsciously analyze everything; our minds compartmentalize everything based on all these seemingly endless variables—some we can see, some we can't. But underneath it all, underneath everything, is this essence, this core connection, and it's why synchronicity is real."

"So where does the quantum physics come in?" Hanah asks.

"Yes, thank you," I say. "These quantum physicists are validating that this interconnected web exists. They're studying the subatomic world (you know, electrons and protons and all of that), and they're seeing that beneath the surface, the world's wonderfully and mysteriously complex. It's the usual scientific story. New technology allows us to see more, see deeper, and from that imagination soars, new theories arise, and new experiments try to make sense of it all, to separate fact from fiction.

"Isaac Newton was a genius, way ahead of his time," I continue. "But he was limited by his technology. His remarkable equations do in fact explain much of the physical world. And his math adds up. On one level, one plus one always equals two. But in the subatomic world, as this quantum physics guy Heisenberg's shown, one plus one sometimes doesn't equal two. There's a deeper level. There's more going on. There's mystery. The Newtonian world, the scientific paradigm of the last three hundred plus years, the one which the modern world's based on, viewed the Universe like a giant clock, one that could be taken apart and reassembled, a clock with clear parts and structure, a clock engineered by God. And we humans, with our brains and our ability to reason, could decipher this engineering, 'cause that's what we humans do—we seek to understand, to control, to create structure. And Newton did. His equations explain so much. It's freaking unbelievable! This model of understanding, however, this paradigm, as they call it, created a kind of mechanistic view of the universe, one in which we, the observer, the interpreter of this clock, was separate from the clock itself. It assumed we were objective observers, and this had major philosophical implications of which we could talk on and on about. The point is that the new science, this quantum physics I'm reading about, is moving toward a new understanding of the Universe, one in which everything, and I mean everything, is connected, an ongoing creation story in which we, every last one of us, are participating. We're not separate. There's no 'us' and 'it'; there's no duality, as the Eastern religions call it. The key seems to be stopping our incessant thoughts long enough to allow insight and imagination to percolate, to see clearly. That's why I'm reading about meditation and different prayers, and that's why I want to go do that meditation retreat in Thailand I was telling you about."

Hanah's clasping my hand again. "You have such a way of explaining things," she says. "I love it. You're going to be a teacher, yes?"

"Who knows," I say. "I just want to keep studying. I do like the idea of learning for a living, and I guess teaching involves that."

"It sure does," Hanah says. "I think it's your calling."

"Perhaps," I say. "Whatever the case, thanks for listening and making me think, and thanks for making me write down my stories. As worried as I sometimes get, I do feel good being back here, and I do feel a sense of synchronicity."

"I love it," Hanah says.

"You've seen the connections all along," I say. "And you don't get in your own way like I do. My brain's too damn analytical."

"I guess we all get in our own way sometimes," Hanah says.

"Yes," I say, "Some more than others."

I want to lie here all night with Hanah. I want to pull the blanket over us, make love under this wondrous sky. But I

don't. We'll be leaving soon. It's just better. And the clouds
have rolled in thick, as if one plump cloud had stopped, and
the others had plowed into it and expanded in every direction
until stars and the crystal clear sky were old and new dreams.
I'm trying to relax and accept life, to listen to God, to be. But
each moment, each second, is a test, over and over and over,
and one lost second becomes lost minutes then hours then
days. I shall try to stay present. And now the clouds are gray.
It'll rain soon. We must go inside.

The next night I'm sitting on the roof, taking in the sunset,
when suddenly there's this tremendous roar, the house shaking
beneath me. Bikers. They're lining their choppers along one end
of the parking lot. Six bikes, three with women. Hanah's still
at work. I'm watching the road. The police can't be far behind.

They're quiet as they're climbing the stairs and standing at the front door, but then Kayne greets them with cold
beers, and now they're all noisily raving about what a good
and proper mate he is.

I'm hesitant to move. Perhaps I should leave while I can.
Just split and come back later. If Kayne's little party doesn't
get busted, great. If it does, I could wait it out, send Hanah
or Peter to see about Kayne. I need clothes, though. I need
my passport. I need our stash of money, and there's no way I
could sneak in unnoticed. I'm like a hummingbird listening
in on hawks and vultures, and no hummingbird in its right
mind wants to fly into such a flock. I'm just a kid from Irvine.
Kayne at least has the belly and the crazy look in his eyes. I'm
probably everything they hate in the world.

I'm sitting and listening and thinking about it for a while, and then I decide to go in. Someone'll have to watch over things. I can always sneak out if I have to. Kayne can dig his own grave. I'm messing up my hair and making my way below.

The kitchen counter's already covered in beer cans. Kayne and the others are laughing in the back. I'm cleaning when one of the bikers approaches. "G'day mate," he says, handing me a beer. His eyes are jumpy, and yet he's calm. He's thin and heavily tattooed, and his dark hair's short, slicked back, with wild and curly graying tufts.

"Name's Sick Sammy," he says. "Appreciate your hospitality, mate."

I'm smiling, raising my beer, guzzling until it's gone. "Shall I call you Sick Sammy or just Mr. Sick?" I ask.

"Mr. Sick," he says. "I like that. Nice one, mate."

I'm stepping into the kitchen, grabbing another beer, watching the others walking toward me. Sick Sammy's introducing me. I'm nodding and observing. Everyone's wearing denim jackets with big patches on the back of a cartoon-looking character in a sombrero, holding a long sword, framed by the words "Bandidos Worldwide." The men all have windblown manes, tied into ponytails or hanging wild like a male lion. Of the three women, two have short leather skirts revealing far too much bruised leg. Everyone's smiling and laughing and talking animatedly.

Sick Sammy's standing beside me in the kitchen.

"They always have this much fun?" I ask.

"Pretty much, mate."

I'm twisting my head to read the saying on his jacket. It's small and etched in cursive.

He's noticing and turning. "We are the people our parents warned us about," he says.

"My mom, I've come to see, was usually right," I say, feeling a moment of shock, realizing that might sound insulting.

"My mum was always right mate. Guess we should've listened to our mums, eh? Never too late, I reckon." He's smiling, watching Kayne talking and laughing and making his crazy Eskimo faces. "Your friend's fuckin' funny, mate," he says. "So what you doing with yourself here, Jim?"

I'm telling him about Charlie's Cafe and about all the great waves, telling him we've been doing the travel thing for a couple plus years. And he's standing there listening to me in a way that keeps me talking, and I'm now going on and on about feeling on this mission to follow my whims, and how I'm wallowing in my studies and writing and trying to figure out what the hell to do with my life.

He asks, "What do you like, mate?"

"What do I like?"

"Yeah," he says. "No thoughts, no analysis, whaddaya like?" He's turning and facing me, not menacingly, but in a way that's causing me to stand tall and breathe.

"I like to read, to learn, to write. I like to surf and have a good time. I like to travel. I like trying to understand people and the world."

"Well," he says, "there you go. That's what you're gonna create your life around. And what are you good at? Again, without thinking about it."

"I'm good with words. I can read stuff and explain it. I see connections between things; I see the interconnection of ideas. And I get along with people pretty well. I'm good at understanding people. I feel for people, you know? I care."

"Good," he says, "you're a good bloke. That's good. And what's your dream?"

"My dream?"

"Your dream, you know, what you *want* out of life. What are you gonna create? What's your vision, your dream? To envision it is to move toward it."

He's asking this like he's asking what kind of beer I like. It reminds me of my tutor, Mr. Cipoletta. The matter-of-factness. The simplicity. The sureness with which he speaks. Dreams, to Mr. Cipoletta, are as natural as animals seeking prey. They're primal. Some actually say we were born with them. 'Cip' often mentioned C.G. Jung. We all have them, he says, but too many take their eye off the ball. And it causes so many of the world's problems.

"No one's asked me that in a long time," I say. "I'm not sure anymore. It was to travel, to wander, and to wander some more. And that's what we've been doing."

"And when do you go home?"

"I don't know. I guess that's what I'm trying to figure out. I just want to keep learning."

"Now's a good time to figure it out, mate. I reckon my head's the clearest when I'm wandering free. It's why we love the bikes. Travel's a gift that can align head and heart. I never make a big decision without giving myself some space to clear my head, to settle myself. Freedom's a gift, mate. Take advantage of it."

"And what about you?" I ask. "What's your dream?"

"I'm gonna own a Harley Davidson dealership. Right off a major highway. It'll have a small pub and coffee area, even a library with biker and touring books."

"And how's it going?"

"Working on it, mate. Working on it."

The counter's filling up with more and more beers and everyone's getting rowdy. There's a big, round, hairy guy named Bongo who says he's always wanted to be in a circus, and he and Loose Lenny, the smallest—yet smelliest—of the bunch, are now showing us their "act," the "helicopter" they call it. Bongo's spinning Loose Lenny by arm and leg, knocking over beers and food and a picture on the wall before dropping him face down onto the couch that cracks at one end. Everyone's drunk and laughing, but Sick Sammy gets angry with Bongo and smacks him around, and it's funny to see a smaller guy smacking around a big bear. Sick Sammy's yelling about having more respect, and he insists on paying for all damages. Even better, while the party continues, he fixes it himself. He gathers the wood, cuts some pieces with a small saw, and nails it all in place. Good as new.

In the morning it's quite a sight to see the creatures passed out, snoring and slobbering, while the birds sing their morning song. Hanna looks horrified as she takes in the damage and the mess. The couch is fixed, but our one picture's cracked, the frame dangling, and beer cans are everywhere, along with several piles of ash throughout the living room. But once again, Sick Sammy surprises me. He's just waking, but seeing Hannah's horror he orders the boys to "hop to and clean up this damn place." He even sends Bongo out for a new frame. Half an hour later the place is good as new, and Sick Sammy starts talking about going on a sapphire run. He says he wants to pay us back for the fun, that we'll make some quick cash and experience an Australian adventure. He's walking off to tell Kayne, and I'm following him down the hall. The bathroom door's swinging open. I'm looking at Kayne from behind, shaking my head. And Kayne gets it, says we've got family coming into town..

CHAPTER ELEVEN

Irvine 1981

Faith: Before going into battle, you must believe in the reasons for the fight.

Companions: Choose your allies and learn to fight in company, for no one ever won a war single-handedly.

Time: A battle in winter is different from a battle in summer; a good warrior is careful to select the right moment to begin a fight.

Space: One does not fight in the same way in a mountain pass as one would on a plain.

Think about your surroundings and how to best move around them.

Strategy: The best warrior is the one who plans his fight.

—Chuan Tzu's 5 Rules of Combat (written 3,000 years ago)

MR. HERRIGAN'S BEEN talking about WWI. He says he's not supposed to talk about it, that it's outside what they tell him to teach, but he likes to talk about whatever he wants sometimes, and he's reading some books about World War I, so that's what he talks about. He usually does all the stuff he's supposed to do—The Renaissance, European explorers, early America, colonies, and on and on, not to mention math and English and everything else—but often he's talking about random stuff like computer technology, spacecrafts, or some crazy story about worms living under peoples' skin or deep sea creatures that look like aliens. He says we might soon be talking through computer screens to people anywhere in the world, that money might disappear, become all electronic, and that we could all eventually get little electronic chips as wallets. He says in forty years we kids might be driving cars that drive themselves or cars that fly, and he says that scientists have been discovering stuff about the universe that'll make anyone—his eyes get all bug-eyed and crazy, and he might be crazy, I don't know—contemplate their lives and dreams in ways we can't understand 'cause they've never been thought of, and hence, don't exist. He talks about space, black holes that suck all matter, even time itself, and alternative universes that leave us laughing and wondering what's real. Most of the time, I've no idea what he's talking about, but it doesn't matter; his enthusiasm—the head shaking and eye popping—is funny, and funny's good. And he's all over the place. One moment he'll be talking about a finger found in someone's Ding-Dong, then a foot-long rat that crawled from someone's toilet, then onto flowers capable of eating one of those big bumblebees.

The other day he told us about some old Chinese guy's rules of combat, and I felt like he was talking directly to me. After class, during break, I asked him if I could write them down. He typed them out right there and handed them over, said he'd bring me a book the next day. And he did. I gotta give

Mr. Herrigan props 'cause he's not a regular boring teacher, and this talking about everything and anything keeps us all alert and wondering what's gonna happen next. The man exudes wonder. Unfortunately, everything else in school still sucks, and any social life and chances with Krissy may entirely rest on the outcome of tonight's Skate Night. Perhaps this is why I'm thinking about World War I and mustard gas clouds. I feel like I'm standing in one of those god-awful trenches, watching those clouds float my way, and I'm tempted to give up on Krissy and on everybody who doesn't understand me and never will.

Fortunately, my reconnaissance and the enlistment of Allan's help are forcing me to stay focused. Allan and the DJ are expecting me. I won't let them down, even if I myself am standing at cliff's edge, ready to give up on the world.

I'm trying on several shirts. The yellow IZOD, the OP with the skateboarder, even pondering the purple Sex Wax T-shirt. I finally settle on a navy blue IZOD and some tan OP corduroy pants that are just thick enough to make my ass look like it exists.

After helping Skip pick an outfit (a green IZOD and black corduroy pants) we're jumping into Mom's Oldsmobile, which still stinks like leftover fries. Mom must have sensed something was up 'cause she doesn't badger us with questions about our day or what we'd learned in school. And she doesn't make us suffer through the Barry Manilow eight-track. She's quiet and focused, like me, and she's playing the local rock station (The Stones' Satisfaction and AC/DC's Hells Bells), and when she drops us off, all she says is, "Just call when you want to be picked up."

"Thanks, Mom."

I see Krissy the second I walk inside. She's wearing a purple sweater, speckled with little white stars, tight Jordache jeans, and gleaming white skates with sparkling topaz wheels. Her blonde curls are pulled into two long pigtails with white bows at the ends. She's surrounded by giggling girls that move as one mass—another damn amoeba. The amoeba's sliding onto the floor, floating into the sea of people. I'm looking for Brian Daniels, glad he isn't with them, when he appears skating backward towards them, all slick and shit.

Allan's head's poking out of the Rentals window. "Hey Jim! Here, over here."

"Is that her?" he asks. "The one in the purple sweater?"

"Yeah, that's her."

"Oh, man, I've seen her before. I see what you mean." He's staring at the amoeba, then blinking and looking at me, and I figure he's either contemplating his own inability to meet girls, or he's just ascertained that she's out of my league and we're about to experience carnage.

"So here are the skates," he says. "Tight and oiled, ready to go. Speed skates are every ninety minutes. There'll be at least two tonight, first one in an hour or so. And you won't believe what I got for you." He's looking toward the snack bar where a pretty girl with straight, dark hair is walking toward us. She's older, fourteen or fifteen, and she looks annoyed. She's stopping and looking me over with dark, sexy, and pissed-off eyes.

"This is Olivia," Allan says. "My big brother's friend's sister. She kinda owes us one and is willing to act as your date tonight. My brother Fred says nothing gets a girl curious like the presence of another woman, especially a pretty, older one. And she was willing to help once she heard what'd happened."

I want to explain that I'm really not the kind of loser who always gets laughed at, and I'm curious why she owes them, but before I can speak, she squares me up and says, "Listen, shithead, you are kinda cute, but don't think I actually like you. I'll hold your hand a little, play the game, but you try and kiss me or anything and I'll kick you smack in the balls. Got it?"

"Got it."

Skip appears. "Have you seen the arcade?" he says. "There are ten Asteroids and six Defenders."

"This is my little brother, Skip," I say to Allan before turning back to Skip. "You gonna skate?"

"Hell, yes I'm gonna skate," Skip says. "I got your back, bro."

"I think I know how you can help Skip," Allan says. "Come, I'll set you up."

Olivia and I go for a skate. I'm staying close to the outside, dragging my hand along the red, carpeted wall and the smooth, rubber railing, lifting one skate deftly over the other. My eyes are half closed, and I'm focused on the sound of ball bearings and polyurethane wheels rolling across the wooden floor.

I'm watching Olivia. She skates well, and she's got a great ass.

She's looking over, and I'm looking back toward the floor, remembering what she'd said.

"So what's all this about anyway?" she says. "Some girl who laughed in your face or something?"

"Yeah, her, the one in the purple," I say, pointing without really pointing, with a nod of the head and with my elbow. "She's nice though," I assure her. "Don't think she meant to laugh. I could see it in her eyes. She was just surprised, and there was an audience, so she nervously laughed, and I've been the guy who was laughed at ever since."

"Girls can be fucking mean," Olivia says. "So who's the guy? The one clearly trying to impress her?"

"That's Brian Daniels. Mr. Popular. He's an asshole."

"I see that."

"And everyone thinks he's cool. Makes me crazy."

Olivia's smiling. "Yeah, I get that," she says, "people are just fucking stupid."

She's grabbing my hand and pulling me forward. "Come on," she says. "I know just what to do." She's turning around, skating backward, gracefully avoiding others, her fourteen-year-old ass moving side to side in slow rhythm to the "Stray Cat Strut." She's really good, and we're obviously attracting attention 'cause I can feel the eyes and see the heads turning, especially when we pass the amoeba and Olivia turns back around, puts her arm around me and whispers into my ear, "I think we got her attention."

We're making the rounds together. Video games, red licorice, some popcorn. I even win Olivia a stuffed "Tigger." Allan gave me tokens, so we're living it up. Then we're doing more laps, together but alone, and it feels good to let the legs and arms rip, to weave through people, to gain speed around corners. I'm feeling loose and ready for the speed skate. We're stopping, standing along the railing, watching the crowd float by. The amoeba's still intact, and Brian Daniels and some other goons are showing off, doing circles and swiveling between people. They keep looking over, such obvious morons, and Olivia's really playing it up, feeding me popcorn and whispering into my ear. I want to kiss her, but I remember what she'd said and that she was old and out of my league. And besides, every time the amoeba passes, Krissy's flashing me tiny glances and my heart's missing beats and Olivia's outta my mind. And Brian Daniels's watching it all, looking stupid and perplexed, even as the song's ending, the lights are dimming, and the DJ's announcing the speed skate.

The floor's clearing, and the first powerful beats of AC/DC's "Back In Black" booms from speakers above. Olivia's squeezing my shoulder. It's dark, and strobelights are streaking erratically across the floor, the ceiling, and the chest-high railing. I take several quick and choppy steps, get up to speed, and swing around the first corner, sliding toward the wall, gripping just in time. I'm back at the rink in Seattle; I've taken these corners a thousand times. The gentle and controlled sway down the straight stretch, the setup—my feet are themselves, they know exactly where to be—the shifting weight, the momentum of right foot and right leg over left, the three powerful steps, the sling, and the sliding, gripping, and controlled exit. I am this moment. All those hours, all those speed skates, have led me here, right now, and I know it. The world's watching; it can't help but watch. I am vortex and mass, the center of everything and anything. Three laps, four laps.

I notice Krissy standing behind the railing at oval's end, and I'm momentarily awakened. A hand's pushing me from behind, the spell's broken, and I'm heading straight for the railing, sliding sideways. I lower myself, slam the wall just below the railing, just below Krissy, and bounce off like a bird whacking a window. I'm shaken, my right shoulder and elbow hurt, but I'm still on my feet, still moving forward. One step, two steps, swaying, the setup, another corner, and the sling. I'm back up to speed and eyeing Brian Daniels, who's looking back. I shoot to the inside, and together we sling around the corner, scraping the wall, our arms and hands wrestling. He's kicking my skates. Bumping and wrestling is expected, but skate-kicking's practically assault. I tell him, "No skates, fuck-wad!" But he just says, "Fuck you," and keeps on kicking. We're rounding the corner, and I realize the song's about to end. He's too strong, pulling me behind him and outside, but this works to my advantage, for as we round the last turn I'm right behind him, ready to push. I'm waiting and waiting, and we're sliding toward the railing. Then, the perfect moment, and I'm pushing, and he's slamming into the railing, flipping out of the rink, end over end. The push slowed me, and I'm cruising out of the turn, catching my breath, rising, and resting my hands on both thighs just as the lights flip on, the music stops, and a low, deep voice begins to speak. I'm passing under the "Sound Garden," and Leonard the DJ is smiling. Then I hear it, the soft, slow beat of the Eagles.

I'm stunned, unsure of what to do, searching for the amoeba. Krissy's standing among the others but looking alone. Our eyes meet. I'm moving toward her, but I'm grabbed from behind.

"Come on now, Champ," Olivia says. "Can't make it too easy now."

She's guiding me into the middle of the floor, which is now again speckled, as if a star-splattered sky was turned upside down and was moving, and I'm looking for Krissy, but it's too dark, and I see nothing but other silhouettes—dark and faceless ghosts—and faceless figures in the dark regions beyond the surrounding oval railing. I'm not sure how long we've been skating, but I can feel Olivia's hand holding mine, and it's sweaty. We're off the floor now, standing in dim lights beside the snack bar. There's a large pretzel shadow on the floor, and Brian Daniels is coming toward us, his fist clenched, his face flushed red. He's stepping on the pretzel, his facial muscles contorting side to side. The lights turn on brighter than daylight, and beyond Brian Daniels, I see Allan and Skip standing together, laughing.

"You're dead, asshole," he says, but the bright light seems focused on him—all eyes are on him—and he's visibly shaken. One side of his tan shirt appears bloodstained, but as my eyes adjust, I realize it's the light-red color of cherry Icee, and I can see Skip's empty cup and his grin as wide as Montana.

Olivia's standing beside me.

"You're fucking dead," Brian Daniels says.

"Whatever, shit-for-brains," Olivia says. "I've got older brothers who are really big and really like to fight, asshole. You come near him, and you'll be hearing from us."

I'm being pulled away. We're standing by the pay phones. "You really have older brothers?" I ask Olivia.

"No," she says. "But you tell Allan if you have any problems. I do have friends. I gotta go now. Nice job there, Champ."

Skip's calling Mom. We're outside. It's cool. We're in Mom's car, in the back seat again. It's silent. We drive home in silence.

CHAPTER TWELVE

Bali, Indonesia 2014

Cloak, noun
1. A loose outer garment, as a cape or a coat.
2. Something that covers or
conceals; a disguise; pretense:
He conducts his affairs under a cloak of secrecy.

—from *Dictionary.com*

C **LOAK #1 — GOD/VOIDNESS/BIG MIND/SOURCE/TRUE SELF.** Like a fashionable robe, it is intended for my personal and private use, but also meant to wear anywhere and everywhere, a cloak meant to stroll around the house, to meditate in, to wear while praying, but also fashionable and functional enough (it can be both light and heavy as needed) to wear at all times. The exterior is navy blue, made of the finest silk, with subtle, white cuff links and an oversized white collar.

There are four exterior (and quite fashionable) pockets, each with silver buttons (real Roman coins), two interior pockets with zippers (from Egypt), a fleece layer within, removable for warmer weather (sleeves as well), and removable zippered sleeves, also for warmer weather.

Forget your body; you are not your body. Forget your thoughts; you are not your thoughts. You are not desires. You are not emotions. You are nothing—Voidness. And yet, you are everything: Eternity, Spaciousness—God. Forget everything. All you see and perceive is imagination, creation, illusion, one big show. And you think it's real 'cause you think it. And once you think it, you become. And once you become, there's friction, duality: subject and object; you and the world. So stop. Cease all thought and judgment. Become God. Settle in. Set up camp. Come back and back, and keep coming back until this place is home. You are That. Beautiful Emptiness. So watch and listen without watching and listening. You are timeless; birth and death are mental constructs. You were never born, and you'll never die. You are not your thoughts. You are not separate. You are not of this world; you are the world. You are silence—The Silence. Eternity. Time itself. Words and thoughts will never understand. All perception's forever limited; all fall from grace the moment they perceive. God is everything, nothing, all love, all hate, every moment, every creed and creation. Inexplicable Nature. Planets spinning in ever-expanding space. Wonder. And in silence—remember, without remembering—the universe speaks an unspoken language to every

Self that's united with itself and with the all-connected Universal Self. It's life's compass, its heartbeat. So listen, just listen. But be patient, for God works in mysterious ways. God may make you wait. God may make you suffer. But there's sense to it all, even if it makes no sense. So get off the thought train, have faith, and surrender.

My stories remind me to stay open to people who may appear unexpectedly. At home, among routines and friends, it's easy to dismiss people. Makes me wonder what magic I might've squandered in recent years. For one needn't travel to wallow in magic.

This was apparent when yesterday I met a young Norweigian man in the monkey forest. He says his name's unpronounceable, so he goes by Lucas. He's tall and tan and fresh. He has long, lean muscles, shoulder-length fine, blond hair, and clear blue eyes. He's asking me what I'm writing, and his openness and optimism, at first, strike the usual chords of disgust. You're so young, so naive, so disgustingly fresh. Experience, real life, and knowledge will beat you down. Better prepare yourself. I know, you see, I'm superior, learned, forged by life's fires. Youth and privilege and freedom are making it easy to wander carelessly. You're right now tuning into God, into a silence and bliss where answers and direction line up like dutiful soldiers. But you'll see; you'll see.

"Might as well be one of these monkeys," I say. "So I write. The act is balm; it's catharsis, cohesive. In a way, it transcends thoughts. But then again, of course, it doesn't. But I've failed in this too, this writing. For what've I to show? More thoughts. More concepts. Piles of shit."

"You say the title is *Confessions of a Cloak Artist*?" he says. "And what are cloaks?"

"My purpose defined," I say. "Thought structures. Worldviews. Cloaks. They're tried and true principles, but they're still what I 'think'. And I'm tired of what I 'think,' tired of what everyone damn 'thinks.' It's all I see, everywhere I look, every word I hear—what everyone damn 'thinks.' Used to believe I was building knowledge. Now I see I'm just another person thinking. And where's that gotten me?"

There it is, my unenlightened state exposed, my anger. Perhaps he'll leave me alone now.

"I don't believe you," he says.

"Don't believe what?"

"That you don't believe in knowledge."

"You're right," I say. "But again, I'm tired of what I 'think.'"

"I understand," he says. "I think I do. So you've written out these cloaks, they're part of this novel you're writing?"

"Yes," I say. "But they've failed me, so what's the point?"

"I see," he says. His large, blue eyes have a glint and a depth that's unusual in such a young man. "So what's wrong with them?"

There it is, as expected. "They just haven't worked," I say. "And if something doesn't work, what's the fucking point?"

"I see," he says. "But specifically."

"Specifically," I say, "they're just more words, what I 'think.'"

It's getting dark, especially here in the shade of the trees. The Norweigian's processing as thoughtful people do. I've written nothing, produced nothing. We say our good-byes. Perhaps we'll meet again. We exchange email addresses, a lone traveler's creed. Used to be phone numbers and addresses. Faceless aquaintances around the world. He wants me to email him if I experience some kind of breakthrough. I tell him not to hold his breath. He's walking away, down the leaf-littered concrete path that winds though bamboo archways. Several times he stops, turns, and looks, as if he's about to walk back. Then he finally puts his head down and plugs forward, up some rain-beaten concrete steps, and disappears.

Lucas, the Norweigian with the unpronounceable name, is back. He wants to read my stories, just like Hanah.

The woman with purple looped earrings is picking yellow flowers from a plump green shrub, whispering words of respect, and dropping them onto the lime-green grass below. She's gathering them, cupping them in her calloused hands, and diligently placing them into several stone bowls filled with rainwater. She's placing one on the table beside me and my books, and she's placing others on various pedestals around the garden. I'm smiling. Lucas is smiling. She's smiling back. Dark clouds drift above the steep Balinese roof and the dragonesque sculptures that adorn each corner. There's a papaya tree. There's a mango tree. There are coconuts lining the ledge just outside the nearby kitchen. A small red and yellow bird sits atop one.

I'm settling into the peace that travel and unstructured time allows. My time is of course still structured, but with more of it, it's easier to get all routines accomplished, to create space. Sometimes I might repeat my morning routine in the early evening, especially if, like today, it feels like rain's coming. I've just meditated, read some of the Upanishads, some Indonesian history, a bit about Woodrow Wilson boarding a ship to Paris in 1918, and a few pages of the poetic and imaginative prose of Italo Calvino's *Invisible Cities*, prose that sometimes makes me feel small but more often inspires magic. It's good Lucas showed up when he did, for if he'd interrupted that, I might've sent him away.

He's looking at my surfboard. He starts asking questions. I've surfed thirty-five years. He's surfed on and off for five, whenever he could get away. He lived in Australia for several months, in Coolangatta and near Kirra. He'd fallen in love with a blonde girl named Mae. He'd almost stayed. Just came from New Guinea where he'd surfed waves too shallow and been forced to stay on land. Went hunting for tree kangaroos with local tribesman, bought a kangaroo to save it, and gave it to a family who'd smiled and promised to make it their pet. Next day they said it ran away. There were strips of hanging meat, but he said nothing.

Last year he'd gone to Thailand for a ten-day silent meditation retreat, walked through miles of steaming jungle, lived a strictly scheduled ascetic and silent life, and read a wonderful book by Buddhadasa Bhikku. He's not bragging. The stories are flowing like rain and rivers. He wandered around India reading Krishnamurti and Osho and Gurdjieff. He's now reading the Bible and has a stack of others at home, the Dhammapada, the Torah, the Koran, the Bhagavad Gita, the Upanishads, Patanjali's Yoga Sutras. He wants to read them all; he wants to read everything. He's asking if I've read them. I'm nodding. He's nodding. His father in Norway was a priest, always talked spirituality and religion. We're sitting in silence, breathing in the smell of sweet smoke and the air, which is cooling. I'm telling him I'd done the same meditation retreat twenty years earlier, had read the same book, had also wandered around India reading everything that came my way, tell him I'd met Krishnamurti's grandson, had chai tea with him along the Ganges river on a sweltering, monsoon summer day.

"Suon Mokk?" he says. "The monastery? The meditation retreat?"

"Yes, Suon Mokk."

He's shaking his head. He's me twenty years ago, except he's better, fresher, calmer, yet to make my many mistakes. I'm wondering if he will. I'm wondering if he can maintain such calm. Will life's fires burn or forge? The world's on fire, and he's calm. And so am I—at the moment. He saw me, however, in my usual unhappy state, yet he's still here. He walked away, but he came back.

The woman with the purple looped earrings is walking up the stone steps, cupping a small saucer with a paper mache candle that's flickering and emitting dark smoke that's now turning gray. She's placing the paper-mache candle on the ledge below the palm fronds, the ledge that distant bright green and terraced rice paddy hills lay beyond. There are large orange flowers with yellow stamens, landing pads for thumb-sized bumblebees; or perhaps thick dragon flies with yellow stripes, I can't tell.

CHAPTER THIRTEEN

Traveling 1992

"Dreams, as we all know, are very queer things: some parts are presented with appalling vividness, with details worked up with the elaborate finish of jewelery while others one gallops through, as it were, without noticing them at all, as, for instance, through space and time.

—Fyodor Dostoyevsky,
The Dream of a Ridiculous Man

JIMMY'S LATCHED ONTO us like a tick, following us to Israel as if it's as natural as the rising and setting sun. And now we're indebted. He's lent us enough money to get to Israel, and he's hell-bent on going with us. Says he's heard loads about hot Israeli women, that it's just the unexpected turn he'd been hoping for, and that he's gotta roam wild before going back to the states where he's gonna live in L.A. and become a big shot. He seems, on one hand, to know where he's going in life, and yet there's something almost childish about him, like he's stuck in this persona he began creating when he was twelve; he's stuck, he knows it, and yet it goes unarticulated; he knows no way out, and until he does, he cannot speak or act on the matter. It makes me wonder where I myself might be stuck, what hubs of regression might lie within, undetected, unrecognized, unabolished.

I like Jimmy. He means well. He's funny and quick to get a party going. But he's more trouble waiting to happen. I can't help but partly blame him for us getting our money stolen. If we hadn't met him, if he hadn't pushed the partying in Greece, it might've never happened, and right now I'd be moving toward Sabrina. Instead, we've lost our money again—all of it—and even Kayne's out of answers. But answers have found us. Next morning, Jimmy's telling some girls about our predicament, and one of them mentions Israel. Apparently, they're build-ing big hotels in Southern Israel, in Eilat, a growing tourist destination at the northern tip of the Red Sea. It'll take us six weeks of nothing but work, but we'll have saved enough to get to Uganda, to keep traveling, moving forward. It's a no-brainer. We'd spend too much money if we stayed in Greece or went north back into the heart of Europe to work, so off we go to Israel. All we'll have to do is get back to Cairo where we already have a pre-arranged flight to Nairobi, and as bad as this scenario is—having to work our asses off and having to wait six weeks to find Sabrina—I'm again in awe of larger powers and destinies, for our pre-arranged flight in and out of Nairobi makes Uganda possible, and thus makes finding Sabrina possible.

I'm remembering Kayne and I standing before that huge map of potential destinations, the major airline hubs lit up like little red lampposts. Paris was an obvious choice, a starting point for a European tour. We'd considered Madrid, considered starting with an Iberian Peninsula tour, but this naturally led to Morocco, and it was clear that we'd have to limit ourselves. Instead, we'd decided to save this region for future trips, to start with Paris, saunter our way through Europe, end with an exploration of Italy, then fly out of Rome to Cairo. Istanbul, of course, was an unexpected side-trip, and so it goes. I remember standing there, staring at Africa, imagining wondrous animals roaming and jungles full of hand-sized bugs. Elephants and gorillas and thick, red earth. We needed a taste, and Kenya was the logical choice. We figured we'd be low on money, ready to shoot off to Australia for work. And now, this choice appears destined, at least that's the story.

It's been a long journey, first on a weathered tugboat to Crete, then on this small modern cruise ship where we lucked into three half-price tickets straight to Alexandria. And here I must credit Jimmy, for he made it happen; he was, in this case, willpower. It was either get to Athens and fly to Cairo or Tel Aviv, or find a way across the Mediterranean and across the Sinai to Israel.

Flights are too expensive, and every ferryman's saying no. But Jimmy keeps talking. He's asking around, talking up newcomers until he's overheard by a quiet Slovenian girl and her flirtatious friend who'd just come from Crete. They say there's a large cruiseship in port there, that they'd just met three Canadian girls who were all excited for having secured passage to Alexandria. Jimmy walks straight to where the Crete ferries depart, and within twenty minutes we're on our way. The sun, the swirling and salty breeze, the wonder of it all; if we'd left ten minutes later we'd have missed the cruise ship, and the Crete ferries were done for the day. A tugboat full of said-to-be modern-day traders is our savior, a boatload of surly men arguing loudly in a multitude of Mediterranean tongues. On Crete, the small cruise ship might as well've been the Queen Mary, so majestic and immovable was she, her tall black hull blotting out the sky. The man guarding the gangway is as surly as the traders and as immovable as the ship. But Jimmy keeps talking, keeps pushing; "no" is not an option.

Horns blow and ropes as wide as us are removed. Jimmy's trying to push past the guard, but he's swatted away, and Jimmy's no small man. The swat, however, creates an opening, and Kayne's darting up the gangway, which is about to be removed. Screaming security guards engulf us, and all are now watching Kayne—who's slipped away—talking to a woman who can barely be seen inside the slit of the black hull. Then the uniformed woman emerges, walking down the gangway.

"It's okay," she tells the guards, "I'll take care of it," and suddenly we're aboard, standing starboard, watching the ship navigate the narrow channel at the edge of a long and jagged jetty, watching the harbor and the isle of Crete slip away as if we'd never been there. The uniformed woman says she'd traveled herself for several years, that she understood the need for improvisation, that she understands. She's matter-of-fact and unsmiling, but our savior nonetheless. We'll have to sleep in an empty staff cabin near the engine room, and we'll have to pay half-price to cover our meals, but we'll be in Alexandria by late morning. Jimmy made it happen. Pure will wins again.

Next day, just like that (it's always just like that, like a shooting star, a plume of smoke, a fleeting feeling), after a night of stars and the sounds of splashing waters and seabirds circling and gawking (at one point, late at night, a group of cooks were outside smoking and throwing leftover food into the frothing and swirling sea), after a night of sleeping on hard, vibrating, and hot plastic mats (we were, after all, right next to the engine room), after a morning spent standing within the spear of the stern's railing watching the hull slice through historical waters, here we are, at the port of Alexandria. There are cranes, like huge erector sets, a round fountain, and buildings stained from salted winds, and I'm feeling and imagining horses and swords and Alexander's chariot parting his giant army into massive columns, like Moses parting the Red Sea. It's late morning, and the sun's already risen red and splayed its rays through so many prisms—what a morning it's been! But now this same sun's heavy, and even the breeze is hot. We'll have to wait until late afternoon to roam and to visit the pyramids, and we'll have to wait till late tonight or early morning to venture into the heat of the Sinai.

On the minibus to Cairo, a feeble old man with sharp green eyes tells us to secure a driver for the early morning.

"The red sun makes the Sinai an oven," he says, "cooks radiators like falafels. And the Cairo sunrise must be seen; you must visit the pyramids at sunrise. It is Allah greeting the day, reminding us of his presence as the one and only God. Today you will explore Cairo. I will make you a list."

"Shouldn't we be heading into the Sinai before sunrise?" I ask.

"Yes, ideally," the old man says. "But you'll have time. Just make sure to be at the pyramids before sunrise."

This is a commandment, and we take it as such, accept it as an extension of this journey's destiny. We follow his list, and make full use of the day: the Egyptian Museum, a long roam through Al-Azhar Park, a mosque, and a bazaar. We sleep like mummies.

The next morning, driving out of Cairo, climbing a hill, we see the black pyramids rising. Then they're turning gold against a dark sky of red and orange flames, and it's hard to deny the presence of something, perhaps the spirits of sweltering slaves, perhaps Allah, perhaps nothing but the sun and the smog, the dust, and the refraction. Vendors are setting up trinket and snack-bar stands. Women are sweeping concrete porches and erratic, unaligned sidewalks. Massive pyramid-shaped shadows engulf camel trains. The sand's steaming. There's a congestion of poetic sounds. Speakers chanting muffled Arabic prayers, the drone of an incoming tour bus, the circling and whistling birds. The whirl of motorbikes, children readying for school—a village awakening. And the pyramids—a magnificent testament to human perseverence and ingenuity. The massive stones, the precise cuts and angles, the perfection.

Kayne says, "What's up there, Skin? You got that crazy look again."

"This is just so cool," I say. "I mean, how the hell did they build these things?"

Kayne's shrugging. "Let's go ride a camel," he says.

"But we gotta go."

"We got time, Skinny."

"You're too big, Kayne."

But he's already walking, and we're following.

The camels are the most emaciated, dreadful looking creatures I've ever seen. Their rug-like fur is spotted with scabs and freckles and bald spots. Flies are swarming in their ears and eyes where sand has hardened into crust. They have long, thin legs with fattened knees lamely turned inward. Their hoofs and dewclaws are battered and caked in clay.

We're dismounting. We're climbing the pyramids. The stones are cold, the golden surface puncturing sky above, and again, I'm wondering how the ancients could've achieved such perfection.

"Better get going," Jimmy says. "Sun's a risin'."

We're appreciating the view. The light's a dim orange and purple-blue. Jerusalem's just over there. And Mecca's there. The driver's waving in the distance below; he appears immersed in the swirling, hazy light and smoke. We're climbing down.

The taxi's speeding off. The driver's visibly annoyed. We took too long. The sun's already risen. There's no air conditioning, so all windows are down, and the pelting breeze is dry and hot. Jimmy's in the front, his knees pulled up to his chest. Our knees are wedged into the back of the front seat. The plastic seats are cracked and duct-taped, a rash already forming on the back of my legs. It's gonna be another rough journey, and I'm remembering the last time I was forced to transcend an unbearable situation.

Bus trip. Istanbul to Cappadocia. I can hear my intestines gurgling. No Immodium. An eleven-hour bus ride. No bathrooms (out of order), one planned stop. I could just meet Kayne in Izmir, but I don't want to miss out, so I'm stepping onto the bus, into the sick waft of sweet cologne. I'm waving off the porter's spray but taking the towel, so gentle is its warmth on my face, the back of my neck, my folded hands. That damn smell's gonna be the end of me though. Everything's swaying, rattling, and humming. There are soft voices. I can feel the uprightness of my spine against the old, beaten seat, and I feel the broken metal coils on my back. I'm awake but feeling asleep, and this goes on for hour after hour until finally, maybe I am asleep, although the distinction—conscious and unconscious, meditation and sleep—no longer exists. I'm not dreaming, not asleep, but also not awake. I'm a mass of unpleasant sensations, my innards at war, spitting and gurgling. I'm inside this body, but I'm not; I'm elsewhere, outside, above, looking down. At myself. At this organism. And I'm in awe, laughing but not laughing at the absurdity, laughing at myself and my usual state of self-absorption. I'm at once amazed at this organism's miraculous structure, its complexity and its simplicity, and yet, I'm also distinctly—and here I pause, for I must emphasize the distinctness of this awareness— aware that I'm not this body, nor this brain or this blood. I'm something else, something entirely beyond my knowledge, my story—beyond everything. And yet, at the same time, within this distinction, I'm also aware of a core and all-consuming unity. But perhaps I'm trying to explain the unexplainable, building castles by piling up rocks?

Back to the present situation.

My throat's parched, almost scorched. We've no water. My eyes are burning. I want to close them, but there's still so much beauty. The red desert rocks, the rawness, the chanting Muslim music. This hub of civilization, this highway for invading armies. The novelty. But I have to close them. I'm dreaming of ice water, the sound of clanking ice, the little beads clinging to the cold, wet glass, the icy water streaming down my throat, filling every miserably hot and hollow space. With every turn, my legs are sliding across ripped plastic and duct tape, my knees cramming against the seat and door. Now my eyes are closing, focusing elsewhere, as if for survival, and time's passing in unconscious intervals; I'm not asleep, but I'm not awake either, perhaps "lucid dreaming" is correct, I can't really say. And here's where things get weird, for I'm in this dream, but somehow know it's not a dream. And of course that leaves questions.

I'm in an old pioneer wagon, my teeth chattering, my head swaying and bouncing violently. I might be a tall four-year-old; I might be a short seven-year-old, I can't tell. There's a woman. My mother. She's prostate, sick. Purple veins streak her sickly white face and neck. And this is the thing, this is the difference: This isn't just a dream, not the usual envisioning of unfolding history. This is real. Why or how I know, I'm not sure, but I know. I'm feeling my thin arms, watching my proportionately small hand caressing fresh, blonde hairs. She's not my current mother, but she's my mother. Again, I'm unable to explain how I know this. It smells of sickness, a sweet and rotten and unexplainable smell, and I'm thankful for the incessant breeze whisking it away. On second thought, the smell's not unexplainable because when the breeze ceases, if only for moments, there's a distinct smell of cheese. I'm looking at this woman. I love her. How do I know this? I just do. Perhaps it's the way she looks at me, for such love can't be contrived. She's looking at me as if she might die, as if it might be her last glance, as if she's taking me in for eternity. I can smell the dust, hear the horse hooves and wagon wheels. The driver must be my father, although he's concealed by the thick, brown bonnet. There's a rifle latched to the wagon bow just behind him. I'm reaching out to open the swaying flap at the back of the wagon, and everything seems to be immersed in a thick and floating fog of dust. The driver in the wagon behind us is a large, muscular man with a dark, brown beard and a brown wool hat. He's wearing a red-and-black wool shirt.

I cannot see the wagon train's end. My mouth's parched. I'm moving closer to the rear, taking a deep breath, and sliding my head through the bonnet's rear slit, stretching to see beyond. Dust overwhelms, but beyond lies waist-high green grasses and softly rolling hills, and the grasses are compressed flat by winds. There are purple and yellow and pink flowers. I want to stop and get out. Again, I'm aware of myself, aware of small hands, tiny fingers and fingernails, thin arms and legs. I'm wondering what I look like. I'm aware that I'm aware, as if I know this isn't real, and yet I'm here, in this moment within a moment, this place and time that may or may not exist. I'm aware that this may be lucid dreaming, a way to lose myself on long journeys with nothing but myself with which to contend. The wagons have stopped, the dust is settling, and I'm jarred awake, as if from a deep sleep but without the dense sleepiness. I'm back in the car, the sounds of rusty doors creaking and slamming.

Jimmy's staring. "You okay there, buddy?"

Some kids appear, asking for money, candy, and pens, but Jimmy's waving them behind us as we walk toward the sparkling water's edge. The kids are tugging at my shorts. I've nothing to give. We're sitting under a canopy, atop Turkish rugs and colorful and ecclectic pillows. We're eating pitas, falafels, and hummus. Kayne's joking with the proprietor. Jimmy's staring again, for I've yet to speak, and I might be moon white for all I know. Finally, I ask, "How long were we driving?"

"A few hours," Jimmy says.

"Was I sleeping?"

"Buddy, I don't know what you were doing. Sometimes your eyes were closed, sometimes they were open. At one point I saw you looking at your arm as if it were some foreign object. You're a strange one, aren't you?"

"I don't know what I am, Jimmy."

"Yeah, exactly. What were you thinking anyway? You got that girl on your mind again?"

"No," I say. "For once, I don't."

"You're still out of it, aren't you?"

"Where are we?" I ask.

"A place called Dahab," Jimmy says.

We're walking back to the taxi. I've only eaten half my food. I give the rest to the kids, divided equally. We're back in the taxi. I feel as if I'm standing beside my thoughts, just watching them like the passing breeze. I'm still feeling the heat and discomfort, but it's fleeting, like watching birds high in the sky. Perhaps it's the novelty, this Holy Land? I'm wondering if there really is something wrong with me. The driver's saying we'll be at the border to Israel in no time.

CHAPTER FOURTEEN

Australia 1994

"The fates lead him who will;
him who won't they drag."

—Roman Proverb

'M DOING THE dragging again. There's something pushing
me—I can't explain it. There's fear, yes, fear of the law finally
catching up to us, but that's not the driving force. It's this feeling I was talking to Hanah about, this intuition. It gets numbed
when I start thinking about details and logistics, reasons for
and against, so I'm going out on a limb here, experimenting,
purposefully moving forward and suppressing all thoughts. It
feels dangerous, even reckless, and it damn well may be. But
we're going, we're leaving, and this boldness is already creating
options; it's creating changes before our eyes, and it's clearly
forcing change and opportunities on others, particularly Peter

and Hanah. And here's where more thoughts enter, thoughts I'm fending off, but thoughts whose wake leave me feeling unsure, guilty, and selfish. This intuition, this urge to move on, feels right—I'm sure of it—and Kayne's game; he's even reveling in my surety. But this seemingly impulsive decision is affecting others. Hanah hasn't said it directly, but I know she doesn't want to be alone with Peter. He's harmless, so I'm not concerned, but it will create discomfort for her. And us leaving is forcing that on her. We've created a wonderful home here, a family, and I'm breaking it up.

It's also strange to say good-bye to Hanah. I've so longed to hold her, to consummate my desires. But I haven't. I didn't. And now we're leaving, and not coming back. The finality of it has made me rethink my feelings for her, has emphasized just how much I've enjoyed our time together. If it weren't for her, I might not have written down my stories, and even now she's insisting that I continue to send them. And that carnal desire never waned. It's thrown my surety out of kilter, made me question everything. It's thrown me into a scenario in which this concept of following my intuitions, this faith in synchronicity, is lost in this confusion. This concept that I can just follow this voice, that I can calm myself and truly know what to do, my own little answer machine, the place I go when I have to make decisions, is now questioned. I'm chalking it up to change, to fear of the unknown, to overthinking.

I've talked to Hanah, apologized, expressed my guilt, acknowledged my understanding of how this is affecting her. I've thanked her profusely. But she insists I follow my instincts. She saw my surety when the decision finally came. And she recognizes how everything has so come together.

She's happy for all of us; she really is. But it's still sad, and she's still unsure of her next step. The whole thing leaves a hole in my chest and a heaviness in my belly.

The decision to leave has initiated a series of synchronistic events. Once again, we post a sign—actually two signs—on the message board at the local hostel. One's for our room, a sublet for two months, the remainder of our lease. The other reads:

> *Two fun and easy-going Americans looking for fun and easy-going travel companions to slowly wander south (we're hoping to fly out of Melbourne). Will contribute gas money. Also open to sharing the expense of a used vehicle with the intention of selling at travel's end.*

The boarders come knocking like starving children. Travelers searching for a temporary home. They interrupt the morning song and the evening glow. Doorbell after doorbell. Swedes and Canadians, Japanese and Americans. Italians, Germans, Dutch and French. But no one feels right. It drives us all crazy, so we take the sign down, figuring we'll put it back up when we're mentally prepared, after a day or two of rest. Then Peter meets two Swedes at the donut shop. They aren't looking for a room, just a donut, but as Peter asks questions in their native tongue, their story emerges. His eyes bulge with the wonder of this chance meeting, his cheeks glowing pink. These Swedes, Oscar and Theo, are here to train Australians in the art of computers.

"You should see these guys," Peter shouts. "They're so alive, so creative. They're talking about some kind of computer network, some way of communicating and accessing information through a computer. They want me to work with them, say they'll train me, and for the first time ever, I don't even have to think about it. The Swedish Stallion's found his calling!"

"So these guys," he continues, "Oscar and Theo, they just got here and they want to travel before working full-time in a couple of months. I tell them about you two and they say you can go south with them. They want to learn to surf. They're buying a used van. And get this! They want to take the room when they return, want to just keep it in the mean time. They got a bunch of equipment and stuff to leave anyway. Their company's paying for it all. It's perfect!"

I'm happy for Peter, but also painfully aware of my own lack of direction, and Hanah has a similar response. She's happy for him and happy that all's working out. But she can't hide the disappointment at the coming changes, and I think it highlights her own confusion as well, questions about the near and distant future. She's uncharacteristically moody, making no effort to hide her feelings.

We're leaving tomorrow, early. I'm alone on the porch, spread out on the couch, one of Shirley's thick blankets on my lap. Smoke from the vanilla candle's swirling and rising and disappearing. The sky's clear; the only clouds are the long and transparent kind that stars shine through. The air's crisp and cool. Hanah's staying at a friend's, says she can't stand good-byes, and she doesn't want to be around with all the coming and going. I promise to keep sending her stories, but this only makes her eyes wet.

Peter and Kayne are working. Our room's empty, the bags packed. More clouds are moving in from the ocean, absorbing the splice of moonlight. It's the same moon and sky of many a night, here and there, over the sea and the desert, the same moon of pasts and futures. I'm listening to the distant hum of cars and the sound of Shirley's television below. It feels strange to have already said good-bye. With Hanah it felt stoic; both of us were clearly suppressing our feelings in the name of necessity. I thanked her, and she thanked me; we've helped one another. Her eyes were moistening again, and she apologized for having to leave. I told her I understood. I didn't say it, but I too am glad to not be dealing with the awkwardness of it all. It's easier just not having her here.

With Shirley, the good-bye had a finality I'll never forget. Even now, an hour later, I can still feel its subtle truth; even now, that heavy sense of death is directly offset with concepts of eternity, of immortality, of neverending change. Shirley and I said good-bye for the last time. We will never see each other again. She's been so kind to us, and something about her presence made us all feel more secure, as if we had family living below. And we did. This woman would've done anything for us. She's family. She'll be dead before we ever return to Australia, but her memory will never disappear; her love can never be forgotten. Her own family's dead. I never did ask her how it happened. She's always felt so real, so present, but in the realness was an undeniable sadness, like a layer of sweat on her soul. She has many friends and extended family, and I know she won't die alone, but I still feel bad leaving. And again, the finality. I get the concepts of timelessness, that energy never dissipates, that it only changes form, like vapor to clouds to condensation to the molecules and compounds that miraculously create life. I get that Shirley's boundless energy and spirit, so encased in her withering body, will simply change form, like the clouds. I get that in a relative universe, from the largest and widest perspective, this change, this shift we humans call death, is little different than the clouds or any other transfer of energy, big or small, and I get that from the perspective of wonder, from the wonder of this thing called human consciousness, Shirley may indeed soon be entering the most exciting portal there is. We spend our lives worrying and struggling against what is, and death's the biggest "what is" of them all. We struggle and struggle and try to control our lives, and meanwhile life, in all its dimensions, just keeps moving forward. People do what they do. Animals do what they do. Energy in all its varieties just keeps on changing and morphing, and life continues unabated, despite us and our ceaseless attempts to control and define, to delineate and understand. Is this nihilism? Apathy? Defeatism? Fatalism? Am I endorsing helplessness? Am I saying that nothing matters? No, I'm not. But yes, I am. How can I explain? How can I make sense of it all? One must just keep doing. Do good, fix things, spread love, and expect nothing. Easier said than done. I see this, but don't know what to do with it. But sitting here, heavy with all these conflicting emotions, I can't help but stew over it all. Shirley was sad to say good-bye. She'd stood there with tears and a huge smile. She'd hugged me like I was her own son, and, even now, I can feel her energy; I can feel the accumulation of her kindness, and I know I'll always remember her. She's inspired me to be kinder. But still, here I am, wallowing in this cauldron of human emotions, this ever-changing brew.

I'm sad and guilty and a bit scared. But I'm also thankful and excited. Sometimes thoughts precede emotions. Other times emotions precede thoughts. Which is cause and which is effect? How can I ever understand myself in the midst of such confusion? I've read about just watching it all occur, not getting carried away by it. But I can't. It's part of the process. I get carried away. I'm wondering if I'll ever be able to just watch it, ever be able understand this ocean of emotions that is I, this ocean whose source is so many mountains and streams and rivers. But that's just it. I can never step out; I am part and parcel. This is the process. So how can I get beyond these thoughts, beyond myself? How can I just watch the show? Perhaps just keep moving. We don't want to leave this special place, this porch and this sky, these people. We'll never forget. But it's time.

The '76 Ford van is dark tan, the color of vomit. There's a white paint splatter on one side. There was one hubcap, but we took it off to complete the set of dirty, black rims. The bumpers are rusted, every window's cracked, and every tire's bare and smooth. A hole in the muffler causes a violent tremble, a fluttering roar, and there's the sound of gas sucking with every acceleration. The hard, plastic seats have bug-infested foam and fault-like cracks lined with dirt. The previous owner was a florist, and the car smells of rotten flowers, despite the constantly burning incense and the Swedes' cigarettes, the little rolled fags that are part tobacco, part marijuana. But it runs. It starts. The radio works, even the heater.

The Swedes, Oscar and Theo, sit in front, talking animatedly through the smoke and the many sounds. Kayne and I sit on the couch that leans against the back doors, our legs spread before us. We felt bad taking the house's one couch, but Peter and Hanah insisted, and we had little alternative with nothing else to sit on in the van. The couch converts the tremble to a soothing and soft vibration, and I can't imagine life without it.

We'd been driving through the familiarity of Burleigh Heads, Currumbin, Kirra, Coolangatta, and Tweed Heads, but now it's unfamiliar, and each moment is new. The hills beyond the dirty windows pass slowly; they are sloping and long, green with little yellow dandelions, and now there are tall grasses the color of cornstalk. I have to hunch near the window to see clearly. There's a baby wearing only diapers, his hair matching the color of the dried grasses. For some reason this stands out among so many images.

Oscar and Theo have yet to stop talking. They pass their little rolled fags back and forth and talk through the haze of smoke. Theo (who isn't driving) will have another rolled before the previous smoke even dissipates. They talk about the world, how it's coming together, as they say, and how this new computer network is sparking an information revolution. Their dialogues are creative vacuums, a game in which an idea is mentioned and thrown around like an object that is smelled and felt and listened to, then taken apart to see if its pieces speak for themselves, then put back together, placed in the corner, and left to be pondered on before being taken apart again.

Oscar's a stereotypical Swede with long and fine white hair, gently tanned skin, and a long, soft-muscled body. His eyes remind me of the Grecian sea at sunset, a thick and rich blue that sparkles various shades of orange and yellow. He seems the deconstructionist of the two, the one to break down a lofty idea, to lay its parts on the floor to see if they can be put back together. This, at first, seems to clash with his innocence and optimism, but as I've listened to his words, his tone, I've come to hear his rationality speaking on its own, his mind a machine unaffected by its own experience. So far I've yet to enter their conversation as I'm tired and so enjoying the new terrain and the little towns passing through the dirty windows.

Theo's the opposite of Oscar in every way. A typical Swede he's not. He's black and short. His hair's cropped on the sides with short, overhanging dreadlocks that are always swaying with the slightest wind or movement. His father was in the diamond business. The family had moved from Sierra Leone to London when Oscar was four. At fourteen, they moved to Lund in Southern Sweden. This, in part, explains his unusual English accent. He has a wide and expressive face with big, deep-set eyes that often appear orange, a face that reminds me of Zaire, our Nigerian friend in Israel. I like him. I like them both. They are, as Peter had said, passionate and creative, and neither have that bullshit, self-possessed look in their eyes. They are brimming with creativity, and I now better understand Peter's fervor, for all this computer stuff is indeed exciting.

Theo's turning to face us. "We need an outside opinion," he says. "Have you heard what we're talking about?"

"Kind of," I say, "Just watching the world go by."

"I need to ask you two something," Theo says.

Kayne's half asleep. "Ask him," he says.

"Two heads are always better than one," Theo says.

"His head's worth two."

"Just listen," Theo says, laughing. "You've heard about the worldwide computer network, yes?"

I nod. "Yeah," I say, "but I don't really know much about it. We've been gone for a few years now."

"Well, it's here, and it's growing as we speak. Once connected, you can get information from what is basically a huge database of independent sites devoted to everything you can imagine. Say I'm looking for information on elephants, so I just go to a site dedicated to elephants, and this site might include information on other sites on elephants. "

"Wait a second," I interrupt. "Explain what you mean by site."

"Each site," Theo says, "has a different computer or online address, a website as we call it. You or I can right now buy a website address and create a site dedicated to elephant research or to whatever we want. It won't be long until most everyone's buying stuff through websites. This is growing as we speak; more and more sites are being added every day, and we're getting better at organizing it all. For example, we're getting better at creating search engines, a central site where you can search for all sites within a category. The search engine would find you most all the sites on elephants. You'll be able to find pictures and graphs and various information on elephants, and you'll be able to copy all of it onto your own computer."

Oscar interrupts. "And like Theo says, it won't be long before you can shop through this system, through this internet. Companies will be paying to have their sites at the top of the search engines, there will be ads throughout the web pages, and companies will be able to see what people are searching for. Won't be long before they're catering advertisements specifically for you."

"Whoa," I say. "You're losing me. And that sounds a bit scary."

Both Theo and Oscar are laughing. "I know, I know, it's crazy," Theo says. "But back to my question, back to what this internet could mean for the spread of information, for education. If you have a computer, or have access to one—through a school, library, or worksite—you'll be able to access most of the information in the world because these various sites are just growing and growing. Encyclopedias are essentially being converted to online sites. At some point, books might even become obsolete."

I'm cringing.

"Don't worry," Theo says. "It's a long way off. I'm just talking, that's what we do sometimes. We're freakin' crazy lost in this stuff. And we see endless potential—for the world, for us, for everybody. And one thing we see is the potential for spreading information, for a boost in the overall education level around the world. We're talking about a technological and information revolution here like the world's never seen. And we're smack dab in the middle of it, right at the beginning, actually, as far as the computers go. You watch. You'll see. It's all happening. And right now. More people than ever, from all over the world, are gonna be able to get an education. And think what might happen as a result! Think how that could change the world!"

They've definitely got my attention, and I'm remembering Peter's excitement as he described their enthusiasm. Their passion's infectious. They remind me of Mr. Herrigan, my sixth-grade teacher, and Mr. Cipoletta, my tutor of many years. They'd both love this stuff.

Theo's raising a finger. "Now," he says, pausing for emphasis, "here are the questions that we have for you on this particular topic. This is where Oscar and I disagree. What might happen if more of the masses are educated? What might the world become? More people will be able to communicate. It will do what the invention of writing and the printing press did before. It will do more! And governments may not be able to control it; we may see the end of information control, of mind control."

"And we may see more," Oscar interrupts, looking back through the rearview mirror. "Remember the catered advertising? And whose to say governments won't spread misinformation?"

Theo's raising his finger again. "Now, this is how I see it. My friend here thinks it won't fundamentally change the distribution of information and/or wealth because there'll still be the haves and have-nots, those who can afford an education and a computer, and those who can't."

Theo's turning to Oscar. "Anything to add?"

"Just that the educated will also be the only ones able to effectively access and process the information as well. The people who can't read still won't be able to read—book or computer."

"Anything else?" Theo asks.

"Just that it won't be long until this worldwide web's inundated with information, perhaps too much information. It'll be like going from having a hundred legitimate newspapers, each expressing various ideologies, to having five thousand, many of which aren't officially endorsed. Basically, there's gonna be too much illegitimate information out there, and too much information in general, and even the educated are gonna have a hard time sifting through it all. I'm not convinced that, in the end, we're gonna be more informed; instead, we're gonna be overinformed, inundated with misinformation that will be difficult if not impossible to regulate, and thereby be less educated overall."

Theo's turning back to us. "We desperately need an outside opinion. Please indulge us."

Kayne's shaking his head. "Homey's got a lot going on up there," he says. "Maybe as much as you, Skinny."

Theo's looking at Oscar, shrugging, and looking back. "So where are you guys heading anyway?" he asks. "Why you going to Melbourne?"

Kayne's now asleep, his big head resting on my shoulder. I'm remembering the look on my mom's face when she first met him, the way she'd said, "He's gonna get you in trouble, but I like him."

"That's a lot to take in," I say, ignoring his question for the moment. "I will say that this computer stuff—these technological advancements, and this internet you're talking about—is very exciting, and it fits right into these other things I'm reading and learning about right now, mainly this concept that we're right now smack dab in the middle of a major paradigm shift, a major shift in the way we humans perceive, understand, and interact with the world. We're witnessing the emergence of a new worldview, and this makes this time in history a major transition period, a hub in which old ideas and technologies are slowly fusing and morphing and shaping themselves into this new paradigm, this new worldview. I can feel it, see it, just don't know what it means; no one really knows what it means. But I can see it. And this internet and computer stuff's clearly a part of it."

Oscar and Theo are both nodding vigorously.

"Yes, yes," Oscar says, noticing the sign to Byron Bay, slowing the van, and turning off the main highway and onto the road that winds down through plump and rolling green hills.

"You're a big ideas guy," Theo says, "a big picture guy. We like that."

"I don't know what I am," I say. "I see big picture, I see little picture, I get lost in it all."

"Yes, yes," Theo says. "But you're better off for it."

"Maybe," I say.

"So please," Theo says, "a bit more about this paradigm shift, this is good."

"All right," I say, stretching my arms and feeling excitement at the sight of the sea and the little town below. "I'll try." I still don't feel like talking much, but they're so genuinely interested that I feel inclined.

"I recently read this book, *Structure of Scientific Revolutions*, by this guy Thomas Kuhn. The basic gist is that it takes a while, fifty, a hundred, two-hundred-plus years for new ideas to be absorbed and instituted, for them to manifest as new technologies and such. It took two hundred years to go from Copernicus to the Industrial Revolution, and another two hundred and fifty to get where we are today. So, big picture, it's going to take a while for quantum physics and all this incredible new knowledge to create real change in the world. This internet, however, might change that; it might expedite this process; it feels like we're gonna be watching it unfold."

"Yes, yes," Theo says. "Exactly. The internet could change everything."

I'm thinking about the Renaissance, the Scientific Revolution, the Enlightenment, the Industrial Revolution. I'm thinking about the creation of America, the manifestation of these movements. I'm thinking about Mr. Herrigan.

The van's slowly winding closer to the town and to the sea.

"Please," Theo says. "This is good. We love this shit."

"I could go on and on," I say, "but Kayne's taught me to know better."

"Please," Theo says, looking at Kayne, who's still sleeping.

"Yeah, well, let's just say that institutions and ideologies are like huge rocks, you know. The winds of time and knowledge will sculpt them, will wear them down, but it takes a long time. And meanwhile, humans are stuck in our own sense of time, struggling against it all. And we're stuck in our own interpretations—which are forever subject to contexts, to cultures and institutions, religions and language, to everything. Basically, quantum physics has shattered the old Newtonian paradigm. The subatomic world has changed everything. Our entire understanding of the universe and ourselves—of practically everything—has been blown apart. But life goes on. Time continues. We do what we do, and history unfolds."

"So how's it unfolding?" Oscar asks.

"It's been unfolding since the science evolved, since quantum physics. Atomic energy, postmodernist philosophy, all this cross-pollination of cultures and ideas, of Eastern and Western philosophy—it's all part of the process. But who knows how it'll all play out."

We're now at the entrance to the town of Byron Bay. Oscar pulls the van to the side of the road, and it's decided that we'll go to the local bar.

"Anything else to add?" Oscar asks.

"Not really," I say. "Just that it's as if we're back in the 1700s and another kind of Enlightenment's unfolding. I can see it. I can feel it. I just don't know what it means. But this is a crazy-exciting time to be alive, that's for sure. We're going to see some amazing stuff in our lives. Our new technologies, including your computers and your internet, are going to crack open the world as never before. I can just feel it."

"It's gonna be crazy, that's for sure," Theo says. "So you never answered my question: why you leaving out of Melbourne?"

"Our visas are running out," I say, "figured we'd check out the coast and fly out of Melbourne. We're gonna surf in Indonesia for a bit, and I'm going to a monastery in Thailand for a ten-day silent meditation retreat."

"Cool," Oscar says, turning back to the road now heading into Byron Bay. "Cool."

We're driving through town. There's a long, two-lane road with shops and restaurants on both sides. It reminds me of Haliewa, Hawaii. I visited there when I was ten with my brother, mom, and grandmother, before we'd even moved to

Irvine. I'm thinking about my grandmother. Like my grandfather, she's now dead, but I can see and feel them both. I can hear their voices, see them so clearly. Their wisdom, their spirit, is forever, as if they're now part of me. Perhaps we'll someday discover that blood, that genetics, somehow connects us to our ancestors. Or maybe it's something else.

Oscar's stopping the van, asking a man about bars, and we're now heading to the outskirts of town. I want to eat, but they all want a beer. I'm still thinking about my grandparents when I see the choppers, all lined up, and I recognize the orange flames on Fast Freddy's tank, Bongo's two oversized chrome pipes, and the big eagle perched between Loose Lenny's wide handlebars.

Kayne's awake and up and in the bar, and just like that I'm being dragged again.

We're greeted like long-lost family. The weight of surrender. Such coincidences, I've found, rarely go unfulfilled; the cycles of experience must complete themselves or one will feel a hole, a dull pang, in unconscious depths. And of course—I should've seen it coming—they're on their way to the sapphire mines, that same experience we'd narrowly escaped just days before.

Sick Sammy's face is matter-of-fact. "I had a feeling you were supposed to come with us. We can only take the two of you though."

"I'd love to," I say, "but we've promised our friends here that we'd continue south."

Kayne's introducing Oscar and Theo, telling the bikers that they'll be living in our old room, telling them they're computer geniuses who are gonna change the world.

"How long will you be gone?" Oscar asks, shaking Sick Sammy's hand.

"Just for tonight, mate," Sick Sammy says. "You'll be on your way in the morning."

"Perfect," Oscar says. "We're staying the night anyway. And we're in no hurry."

"It's done then," Sick Sammy says.

Kayne's drinking out of Bongo's pitcher.

Everyone's raising a toast to another fuckin' sapphire run.

I'm handed a tequila shot, along with a lime and a salt shaker. Everyone has a tequila shot, and I'm slamming it, along with everyone else. It reminds me of Greece. Shot glasses are slamming on the bar and tables. I'm looking around. No one else is looking around. Everyone else is just laughing.

We're roaring up the road we just came down, away from the precious sea, heading inland with a bunch of hairy bikers. Bongo has the belly of a silverback gorilla. For a while the road's straight, but now it's winding left and right, long and leaning turns punctuated by shorter "s" turns, punctuated then by long stretches of straight highway, then back into turns. The turns force me to hug Bongo, but I'm unable to clasp my hands around his belly, so I'm left clutching and shoving my chin into the sombrero on his "Bandidos" patch. If I throw up, I'll have to avoid the patch.

We're slowing, coming into another town with an aboriginal name. A market, a pub, a barbershop. A school with a football field. Engines are flaring. Kayne's waving and yelling at people who're gawking and waving back.

We're stopping for gas. There's a family in a blue VW van. Kids are smiling and waving through slits in white curtains. Choppers are gassed and wiped down. Tires are checked. Everything's done meticulously.

I'm standing beside Loose Lenny, stretching my arms. "So what's this sapphire run all about?" I ask.

"Oh, mate," he says. "A fuckin' blast I tell ya." His eyes are like barbed wire, the veins sharp and twisted. "We go in late, when it's darkest. You'll be watching for the trucks or the bastards on wanker little dirt bikes. We go down the mines, get into the machines, and pick out the extra sapphire. You gotta kick 'em and hit 'em and shit, but the sapphire's in there, it's fuckin' in there."

"So what if those trucks or bikes show up?"

"No problem, mate, that's half the fun. Government won't let 'em have real guns, so they shoot these pussy-ass pellet guns at us that sting when they get you, but it's just a sting, I reckon."

"And what do you do with the sapphire?"

"Got friends who pay good money for it."

"I don't get it," I say. "Why would they just leave the sapphire in the machines?"

"Don't know, mate. Guess they're worried about breaking 'em, the machines, you know, so we save 'em the trouble."

Sick Sammy's giving a "round 'em up" signal, and it's back to the highway and the rolling, light-green hills. There are cows and horses, rusted-out jeeps, tractors, and tractor parts. There are crude, wooden fences crisscrossing hills, accentuating topography and wild flowers, and I'm soon surrendering, accepting this lack of control, enjoying new terrain, the winds and the vibration, the long stretches of road, the swirling overload of senses. We're riding and riding. Out of the green hills and onto the straight and flat highway that appears to stretch into the big orange sun. We're heading inland, but it feels as if we're heading across a huge bridge toward another shore, or toward space. The rolling green hills have given way to scattered rocks, sparse trees, dry earth, and tumbleweeds. The air's feeling like it might sand one's skin off.

We're pulling off the highway, the bikes parked in jagged order, and Bongo's cutting up who-knows-what drugs on a plastic mirror, the lines all evenly spaced, and I don't want to fall asleep and look like a pansy, so I'm sniffing it up, and off we go, howlin' and whoopin' it up. Kayne's waving his arms like he's an airplane, and I'm hugging and hitting Bongo's shoulders. I can practically see the sun's deep orange gases swirling as it slips below the horizon and everything except headlights becomes black and it's ten degrees colder. There's a sliver of moon, the stars spread like spilt salt, and I'm starting to like the middle of nowhere; it feels like the moon or Mars, and it's doubtful that cops would ever be in such a place.

We're stopping again, covering lights with small patches of leather, and slowly and quietly heading up a rising black hill. At the top, on a flat section, we stop, turn off the bikes, and push them across a long plateau stretching to what looks like the edge of a small volcano. Below are several rusty and dilapidated shacks lit by floodlights at every corner. Deep stratifications weave up and into the dark hillside below. To our left, a dirt road winds down into darkness, and I'm wondering about the route it takes to the bottom. I can hear myself breathing, and there's the sound of boots crunching dirt, but otherwise the silence is intense and beautiful and all-consuming.

Sick Sammy's whispering, "Birdmen, you stay here." He's pointing down and to what looks like the base of a ridge where a dim light reveals the shadow of a small cabin. "You see anyone coming and you whistle and yell like you're on fire."

"Got it," I say. "Looks empty though."

"Somebody's there," he says. "Just a matter of how many. We haven't come for over a year, so we should catch 'em off guard. Might stay quiet. But it might not." He's handing me a whistle.

He's signaling the others, and just like that they disappear, walking into the blackness below. I'm wondering where the hell we're gonna run off to in this one-highway town, and what the hell we've gotten ourselves into, but it's too late for that.

"Pretty crazy, huh, Skinny?" Kayne says. "They must know what they're doing."

"Guess we're gonna find out."

"Remember those construction workers when we were twelve?"

I'm nodding.

"Just like this," Kayne says, "except it wasn't dark."

"And you just had to start throwing rocks at that guy!"

"He had a ponytail, Skinny," Kayne says, laughing softly, "a ponytail!"

"Shhh," I say, whispering, "yeah, well, that was great, Kayne. You hit him, all right—and the car."

"Those guys were fast."

"They caught me before I could even move," I said.

Kayne's shaking his head. "I wanted to keep running, but when I saw ponytail man and that other dude pulling your arms off, I had to stop."

"They were pissed."

"I had to walk our neighbor's dog for three months to pay that off," Kayne says. "Then your mom caught me, Kevin, and Ben smoking a joint in your patio. Remember that?"

"Yeah," I say, "but you didn't run like Ben and Kevin. You stayed. Even Roger respected that."

"Your mom's funny, Skinny."

"Yeah, whatever, Kayne."

I'm wondering how it could be so silent below. Then they appear, one by one emerging from the blackness. We're watching them, and we're watching the cabin below.

Everyone's smiling, laughing silently with one another, and waving around little bags of stones, like sacks of gold. Kayne and I are standing and dusting off and backing out of the cabin's sight. Sick Sammy's whispering, "Caught the buggers sleeping."

"What did you do with them?" I ask.

"Just tied them up real good, mate. They'll be fine."

We're walking the bikes back across the long plateau, then coasting down the hill. The breeze feels good. At the highway, engines are roaring to life, and we're shooting into star-splattered blackness and back toward the hills and the sea. I'm waiting for someone to appear—the police or one of those trucks—but minutes become hours, and we're becoming numb, one with the cold night. Then, like distant planes approaching: sirens. Then, from all sides, from lonely roads to nowhere, flashing lights. A roadblock. We're surrounded.

CHAPTER FIFTEEN

Irvine 1981/82

"He who dies with the most toys wins."

—Unknown

WORD'S OUT THAT the Murphy boys got a minibike and that they're hellbent on breaking every rule in Irvine, every damn regulation ever passed by city or association, and, even better, any and all are welcome to partake; any and all can give her a whirl. It isn't that no one else has such things. Most garages in Irvine boast any number of toys. But apparently no one allows others to play with their toys with such reckless disregard. We know our time's limited, that the powers to be will shut down such fun in no time. So we're embarking on an altogether different path.

Mom brought it home last week. Dad chipped in for most of it, a reward, Mom says, for getting decent grades. And I have Mr. Herrigan to thank for that. His curiosity, his wonder, his kind efforts in general, made me want to do well for him. I didn't do it for me. I didn't do it for Mom, Dad, or the minibike. I did it for him. He wasn't telling me to do it, wasn't insisting on anything, wasn't even plying me with guilt—even after I didn't bother trying on the first few tests and quizzes. He'd just smile, sometimes saying something like, "Oh, you're a piece of work, aren't you?" Or he'd say, "Give 'em hell, Murphy." I have no idea what he's talking about, but there's always this sense that we're in this thing together, that it's us against the world.

Once, later in the year, I ask why I'm "a piece of work."

"Spunk, spark, intelligence, wit," Mr. Herrigan says, his face crinkling into a smily frown, his right eye twitching as his head turns and tilts. "It means you're thinking for yourself."

"Is that good?" I ask.

"Is nature good?" he asks.

"Nature?"

"Yeah," he says. "Trees, the ocean, that orange on your desk. Are they good?"

"Yeah," I say. "I guess so."

"And so is thinking for yourself," says Mr. Herrigan. "It's natural. And yet amazingly rare. Thank you, Mr. Murphy. I celebrate you."

He walks on, passes out papers, tells the entire class that Mr. Murphy's a free thinker, that he wants to thank all of us for listening and learning and thinking, that we give him faith. And faith, he goes on to say in that comical and serious and over-the-top way he does (he stops and stares up and off into the corner, as if he's one of those religious figures looking up and into light from a sacrosanct sky), is gold, gold, gold!

Frank, a large boy who sits in the back and who's always pushing the rules (standing or talking or making stupid noises), raises his hand, swinging it as if he has something urgent and brilliant to say.

"Yes, Mr. Fanning," Mr. Herrigan says, standing tall and still in the manner he employs to exert calm and control.

"Does that mean that I can think for myself and talk when I feel like it?" Frank asks.

"Thank you, Mr. Fanning, for your insightful political science question."

There's snickering. Mr. Herrigan calmly waits for silence. "I'm actually being quite sincere, Mr. Fanning, for that is a legitimate and important question."

And this is another thing about Mr. Herrigan. He's always respectful, even to an idiot like Frank Fanning, always calm and cool, quick to smile and laugh. He employs the perfect balance of seriousness and fun, whatever the situation dictates. If a kid's ever out of line or disrespectful, he just stands there, calmly staring, as if he understands everything, maybe asks the kid if they're ok, what's going on, or tells a personal story about himself acting out. The point is he's been there, we'll all be there, and it's ok. We're in this together. And we're better if we have respect and understanding. At worse, he'll walk over to the kid, have a calm, private conversation. He never denigrates. He gives respect, so he gets it.

"Our government needs free thinkers, Mr. Fanning, even wants free thinkers. But that doesn't mean we can do whatever we want. Rules and procedures, law and order, are essential for just this reason, to create a safe, secure, and respectful environment. In this class, for example, I'm the government. It's my job to create law and order, to fairly apply the rules. If I do this, then we can be productive, we can maximize our wonderful time together, and we can feel safe to express and debate ideas, just like we're doing now. If I don't, if I'm wasting your time, or if I, the government, am being unjust or unfair in my application of the rules, you all, the citizens, have a right to rebel. You could all stand up, refuse to participate, walk out, and raise all hell. And you'd have every right to do so. It would be my fault. It's my job, as the government, to preserve law and order. Everything that happens in here's my fault. Remember us talking about Locke and Hobbes?"

This week Mr. Herrigan has been telling us stories of John Adams and his young son, John Quincy Adams, traveling across oceans to faraway European lands. Adams was attempting to secure favors from the French and the Dutch and whoever was willing to help America in its great and courageous rebellion, and young John Quincy was there for experience. Young John Quincy crossing seas, absorbing French aristocracy, witnessing cultures and poverty through his own youthful eyes. He studied languages. He studied classics. He studied as if in college. He traveled and traveled. He saw death. He saw beauty. He experienced adventure. He was the age I am now and the age I'll be in the next few years, and I'm wondering if these stories are why I'm speaking so. I'm him. I'm potential. I'm not just a child, a stupid kid. I'm something else, something bigger, and I have powers to define myself.

My hand's rising. When Mr. Herrigan points to me, I'm momentarily surprised, as if unaware it's raised. I'm speaking words that seem to speak themselves. "You say, sir, that we have the right to rebel if our government's unjust and unfair. But is that really true? Even teachers are rarely fair. It's why we kids get upset. We sense bullshit, and we don't like it."

There's more snickering. Mr. Herrigan's still standing, calm and tall. His head's tilted. He appears amused.

"Yes, Mr. Murphy. Bullshit it is."

More snickering, then silence, the students waiting for more words to drip from Mr. Herrigan's mouth. Every once in a while he'll do this; he'll play along with a transgression, as long as it's an intelligent one. Again, it's us against them.

"And said with such eloquence," he says, "such reason. So nice to meet you, Mr. Murphy, although I've always known you were there. Wonderful. This, Mr. Murphy, is the beauty of America, the beauty of our system of government." He's talking slowly, with that intense, almost crazed look in his eyes. "Remember, the Enlightenment took a long, hard look at humans and at government. These thinkers were determined to create a better system, one that took human fallibility—the imperfections of humans that you speak of—into account, to create a system with checks and balances, with stopgaps. The Second Amendment's meant to ensure that our populace stays armed and ready to stand against an unjust government. It's imperfect, but important, and effective in this manner. At every level—federal, state, and local—there are rules and procedures. Every branch—executive, legislative, judicial—at every level has rules and stopgaps to prevent abuses of power. It's the best the world has to offer, the best the world has come up with."

Mr. Herrigan's pausing, his breath rising in his chest, his head tilting back and swaying—his entire body's now swaying side to side. "But you're right, Mr. Murphy, it's still imperfect, people are imperfect, the system is imperfect. We need to keep questioning. We need to keep changing, evolving. Such is life. Adapt, evolve, grow. And with bright young folks like all of you, that's what we'll be doing."

There's my hand again.

"Yes, sir."

"But how do we accept all the unfairness?" I ask.

"You don't, Mr. Murphy. You mustn't accept anything. And sometimes it's best to rebel, to stand up and say no. But often that is anger speaking; it's an emotional reaction. Sometimes anger has its place. Usually, however, the wisest move in any scenario doesn't stem from anger. If we can remain calm, we can pick our battles wisely. There's a time to fight. The key's knowing when. Most people choose to fight too quickly, and most fights are a waste of time. Much of the news, the fights we see everyday in every country, are unnecessary and unwise fights. It's hard not to get angry. I know. I get it. Stupidity's hard to swallow. But if you really look at yourself, we're all guilty of being stupid at times; we've all acted out of stupidity, as you say, out of our own confusion. So let's start there, from a larger perspective, from a place that sees that we all make mistakes. But again, I get it. And sometimes a response is necessary. Usually, however, if we act on that initial anger we create more problems than we solve. If we take a hard look at ourselves, at our anger, we see that our desire to respond, to fight back, is more about us than it's about them; it's our own ego, our own pride, and the correct response in any given situation rarely comes from pride and anger. Anger usually leads to more anger."

There's my hand again. "But how do we not get angry? It just happens."

Mr. Herrigan's tilting his head again, his pursed lips and twinkling eyes revealing the tiniest of smiles. "Yes, Mr. Murphy. Very perceptive of you. You're on quite the roll. I know it's difficult to understand. Let me try to explain."

He's walking to the chalkboard, making a large circle. "Here's someone's brain, could be the brain of any one of us." He's making a bunch of squiggles inside the circle. "Here are our thoughts, all the stuff we're always thinking about, the many ways we imagine the world to be, the stories we tell ourselves, our own little realities." He's drawing a stick figure body. "And here's our body. For the sake of discussion, let's say that emotion is here." He circles the midsection, the stick figure's hips, torso, and chest. "So here's the process. Something happens, let's say some jerk on the street bumps into you, pushes you away, curses you. You immediately tighten up. You immediately turn your angry gaze onto this jerk." Mr. Herrigan's acting this out, his body tense, his eyes raging, his face snarling. "The anger's rising," he says, pointing to the midsection stick figure. "And you're thinking, 'How dare he disrespect me like that.' And it's true. It's unacceptable. This guy's being a real jerk. But here's the thing, here's the key. There's this moment, this crucial moment, when you either breathe and remain calm, or you straight-up react. And this is the moment of moments, the place where we can all gain control over our lives. If you react, if you don't crawl into this small gap between thought and emotion, then you're not in control. Perhaps you turn aggressively toward this jerk, perhaps he gets in your face, perhaps he even hits you or you hit him. Whatever the case, he now has control over you. If the two of you actually fight, you both reap the consequences. It doesn't matter whose fault it was; it takes two to tango. And this is where most people are in the world. They react to the world around them, create all these reasons why they have to defend their self-respect or the self-respect of others. Anger and/or pride consume them, and they just go through life reacting and dealing with consequences. And for every cause, there's an effect. It's an eternal law. Everything we do matters. And again, here's the thing. It didn't have to go any particular way. If you, for example, had just had the ability to stay calm, to understand that this jerk bumping into you is nothing personal, then the problem would've ended there. In fact, if you could magically see into this guy's thoughts, you'd most likely see that he was simply upset about something. Perhaps he'd just broken up with a girlfriend. Perhaps his young daughter had just been killed. Perhaps he'd just lost his job. Or maybe he's just a flat-out jerk. You see, if you can stay in that calm space between thought and emotion, then not only do you gain control over your life, but you naturally cultivate love and compassion. I know it's hard, but if you can do this, you will avoid many problems for yourself and many problems for the world. Most everyone ..." Mr. Herrigan is circling his hands above his head, "... is always blaming everyone else for their problems. But when it really comes down to it, most problems can be avoided, and if they're not, it's most often our own fault."

There's my hand again.

"Yes, sir."

"But what if some guy's beating up a girl right in front of you?"

"Yes," Mr. Herrigan says, "this is a common misunderstanding. There are clearly times to act, and if we can cultivate clarity of mind, we'll know when those are. In those cases, you tackle the guy and save the girl. There's no need to think about it. That's the right thing to do. You don't, however, have to beat him to a pulp like you may want to. Whatever the case, if we can stay calm enough, if we aren't slaves to our thoughts and emotions, we can live in peace, and we can spread peace."

My hand again. "But how do we do that? How can we stop thoughts?"

"Some people pray, Mr. Murphy, some meditate, some just ceaselessly watch themselves and seek to serve others. We all have to figure it out for ourselves. Only we can do it; only you can decide how your own spirituality unfolds; only you can explore the depths of your own consciousness. It's not my place to tell you anything on this matter; it's really no one's place. In the end, we're all responsible for ourselves. We will, of course, absorb whatever knowledge is available; we'll usually align with the traditions and cultures around us. This is natural, and this is good. People need guidance, traditions, and moral structure; religion's good, Mr. Murphy. But people are often too quick to claim truth, to grasp it like children grasping their favorite stuffed animals."

He's grabbing a small, stuffed, blue Cookie Monster and hugging it to his chin. His face is contorting, his eyes wide and fluttering. He's petting and hugging the toy. He has our full attention. He's whispering to the toy in a silly and exaggerated voice: "You are the only truth, you and only you. I shall hold you and protect you. Don't worry, I shall spread your message. Yes, there's only you, my dear little one. Don't worry, I'm off to let everyone know!"

He's back. This is another of Mr. Herrigan's ploys: he draws us in with attention-getting silliness (our eyes become glued to him), then he stops and becomes momentarily serious. "And this, my young and thoughtful travelers, is where we all must be careful. We're all capable of falling for this charade, this ruse, this chicanery!"

His arms are flailing.

"We find something we like, something that works for us, usually something from the familiar world around us, and we grasp it, assume it's some kind of otherworldly truth, and next thing we know, we're selling it to the entire world! And we may mean well. Most people, we must never forget, mean well. Their intention's simply to share this beautiful thing they've discovered for themselves. If it's good for them, they figure it must also be good for others. But others, you see— other people, other cultures, other religions—will rarely see things the same, and if we fail to understand this we end up in conflict. And this, my beautiful friends, my fellow travelers, my fellow stargazers, is our purpose here; we're here to gain perspective, to step back and see this wondrous world splayed out before us, to see the endless variety, to better understand it, to better learn to think about it, to somehow grasp that we can believe what we believe, yet still accept others who don't. It's okay. It's good. It's beautiful. There are many avenues to truth, to God, to government and peace."

His arms are wide; he's embracing the world; he's on one of his rolls.

"We are all so wonderfully different, and yet so wonderfully the same. We've all just got to get over ourselves a bit. And no one can do it but us. We alone, ourselves, are responsible for our minds, our anger, the way we are in the world."

As if stopping himself, realizing that he's lost track of time, Mr. Herrigan smiles, his head swaying ever so gently. "But we must move on." He's pointing to the board. "We must get back to our schedule. Good conversation, though. Any parting thoughts?"

My hand again. "But most people seem incapable of doing that," I say, "of having this perspective you speak of. Why is that?"

Another of Mr. Herrigan's smiles. "Indeed," he says. "Indeed, Mr. Murphy. It does, at times, seem like that, and it's easy to feel hopeless. But hope's all we have. I, for one, gain hope from all of you. I see your goodness, your curiosity, your desire to do better. We all want to be better; we all want to be happy. But we all have to own it; we have to exercise our minds, train ourselves to think. We can't help what others do—we just can't. So don't worry about everyone else. Just worry about yourself, that's all any of us can do."

This interaction was my first experience with pure action and pure thought. Mr. Herrigan's explanation of a gap between thought and emotion would affect me and my future actions more than could be forseen, conceived, or even imagined. My hand kept raising itself, and words followed suit. There was no space or time for nervousness. I'm not sure why this happened, not sure if something happened in the hardwiring of my brain or in my ever-changing adolescent biology, but never before had I experienced such calm and clarity when speaking in public. I have yet to wrap my thoughts around the entirety of this experience, and I have not consistently reproduced this calm and clarity. It comes and goes, and I've yet to feel its owner. Nor have I digested the complications of Mr. Herrigan's explanation. For example, how can a person just know what to do without thoughts to guide them? How can one ever truly live outside their thoughts? These questions disappear as fast as they arise, for my own mind can only think about one subject for so long, and such abstractions seem better left to the winds. But here I am, after all this time, and I remember this interaction verbatim. And somehow I know I'll never forget Mr. Herrigan. His perspective—the complex, multifaceted, and wondrous world he's shown us— has changed me. I don't quite know how, and it's yet to quell my confusion, but something has changed. Mr. Herrigan's the reason I got good grades. And he's the reason we now have this gleaming new minibike, ready and waiting for adventure.

The minibike's actually used, but its fresh paint, shiny polish, and new leather seat make it look good as new. It has fat, knobby tires, about one foot in diameter, a red tank with black pinstripe trim around a Kawasaki emblem and the edges, and gleaming chrome handlebars that independently extend from the front shocks in a U shape. The first few afternoons Mom's taking us to parking lots and grading papers as Skip and I take turns steering through obstacle courses of Mom's pink Tab cans, and timing ourselves on hundred-yard dashes. This is familarizing us with the agility and speed of the mini-bike, but we've got much bigger plans, and all of Irvine now knows about it, all except Mom and the adults. Hell, at this point the whole thing's taken on a life of its own. I've been approached by no less than five random people about the Minibike Games. Now that the date's set—day after tomorrow—who knows how many people'll show. Mom's taking a class, and she'll be gone for entire afternoons and evenings. It's all miraculously come together.

Couple of weeks ago she sat us down and made a ceremony out of the fact that the usual babysitter's unavailable, that she can barely afford it anyway, and that we're now old enough to be left alone. She had Dad call for emphasis, really laid it on. She so appreciates Skip and me being so understanding. She's noticed how we've been doing our chores without having to be asked, she's proud of my improvement in school, and she knows I'll do well at Benjamin Franklin Middle School. I'm setting such a good example for Skip. Really good. And she's sorry she has to be gone for so many afternoons and evenings. So sorry. She'd rather we had a babysitter to help, but it's just not working out. She's leaving meatloaf and raviolis in stacked Tupperware in the fridge. It's all set up. Peanut butter and jelly sandwiches with bananas for lunch. She wants Skip and me to eat at 6:00 p.m. She wants us showered and ready for bed by the time she gets home at eight. She's going to miss us. She loves us. She trusts us.

I still see Krissy around. Olivia was right. My non-interest seems to have increased her interest, and the few times I've seen her at the skate rink, I've had to strategically avoid her. I can feel her eyes following me, and she inevitably finds her way into my line of sight. She waves, all cute and all, and I nod, force a half smile, break eye contact, and act as if I see someone or just remembered something. Usually this works, but the other day she caught me walking in, all alone, no one around and nowhere to go.

"Hi," she says.

"Hi."

"You skating tonight?"

"Yeah, you?"

"Yeah."

"Who you with?"

"Just some friends. Don't think you know them."

"No."

"No."

"Great place huh?"

"Yeah, great."

Seems like yesterday that I first saw her, and I'm now seeing the futility of dreams, the stories I've created. I thought all happiness depended on her acceptance, her validation, thought all good had died when she laughed in my face. The world had halted, and stars shed tears. But now there's nothing. UPP Elementary's the past. Benjamin Franklin Middle School's the future, hence the importance of the Minibike Games. I'm wondering if I've learned anything, wondering if dreams will again consume me, swallow me whole. For once I'm feeling calm. But can that last? Will calm ever last?

Kevin Newberry, the kid with the parentless house, the house with stained carpet and holes in the walls (we made some ourselves one day), the house where I first smoked weed with Ben Needleman, is finally going to take me to Santa Ana where he buys his weed. I really don't want to go, but I feel kinda bad for blowing him off so much, and he's got me cornered. He's such a meathead and deserves all the blowing off he gets, but he's been nice about sharing his weed with Ben and me, and nice about letting us partake in all forms of debauchery in his house, this hangout, this mysteriously backward place where adults and the outside world don't exist, so I guess I gotta go. And I am, I must admit, somewhat curious.

    There's an explorer in me seeking jungles and swamps and forests who wants to be shot into space, and Santa Ana's an urban jungle, raw, real, and dangerous. But I want control. I want to steer the ship. I certainly don't want to be at the mercy of meathead Kevin Newberry. He's like an unmoored ship; the winds are indifferent and the ship's indifferent, but the havoc wreaked will not induce indifference. But here I am, on the ship. I accidentally told him last night that I had the day free, that my mom would be gone all day. He takes this trip every week, buys hundreds of dollars' worth of ten-dollar dime bags, takes a little out of each bag, then sells them for twelve. He's been bragging about what an adventure it is, that he's in with the gangsters, that they've got cool guns, and that he's gonna himself buy a gun. And all along he's always saying, "You should come," and I'm always saying, "Sure, if I ever get a chance," and then it slips that that chance has come, so here I am.

And like I said, we've been using his backward-ass house and using his weed, and we'll continue to, so I feel obliged. We smoke in his house. We've smoked in every room. We roll joints. There's a three-foot bong in the garage. I'm not sure how it happened, us smoking weed all the time, it just did. Kevin (the type of kid Mom told us to stay clear of) has it, we have hours alone in his house, and we're curious. It's fun. It changes something within me. That invisible film oozing under one's skin, the smoke seemingly floating between brain and skull, numbing some thoughts, heightening others, rewiring brain circuitry. And that's just it—it's different. How, exactly, I'm not sure, but I like different. I want experience. I want adventure. I stare longingly at the moon. I'm Tom Sawyer. Not that I thought about any of this. Like I said, it just happened. But now I see that doing and being something different is part of it. And there's camraderie in it. New people are always coming by, some our age, some older, some cool, and some not. But the cool ones are cool, and I've found myself bumping into people around town. The uncool ones I just wave to or perhaps show respect with a quick hand slap. But the cool ones I stop and talk to, ask questions, listen to whenever possible. People, I've come to understand, like to be listened to. So I ask questions and listen.

Yesterday, this kid named Kayne came by. He looks like an eskimo and is as big as Kevin, only he isn't fat, he's solid as the walls. I know because Kevin made us wrestle. This is how Kevin exerts his feeble power. He has the smoke and the house, so he makes demands. And I love wrestling; Skip and I are always wrestling. But this Kayne kid's a rock. I couldn't even wrap my skinny arms around him. But I tried, gave it my all. He pinned me, but not before I executed a couple of moves and extracted myself from a few of his, and although it ended in defeat, this Kayne kid was huffing and laughing and shaking his head, said I was a scrappy little shit. And he's in for the Minibike Games.

Mom would, of course, disagree, but I say hanging at meathead Kevin Newberry's house is a net positive. The house and the weed bring people together. We get together, roll joints together, inspect the magical and insidious plants together, smoke together, and do stupid shit together. Like I said, the other day we punched holes in Kevin's bedroom walls, took turns with a screwdriver, no real purpose, just did it 'cause Kevin insisted and because we could. Real senseless shit. Normally I don't like senseless shit, avoid it and avoid anyone doing it, but here it's unavoidable. Kevin insists. Says it's his room to do as he pleases. He just covers the holes with a large Ozzie Osbourne poster. Not that it's even necessary because his mom doesn't seem to notice anything. She's come home a few times late in the afternoon, the smoke still floating through the house, and she doesn't bat an eye. She drives a city bus and she always looks exhausted. Like Kevin, she's overweight with sickly, white skin, and when she's home, she just sits on the couch, drinks vodka in a small glass with ice, smokes, and watches game shows. She's never said a word to me, hardly talks at all. Kevin's all proud, saying that smokers already smell of smoke, that they don't recognize the smell of marijuana, and that because my mom smokes, I don't have to worry about the smell. I, however, remain unconvinced, for Kevin Newberry has never experienced the suspicious and microscopic gaze of my mother, never experienced the daily questions of specific whereabouts and specific activities. Indeed, I've become an expert at creating stories so convincing that I've come to believe them myself. I know it's a lie and that lying is bad, but it feels more like an innocent fib to save Mom concern over stuff she doesn't understand. The positives of Kevin Newberry's house and the weed seem to outweigh the negatives, so I justify the charade. I wash up, use Visine and mouthwash, allow time to pass, and make sure I'm ready. Fortunately, she's always tired herself, ready to eat and relax, and I'm usually able to remain aloof by watching TV, playing video games, or reading in my room. She always likes it when I'm reading.

Kevin Newberry's driving his mom's beat-up yellow Capri. I've inquired as to how he always has access to his mom's car, but he just waves me off and says he can do whatever he wants. I wonder if his mom's really that stupid. He's sitting on a cushion to make himself look taller. He's such an idiot though, driving like a maniac, despite being licenseless and thirteen, and I can't believe I'm sitting in the passenger seat.

The streets are full of gangster-looking guys with brightly painted cars that sit low to the road. The guys are full of tattoos, and wear shorts with knee-high black or white socks and wife-beater tank tops. Most are wearing thick, silver chains around their necks, and bandanas on their heads. The house looks empty. The lawn's yellow and brown, littered with trash. Cigarette boxes, candy wrappers, bottles of Mexican soda. The windows are boarded. I don't want to go into the house, but I also don't want to sit in the car alone. So in I go.

There are two tattooed guys inside the first empty room. Both have handguns in their belt, and both are staring at me through hollow, angry eyes. The man behind the door has a gun, a rifle with the end sawed off. His face is badly pock-marked. He's nodding to Kevin, the closest thing, I gather, to a greeting. I'm remembering Kevin telling me about the guns. The weed's in the next room, the dime bags covering most of the floor. The man sitting on the floor's counting them out. We're leaving. Not a word said. Back in the car, Kevin says, "Places get busted every week, but the guys're usually the same." He's so proud.

"Now you fuckin' tell me," I say. "Let's get the hell outta here." And off we go, back to the safety of Irvine.

I've learned, even at this youthful age, that high expectations breed failure, for future stories rarely live up to expected glories—wonders beheld and woven by imaginative minds. An iota of curiosity and wonder wreaks wonderful havoc, I know, and yet I'm undecided if or how I'll manage future stories, unsure whether I'll allow wonder and imagination (or fear for that matter) to run its course, to build illustrious futures unable to withstand reality. Krissy Porterman was not who I imagined. All I'd expected and thought was fiction, utter nonsense, and yet I'm unsure I'd want it otherwise. Low expectations, on the other hand, tend to create possibilities. UPP Elementary, despite its many social vipers, was memorable. Mr. Herrigan was as good as teachers come, and even I, one forever suspicious of education, am thankful for my year with him. I told Mom this. It brought tears to her eyes. She wrote Mr. Herrigan a thank-you letter, and she wrote the school district to commend him. In short, my thoughts, my imagination, the stories I tell myself, rarely unfold as expected. I'm not sure what to do with this understanding, not even sure there's anything I can do, but that's what I'm seeing.

The Minibike Games provide another example.

Forty-two kids. Bonita Canyon—just remote enough. No adults. No cops. A dirt track, designed by Ben, Skip, and me, complete with berms, small jumps, and one bigger jump. The plan is to give every kid a shot at the course. Everyone gets one quick warm-up lap and then gets timed for two laps. Top times get first crack at the jumps, and this is important because the minibike will not likely survive the inevitable crashes. And all the fun, at first, is exceeding expectations. It's funny as shit to watch kids of every shape and size, every talent level, every grade of aggression, navigate the course. There's only one jump of merit. If hit properly, with necessary speed, one launches a good five feet in the air to land soft and snug on a landing pad of equal size. If hit improperly, tentatively, one comes crashing atop this landing pad, most always in comical form, and the roars of laughter exceed even the Van Halen blasting from Ben's oversized boombox.

I clear it and clock a top time, as does Skip, proving that practice does indeed pay. Ben Needleman lands atop, crunches his balls, and nearly flips over the handlebars, and Kevin Newberry doesn't even catch air. The fastest run, amazingly, for he's so big, was clocked by that new kid, Kayne. I like him right away 'cause he's really going for it. He doesn't hesitate and act all pussyfooted like most kids. He's barreling through the track, his mouth and eyes wide open, his cheeks bulging, and he catches more air than any of us, clocks the fastest time of all. Hilarious! When I write his name atop the leader board, he corrects me.

"I go by Manatee," he says.

"Manatee?" I say. "What the hell is that?"

"It's a sea cow."

"A sea cow?"

"That's right."

"Okay," I say, shaking my head. "Manatee it is."

We're thirty-three kids in when the fun and laughter ends, when the exceeding of expectations ceases. And here I must explain. Following the Skate Night and Brian Daniels flipping over the wall, I experienced a slight boost in social stature. Nothing much, just from not existing to kind of existing. Part of this boost came from the spreading of the story—my besting of Brian Daniels—and the fact that I'd had an older girl on my arm. But Olivia, that older girl, bless her heart, had taken further steps to ensure my safety.

She'd started a rumor that I'm a black belt in karate, an apprentice to some master back in Seattle. And people, I must say, have been looking at me differently all summer—looks of curiosity, even slivers of skeptical fear. The unknown. No one knows for sure, and despite my stringy arms, no one seems intent on finding out, including Brian Daniels. All summer he's been ducking around corners like a little girl. And I've almost come to believe the story myself, thus revealing the power and delusion of self propaganda, the fact that one seems able to convince oneself of anything if it's spoken and thought enough times. I remember Mr. Herrigan quoting Adolf Hitler in an effort to make this point. Apparently Hitler well understood this psychology, realizing that if he said something—anything—enough times, people would come to believe it, and he thus set out to do exactly that. So if Hitler could convince millions that such hate and evil was sound and logical, I guess it's understandable that Irvine's youth were equally gullible.

Tommy Dickson's a long-haired, muscle-bound, dirty T-shirt-wearing rocker, an eighth grader, the school tough guy. I don't know who he is at the time 'cause I've yet to start school and he lives in the one remotely shitty part of Irvine. It's clear, however, by the way the crowd parts, tightens, and hushes that he's predator and fear. He's walking with a side-to-side swagger and an ingrained scowl. He comes straight for me, stops a foot away. His two follower morons are standing just behind him.

"So you're the little Murphy boy I've heard about," he says. "Remember Brian Daniels? He's my friend's cousin. Black belt, my ass. You could be the best fighter in the world and I'd still kick your ass. You call these arms?" He's pushing me and slapping my bleached blond bangs aside. "And this girly, white hair. What kind of pussy are you, anyway? I've heard you may actually be a girl. It's true, isn't it?"

I want to say, "Well, how quaint you are, how tactful. And look at you, you piece of rumpled shit." But I don't. I'm looking right through him, as if he's barely worth my attention because I don't want the animal to smell my fear, and I can feel it brewing, feel it breaking through the carefully crafted facade. It's been building all summer with everyone asking about karate, to show them some moves, to reveal a few secrets. And I've felt no choice but to go along, to play the humble and sensitive tough guy, to wallow in those fear-induced glances, those curious gazes. I'd learned just enough to get by. But Tommy Dickson is reality—a hard shot of it. And just like that a terror overcomes me. To be deemed a wimp in junior high's tantamount to having leprosy, and in my case it's even worse 'cause it'll also carry the stigma of having deceived the general public. They'll be lining up for shots at me.

I can almost hear my heart pounding. If I attempt to speak, words'll surely become trapped in my parched and contracting throat. I've no choice but to continue to stare, to act as if this animal is insect or barking dog. But moments are ticking, and I've nowhere to go. Then, a voice.

"Hey, Moron-boy, why don't you leave him alone. He ain't got time for you. He's not allowed to fight, although his sensei would probably let him kick your stupid ass."

Tommy Dickson's sizing Kayne up. "Who the fuck are you?" he says.

"I'm Manatee."

"Manatee? What the fuck is that?"

"A sea cow," Kayne says, smiling a big, stupid-crazy smile.

"Whatever," Tommy Dickson says. "Give me this thing."

He's hopping on the minibike, starting it, shooting down the track. He's coming out of the first berm and veering off course, and he's heading for the largest of the wooden side jumps, the one we've yet to hit. He's gaining speed, too much speed, then he's slowing and jumping off, and the minibike's twenty feet off the ground. It's landing and bouncing, flipping and flipping again. There's a plume of dust and a collective gasp from the crowd, and Tommy Dickson and his two moron buddies are already walking away. The handlebars and brake levers are bent, as is the gear shifter. The grips are ripped. The tank's dented. It smells of gasoline.

I've invited Kayne over 'cause I like him, and I'm curious what Mom'll say. She's always approving or disapproving of any new friend, and although I ignore her and act like she's wrong, I've come to see that her assessments are always accurate. She didn't like Ben Needleman or Kevin Newberry. Both were blacklisted.

We're eating cinnamon Pop Tarts and watching *Land of the Lost* when Mom walks in. I'm introducing Kayne, telling Mom he prefers to be called Manatee, and she thinks this is the funniest damn thing she's ever heard. He's leaving and Mom's staring at the door, smiling and shaking her head. She turns. "He's gonna get you in trouble," she says, "but I like him."

CHAPTER SIXTEEN

Indonesia 2014

"There are two ways to live your life. One is as though nothing is a miracle. The other is as though everything is a miracle."

—Albert Einstein

CLOAK #2—LEARNING/WONDER/INFINITE CURIOSITY. Like a Navy pea coat with a removable, light leather vest within, complete with another removable vest made of light, breathable cotton, each piece intended to be fashionable, functional, and adaptable to any and all environments; at any given time, depending on the weather, at least one piece of this ensemble is available, and if not being worn, this piece will hang prominently, like one might hang a cross or a family heirloom. The jacket: navy-blue in color, is made of strong

Merino New Zealand wool. The leather vest: brown (raw umber) in color, is made of light aniline sheepskin. The cotton vest: light blue (periwinkle) in color, is made of end-on-end weaved cotton. It is double-breasted with four handmade buttons carved from a fallen sequoia redwood tree.

Keep learning, growing, and stretching yourself, inward and outward. Your hair's on fire; the whole world's burning, and learning's a balm, an elixir. Wallow in Wonder; have faith; stare into miracles. Live in the Big World; break down all petty thought-walls. Forever seek sequestered spaces to create, for creation is life. Place gates and twenty-four hour guards at entryways to mind and soul; only the vetted shall enter. Seek depths where all's swallowed; avoid slimy shallows. Learning is persistence and expectation, complete saturation; we too can stare into the world and refuse to look away. We are organic creation, an ant working on knowledge till death, then laughing as beasts and elements fertilize. Fill yourself, then empty, like the garbage. Stretch your skin and mind, watch it wither and adapt, then stretch it again. Do what you fear, then do it again. Losing is sometimes winning and winning is sometimes losing. Big picture and little picture, all one picture. So just keep learning, creating, moving. Let go. Laugh. You may understand nothing, but you can see everything. Don't worry about the morons; the world's way deeper. Ignorance is ego's playground; knowledge is a key. You are Scientific Method and yet you are Faith in vision and wonder shooting lightspeed through galaxy clusters as time laughs itself still.

It's midnight, 12:47 p.m., and the white, rusted 1990s Toyota minivan is rumbling through gunmetal, liquid night. No less than ten boards are stacked atop loose racks, and the entire van's laden with old and new surf decals. I'd pointed out the wobbly racks and two loose bolts to our Javanese driver, but he'd just flashed a pockmarked smile and said, "No problem, very strong."

Lucas is beside me, calm and still. There are four ex-Californians who now live on Maui, three guys and one guy's girlfriend. A joint's lit, a smoke that could send us to a piss-and-rat-filled Indonesian prison for life. It smells good, sweet. I'm thankful for the generosity—it's a special moment, a fresh and exciting journey worthy of celebration—but I pass it along, am feeling calm and clear and don't want to numb it. The rusted minivan's rumbling along, and I'm remembering so many other adventures in old vehicles, being shot through ever-changing and vacuous time toward newness, through so many gray and reflecting nights. At moments, the moon appears through slits of curving jungle. At moments, ghostly apparitions appear through bug-laden headlights: a swooping bird; a dead, splattered dog; some papaya rinds.

We're pulling off the winding highway and entering a well-lit and wide patch of grey concrete that stretches to the moving seas and the dark volcanic shadows beyond. The ferry's waiting, its rear hatch like the large, open mouth of a whale shark. We're entering like plankton; the hatch is creaking and lowering and locking shut. We're standing outside the car, in the dimly lit chamber, watching the well-lit land slip away through round, salt-infested portholes. The ferry's swaying and sloshing and uttering its low, guttural rumble, but it's also slicing into the silence of shadowy seas shimmering dark and silvery under the moon's other-worldly light, and it's slicing toward wide and dark volcanoes. We're walking up metal steps and onto the dimly lit deck where many hollow-eyed Javanese are staring apathetically, half asleep. Most are probably returning from work, and I remember a conversation three days earlier with a Balinese woman who spoke about Javanese immigration into Bali, temporary and not, and its repercussions.

I buy shelled peanuts and we're passing them around and we're all standing at the rail and flicking shells into the moving silhouettes below. It's loud—the rumbling engines and the sloshing and splashing waves—but it's also quiet, as if the silence within these sounds is deep and consuming.

Lucas has read the first hundred and fifty-some pages of my story, has tasted each of the four story lines, including the one he's currently part of, the one evolving as we speak. He wants me to read some or all of the future stories to him aloud, just as I'd done for Hanah. He thinks, like Hanah, that they are somehow more alive when read aloud, and that I'll derive more insight as a writer from the process. He also thinks, like Hanah, that past, present, and future are one, reflections from the same mirror, indelibly linked, and that all hold lessons and maybe even answers. I probably won't read them aloud, but I'll continue to share, for the writing's flowing, and his enthusiasm's much appreciated.

The bright lights below the rising dark mass of one volcano's getting closer and closer, and we're now turning, the engines whining into reverse, the ferry tapping the tires hanging along the dock. "Easy," says our driver, as if relieved.

Apparently, it's often rough and churning. Earlier this year, a ferry capsized and sunk, and many of the passengers were never seen again. Our driver had witnessed it from the shore, had been on the first rescue boat. He didn't want to say anything else about it.

"We must get to the van," the driver says.

Engines are firing. It smells of fumes. The hatch is opening, and we're driving, into the Javanese night. Something's happened. It feels different. We've entered a new land.

We're awakened to a hypnotic and crackling Arabic call to Muslim prayer. Fog's floating so thick that the bustling street scene—mainly men dressed in white thobes—is passing in and out of view. We've traveled through a portal, awakened in another space, another land. Huge burlap sacks are stacked along the road beside haphazardly parked motorbikes and beside other motorbikes lined up in perfect unison, and men and women are lifting sacks and strapping them onto too-thin seats and riding off looking like circus acts. We're all half-awake, and the fog, the fumes, and the haze are now swirling like little dust devils lit yellow and silver, green and blue-black. I want to stop, get out, stand in the middle of this exotic and surreal scene, but such unchecked voyeurism's unsavvy, not to mention insensitive, so I keep my mouthtrap shut—we all keep our silent-in-awe mouthtraps shut—as we slice through coal black night.

It's now cold. The driver's closing the window, turning on the heat, which sputters as if awakened, as if spitting cobwebs and jungle bits. We're parking beside a shack at the end of a beach, emerging, stretching and absorbing all that's occurred and all that's occuring. Night's becoming day. Dawn's burning through gray darkness. The stretch of sand along the silent, calm sea's turning the brown color of Javanese skin, then like the yellow-brown of wet grizzly bears. The sky's looking like swirling oils, reflecting greens and blues from the sea; it's about to explode an entire color spectrum. Fishing boats that before dawn had been graphite ghost ships against waning moonlit seas, sands, and jungle—this inlet— are now revealing colors, first deep pastels of green and red, yellow and orange, and now they're bursting flourescent under equatorial sunlight. Also illumined are a plethora of grease-caked machines, some hung on boats' sides, others stacked aside on tarps, as well as Vikingesque sculptures on every bow and stern. Such moments, these moments, overwhelm senses, tap something beyond understanding, and thereby leave one feeling calm, slightly confused, and yet exhilerated. Such moments, if reflected upon, usually come via extensive travel, planning, and effort—in this case an eleven-hour flight, then a six-hour flight, then another two, not to mention this bumpy, six-hour bemo ride in the thick of a liquid, ephemeral night, from which we'll now board a modern and impressive speedboat with two barrel-sized engines, and shoot rocket-speed across salt-spraying seas toward our dreams' destination—Grajagan, G-Land. But we're here, finally here, and all efforts thus expelled are yesterday.

They are yesterday, yes, and yet as I'm climbing off the boat, wading through the warm waters, and walking the long stretch of beach and the long, muddy path through the humid jungle tunnel, I'm aware of all of these moments, as if draped in a thick quilt of already expelled energy. I may sleep for a day. At the surf camp, groggy and unshaven surfers are greeting us with indifference, and Lucas and I are led beyond the relatively upscale bungalows to the back, to a rectangular, half wood, half thatched hut called simply "Budget," to the place where I'll continue attempting to meet myself again.

CHAPTER SEVENTEEN

Kenya/Uganda 1992

"I think we're all addicted to something.
Some people are addicted to drugs.
Some to power. Some to sex. We're
all addicted to something."

—Bill Clinton

O NCE AGAIN ALL has colluded toward a single point of emphasis, in this case to find Sabrina, the dream girl, the archetype, this blossoming potential, this romantic excursion unraveling in mind and material. Yes, I do realize this romance is figment, and I'm not unaware of the power of dreams to sway and neutralize, to sweep all desires into neat cognitive boxes. I'm aware, yes, but I've also surrendered, accepted, and settled into a time space where one month or one year or three years are relative to a purpose that's now beyond me. I'm convinced there's a reason we lost our money, were forced to work as slaves, forced to forgo the search, forced to surrender to time's unwinding.

If we hadn't lost our money, we wouldn't have experienced the intensity of Israel, the drippings of history, the magnanimousness of religions coexisting within Jerusalem's stained walls. To stand on Mt. Sinai is to become Moses. To see where Jesus was crucified is to become his blood-stained skin. The tears and prayers of King Soloman's wall. The Dome of the Rock's stairway to heaven. If we hadn't lost our money, we never would've experienced the humility of standing on streetcorners competing for employers' attentions, that alien existence, the fourteen-hour days of hard labor, the existential weight of being imposters. The Nigerians and Ukrainians who can't envision a future at home are stuck working for unforseeable stretches of time, stuck fomenting happiness from the hopelessness of slavery. We too are slaves, are treated as slaves, have garnered the subtleties of such dehumanization, and thus garnered compassion, perspective, and understanding. But we're imposters, and we know it.

Eilat, Israel. We're digging a suburban pool for twelve days straight. And with growth comes slaves. Our skin's red and hard, like leather. We buy wide-brimmed hats and long-sleeved cotton shirts and pants, and work with Nigerians who've been standing on streetcorners for years. Zaire, a man with large, deep eyes, muscles like Popeye, and an infectious smile and spirit, is showing us the room he shares with eight others.

There are empty cans, bloodstained and scattered sheets and old pillows, and the stench of eight mens' sweat. The shower's outside, a hose draped over a ledge behind a wooden outhouse. There's a hole for human waste. Even upstairs, with both windows open, the smell's trapped in the rising heat. Zaire's just laughing his infectious laugh. "You said you wanted to see it," he says.

I do want to see it; I always want to see it. Yet can we ever truly understand? We can always go home. We're mother-fucking imposters! And it's weighing heavy.

We're stuck in the hostel's room of dorm beds, but there's air conditioning and a proper toilet. From the second night on, after the safe full of passports and travelers' cheques was robbed, Kayne and I sleep in the lobby, on two hard couches, and, in return, stay for free. There are two Ukrainian guys who've been there longer than us who lobby for this trade, but the Israeli owner says they can't be trusted. Sometimes it feels as if being American carries diplomatic weight, as if our morality's backed by the U.S. government, despite past indiscretions, and despite ourselves.

On the thirteenth day, we're back on the street corner of slaves, and we are swept up by the foreman of a rising hotel, these monuments to growth. We've joined a team of twelve others, the cleanup team, the "do whatever the hell we tell you to do" team. Four Nigerians, two Ukrainians, a South African couple, a silent Japanese guy, a Croatian, an Aussie, and a Hungarian. Thirteen-hour days with a half-hour unpaid and unprovided lunch. Nine shecks an hour. To sweep, clean, dig, and carry for hours on end is to elongate the present into chunks of time. Four hours, if assimilated, if settled into, can become minutes. Long days of labor force time's realignment. Such is the life of slaves. We've been slaves for a few seconds. And we can always go home.

To search for Sabrina is to steer Don Quixote's horse onto unforeseen paths. And here we are, in the Africa of dreams, barreling down an orange dirt road in a government Land Rover, having swallowed a thick chunk of Nairobi's intensity, like swallowing molasses. Here we are again. Searching. Will I ever stop searching?

The government's white Land Rover is making its way through the crowded streets of Kampala and onto the highway, past the many shacks and fruit stands, and onto another orange dirt road. Kampala's hot and dusty and, in one area, lost in a sea of white minivans and swarming masses. Women embracing babies and half-naked children. Men walking aimlessly, staring through bloodshot eyes. Now, plants are shimmering shades of orange and green and yellow under a smoldering sun. Children are waving at the important-looking vehicle.

Yesterday we were slaves; today we are dignitaries.

The air's glowing orange, as if a reflection of the road, as if the sporadic rains have left the mud exhaling. The official white Land Rover's scraping lime-colored palm fronds and smacking large clumps of small green bananas.

The woman at the end of Latema Road, the contact for Schools for Uganda, says that Sabrina and her friends may still be in Baale Waalungu, or they may have moved on, she can't know for sure. The Land Rover's barreling toward a dream—fantasy and reality colliding, a moment of archetypal truth. Can love at first sight exist? Is Sabrina indeed the true love I imagine? Or have I created this entire story out of deep, unconscious yearnings? Sure, this yearning's been different; I've been utterly swept away by its strong winds. But do desire's stories ever intersect with reality? Might this just be another construct doomed to implode or explode on contact with another? Such questions are swirling as the Land Rover's pulling into the village, past a small palapa, between a few concrete houses, and into the relative plaza where a sea of faces explode with excitement and cheers, as if the president himself has arrived. Doors are opening, all hands reaching for the mzungus, the whites. Women are singing soaring songs. I'm shaking hands and trying to match smiles, but I'm an imposter, I've done nothing worthy of respect. A week ago we were slaves. And now we're heroes just because we're Americans who donated a measly hundred and fifty-some dollars for cement, bricks, and corrugated metal. And worse, we've only done this because it's the best way to maximize our depleted funds.

We're sitting in a large circle. The singing's stopped; all are silent. One by one, each person's introducing themselves.

"Hello. My name is Kiria Samuel, and I am the Headmaster and the Commissioner of Public Works. I am very glad to be in your company. I welcome you to our village."

It takes an hour. Everyone's a commissioner of something. I'm scanning for signs of Sabrina, settling into the disappointment that she's not here, wondering how we can get to the next village, when Kirsty, the Finnish woman who leads the Schools for Uganda groups, sits beside me. "One of Britain's bequeathments," she whispers, "bureaucracy."

I'm smiling, an attempt to guise my brewing disgust. "Is there anyone else here?" I ask.

"Yes," she whispers. "Four others. They went into 'town' today."

"Is one named Sabrina?"

"Yes. How did you know?"

With Africa so thick and dense, like mud, she looks like a feather gliding up the red clay road. And with the lavender red sky and the road that appears to drop off entirely, and the way she's smiling and laughing with the playful children, perhaps she is a dream. More beautiful than even imagined. And is that possible? To be better than imagination? That long, silky black hair that I'd first seen in dim light, in the shadow of dreams, is swaying back and forth as her head turns to meet the childrens' smiles. She's wearing those same denim cutoffs, her olive legs long and smooth and softly muscled. She's wearing a navy-blue cotton shirt, unbuttoned and swaying over a thin white tank top.

She's looking at me staring, and now she's staring herself, moving closer until this journey across continents, across ever-shifting planes of reality concludes. And here we're entering that space of dreams and archetypes, a moment forever imbued with meaning and purpose, a memory where all subtle interludes stand still, where all mentation ceases, a moment of pure mystery and bliss. Two souls have merged; it's happened because I made it happen, and all previous actions, however illogical, are justified.

Her skin's shining, glazed in sweat, the smell of tea tree oil. Her green eyes have gold, ocher, and copper flecks. Her hair smells of coconut and hibiscus.

There are three other guys standing in the shade of a palapa, but for now, they're beyond dreams' reach.

"You must be Jim," she says.

"Yes."

She's offering a soft, lithe hand. "Sabrina," she says.

I nod. "Yes."

"You found me."

"Yes," I say again, still holding her hand.

"Why?"

"I don't know." I'm whispering. "You must think I'm crazy."

"No," she says, "I don't. You don't seem crazy at all. But how did you find me?"

"I don't know," I say again. "We found clues. In unexpected places. They found us."

She's humming. "Hmm."

I want to stand here forever; I want this moment to never end. Thus, with thought, with want, the moment does end. I've sliced it up, divided it. Worries about such perfection ending are already creeping in. But something's happened, and we both know it. And as we're walking over to the three other guys, it's clear they know it too. They're all staring. John from Detroit, Danny from Connecticut, and Leo from Rome. I'm so enchanted that I'm unaware of Danny from Connecticut's jealous eyes, am unaware of the way John from Detroit, and Leo from Rome are watching me and Sabrina, the way they're watching us and watching Danny. We're called to lunch, so we're walking in that direction.

It's been three weeks. The purpose of Schools for Uganda is to rebuild schools, and all we're doing is carrying bricks from one place to another, and on our damn heads. We wake up, eat some manioc, hang out until something or someone inspires movement, and off we go, down the orange and red clay road, talking and singing. There's no real schedule, no clear goal for the day. The birds are always crowing and circling above, as if laughing at our stupidity. Flies are always swimming in the sweat pools of our ears.

Once at the twenty-foot pile of bricks, we stack 'em on our heads and turn around. Little kids carry one brick, mzungus two, women and men three to five. And it's hard carrying shit on your head. My head's too damn small and hard and round; it feels like my neck's caving into my back. I'm now using two canvas bags. Kirsty's nice, but it annoys me that she never questions anything. Throughout our walks, she just smiles and babbles on about how some woman had dropped a basket of cassava in the mud or how her palm-knitting lessons are going. Everything, no matter what the hell they're doing, is just fine with her.

Normally, this kind of inefficient shit would drive me crazy, but I'd follow a bunch of armadillos around if I could do it with Sabrina. To describe this blossoming love, these flowing, sequential moments of pure bliss, this feeling of universal grace—as if God himself has scooped Sabrina and I up, each in one of his soft, celestial hands and had brought us together across light years, across past lives beyond time— is to enter a realm of sentimentality that should always be avoided. And reality, of course, always wins. Sabrina's from Connecticut, not Santa Barbara. Her mother's Italian, not Dutch, and her father's a Serb from the former Yugoslavia. He's a tax accountant, not an anthropologist. Sabrina's never even heard of Margaret Mead, Simone de Beauvoir, or Liebniz. Like her dad, she, too, is planning on studying accounting. She's scared of the ocean and of sea life in general, and has no interest in surfing. And there's no younger brother; she's an only child. But none of this matters, and we've even shared a laugh over my stories, for I've conveyed my erroneous predictions over yet another cassava-and-peanut-sauce lunch. Even as we're rarely alone, I'm lost in infatuation, wallowing in Sabrina's beauty, in every smile and sweet word. That she has no interest in philosophy or literature means nothing. That we're constantly surrounded by others, something that would normally drive me insane, means little under the trance. She's beautiful and she's sweet. She's kind and loving. Several times we've stolen kisses by slipping into the thick, green banana fronds. Under the spell, I'm a man of action. On the first day, at the first opportunity, I'd taken her hand, pulled her into the humid banana forest, pulled her to me with both hands, and kissed her. Her lips are imperceptibly plump; until they slowly parted, I hadn't expected such pliable flesh. I stopped and stared into her eyes, then acted on their invitation, stroked her soft hair, and kissed her passionately. I've stolen kisses everyday since. But yesterday things happened, and the spell's lifted. For three weeks I've been content. Now I'm wondering if I'll ever be content again.

Yesterday's slipping into the banana forest didn't go unnoticed. Danny from Connecticut's waiting on the red-clay road when Sabrina and I re-emerge, the others almost out of sight atop a hill with only a periwinkle, dusky sky beyond.

"What're you doing?" cries Danny from Connecticut. "We might've lost you! It'll be dark soon! You realize what kinds of animals could be out here?"

Danny from Connecticut's glaring at me. I feel like it's not the first time, but I hadn't noticed before, or, should I say, cared. He's taking her hand, fixing his glare on me again, and pulling her up the red clay road. He's a short man, looks like he lifts weights but does little cardio, and he's handsome in a round, baby-faced way. His hair's short and dark. He's wearing khaki shorts and a thin, button-down shirt of pastel orange. He's wearing Stan Smith tennis shoes, stained with red dust, but I can picture him usually wearing penny loafers.

"What a dweeb," I whisper, allowing myself to drift behind, the sky darkening into orange, red, and purple streaks, emphasizing my still-entranced state, and producing a rare moment of solitude. I can still taste the cherry lipbalm from Sabrina's deceptively plump lips.

At first, I'd found Danny from Connecticut's intrusions somewhat amusing, an inconvenience combined with a touch of pity. His desperation's transparent. That he loves Sabrina is now obvious, but while under the spell, I'd hardly noticed. He's short and boring. Before yesterday, his words were like whispers consumed by background noise. But then I watched them walking. The way they talked. The way they touched. What if I've just been wrong? Lost under the spell? Danny from Connecticut's been traveling with Sabrina for months. Perhaps their friendship could blossom into love? They do live in the same state. I hadn't even considered logistics. Where's Sabrina going from here? How could we be together in the future? We're heading different directions.

The fact that previous assumptions were wrong is suddenly not so amusing. She's not intellectual. She's not, it seems, spiritually minded. She doesn't want to understand everything, deconstruct every idea. Hell, she's methodical, wants to add numbers for a living. But she's kind and caring, and as beautiful as they come. Nothing's perfect. We must be flexible, adapt. I need to stop thinking. This is crazy. But it's too late. The well's poisoned; to clean myself requires distillation—dilution of invisible forces.

We're packed into the largest hut, the children outside playing and occasionally peeking inside the doorway and the two screened windows. Dusk's now starlight and moonlight.

Smoke from a corner stove is translucent, funneling and swirling grays and shades of fuchsia, like liquid glass twisting. It smells of mint tea, peanut sauce, smoke, and strong hair product, like shoe polish.

Three of the elders are sitting in positions of honor in front. One, a toothless woman with a permanent smile, says, "Tell me about your family." It's a question to no one in particular, but Danny from Connecticut seizes the moment, tells the silent and gazing group a story about how his grandmother fell in love with his grandfather, a classic American small-town love story, a story full of adventure (the grandfather was hunting coyotes that'd been threatening her family's livestock), piety (they'd both been going to the same church their entire lives), Protestant work ethic and individualism (the grandfather, seventeen years young, was building his own cabin down by the river where the beavers, foxes, boar, and hedgehogs roamed), romance (they'd both fancied one another for years, and sweet and comical examples followed), and drama between families and romantic rivals (the patriarchs—the grandfather's father and the grandmother's father—had once, decades before, dueled over a girl who'd soon thereafter up and died from a bee sting). The grandfather had courted the grandmother for months after they first spoke in the fields near the stream where animals roamed. His competition was a village rival, a boy from the wealthiest family in town, a family affiliated with steel plants in Pittsburgh. The grandfather had long hated this rival for his bullying of weaker boys, for his pettiness. He'd wanted to fight the boy, but knew the grandmother would disapprove. In the end, the grandfather won the grandmother's heart with a poem, and Danny from Connecticut ended the story with its last four lines:

If providence keeps playing His heavenly flute
We are destined to together dance with songbirds
Our future home has an oak with a nest
We will marry, our children shall play in its shade.

Such elegance. Such character. Such American brazenness. And with the added touch of Christian piety. The group's erupting into cheers and laughter, and Danny from Connecticut's no longer boring. Who knows how many other stories he's told? The spell's broken. I'm standing beside myself, terrified, aware of all eyes focused on Sabrina and Danny from Connecticut, the two of them together.

There's no water in the village. The nearest well's twelve kilometers away, and the big five-gallon jerricans have to be filled daily. Until now, wanting to stay by Sabrina's side, I've avoided the trip. Danny from Connecticut's gone three times, and now I'm seeing that I'm also expected to go. There's no way around it.

The well's crowded. We're waiting our turn. Kayne remembers hearing about cold lemonade, Coke, and fresh bread with butter. The town's a distribution hub for the villages. The jerricans are full. We're strapping them to the racks. We're leaving the bikes with a woman, and going in search of luxuries. There's a small supermarket in a large wooden shack and another outdoor market with tables of dried fish, peanuts, cassava, bananas, assorted fruits, and random items. There's a bicycle-repair shop and a beauty salon called "Californya." The proprietor says we're the first "Californyans" to visit, takes our picture with an old instamatic camera, and makes a big deal about placing the picture in the salon's entryway. We're pointing to our ridiculous-looking hair, insisting we're not good representatives of her services. But she's just laughing. "We love 'Californya,'" she says.

We're walking through a junkyard of rusted bicycle rims when we see it: a tractor and small trailer. We're back in the outdoor market, pointing toward the junkyard and the tractor. Women are yelling back and forth, then yelling at others who can't be seen. Finally, a man appears, grinning.

"Yes," he says, "how can I help you?"

"Is that your tractor?"

"Yes."

"Does it work?"

"Sure, it works."

"Can we use it to carry bricks?"

"For the schools?" he asks.

"Yes."

"Sure," he says, "just pay for the gas and it's all yours."

For three days, our last three days before leaving Uganda for Kenya to board a flight back to Athens (another hub) to then board another flight for Brisbane, Australia, I'm talking about the tractor to anyone who will listen, talking about building the school and future schools in weeks instead of months or years. Everyone, including Sabrina, is smiling and listening, even while usually talking about other things, about birds or children's games or the way bananas smell when the afternoon breeze blows. Uganda was destroyed by brutality, orphanages are overflowing with children who may or may not have inherited AIDS, the government's still unstable, but no one's quick to create change. Yesterday, while talking to Kirsty, I noticed Sabrina watching me, smiling.

For the first time I'm looking forward to a meeting. Even the annoying introductions seem proper, and instead of singing a silent song or staring at an ant carrying a leaf, I'm listening to each and every introduction, thinking about which commissioners I could still lobby, although I'm expecting nothing but nodding affirmations and cheers of halleluja.

When it's my turn to speak I'm standing, dusting off my legs, and looking around at all the surprised faces. I'd introduced myself the first day, uttered a few thankful words on other days, but never have I stood as if prepared to really say something. Normally, my annoyed state leaves me incapable of thought, let alone complete sentences. I'm introducing myself, thanking them for their hospitality and graciousness, following protocol. Then I get to the point.

"We arrived here a month ago with a goal," I say. "We were told about the civil wars that have destroyed so many of the beautiful villages of Uganda.We were told that the children have no schools to learn in, that they're gathering around the pub or moving from house to house. We were told that the teachers have no supplies to teach with, that their frustration grows daily. And we were told that we might be able to help, that our money would go for supplies, that we ourselves could help build a school. But we haven't; we've yet to do this. We came, you see, with this goal: *to build a school for the children, your children.*"

I'm remembering how Mr. Herrigan would pause for emphasis.

"Twelve kilometers from here is a tractor. It has a trailer. It works. I've already made arrangements for us to use it tomorrow, and we've already collected money for gas. In two trips, less than a day's work, we'll have all the bricks we need. No more walking. It's time to start building. It's time to build your school!"

I'm waiting for an eruption, for wild enthusiam. But it never comes. There's polite applause, smiles all around, and I'm many times thanked for my interest and passion. A few more words are said, but once the meeting ends, the matter disappears like chocolates around children. I'm walking away sure that logic will prevail. Surely they must understand; surely someone will grab hold of this obviously superior idea. But nothing's happening. At the pub that night, the men are smiling, as if offering understanding and condolences. Then it's back to the politics or gossip of the day.

The next day we're walking as usual. The whole damn village. And no one says a word about the tractor. Maybe it's in the works. But deep down I know better.

We're leaving. The good-bye gathering's even more festive than our arrival, and as the Land Rover's driving off, I can see—behind all those singing and smiling faces—our lonely stack of bricks. Kirsty's touching my shoulder. "Every person in that village is going to be part of that school," she says, "and will have contributed to its building. And they'll laugh about all the things that happened on the trail, how funny it was to watch the mzungus carrying bricks on their heads. They'll laugh and laugh, and they'll never forget us."

Sabrina's nodding. Beside her, Danny from Connecticut's glaring blankly, guarding her from my longing to explain, to communicate.

"Maybe you're right," I say, "if it ever gets built."

Back in Nairobi, we've only hours before our flight departs. Danny from Connecticut's standing guard. I'm telling him I need to talk to her. She's nodding. He's glaring. We're walking around a bustling street corner.

"I love you," I say. "I've loved you from the moment I saw you."

"No," she says, "you love something I represent; you don't love me."

"How can you know that?" I say. "I may not understand why, but I know what I feel."

"We're just traveling," she says, "crossing paths. We're not meant to be."

"How can you say that? How can you be so sure without trying?"

"You found me. I'm not sure why, but you did. But circumstances prevail. Reality prevails. I'll never forget you. But we're not meant to be."

"And you're meant to be with him?"

"I don't know. I'm just traveling."

"That's part of why I love you—your freedom, your wanderlust."

"But I'm not that. I'm that now, but I'll soon be home, and I won't be that. It's you that's wanderlust; you may always be. And you don't even know me."

"I know enough. I know how I feel."

"You're living a story; you're your imagination."

"You see," I say. "You're so thoughtful—I love that! Just tell me we can talk when I return home. Just give me your phone number. That's all I want."

"No," she says, pulling away, tense. "No reason."

"Perhaps imagination's real," I say. "How will we ever know without trying?"

"Good-bye, Jim."

She's walking back. Danny from Connecticut's staring. They're getting into a waiting taxi. She's gone.

CHAPTER EIGHTEEN

Traveling 1994

"There are no ordinary moments."
—Dan Millman

TRAVELING AGAIN. TIME still slipping like clouds and vapors, like weightlessness, a love song to space and dreams and imagination. A month of planes and ferries, of floating among aqua waves and surfers, of full moon parties on slanted strips of moonlit sands, of hallucinogenic jungle parties where nature's lushness fuses with flourescent lights and echoes from the black holes of travelers' hearts, from bottomless wells of desire; if one falls in completely, becomes untethered, the fall may never end. Indonesia, Malaysia, Thailand. Space is expanding and evolving from all sides, but it's also devolving, contracting; evolution and devolution colliding, momentarily yet completely.

Back in Australia, at the mercy of cops, there's about three hours when freedom and optimism was impossibility; an hour in the back of a squad car, watching the bikers being questioned, and another two hours in a sterile white room with only a table and a wall fan that hummed back and forth. At first, the cops were more interested in the bikers. But we didn't know anything, hadn't seen anything, had simply gone for a ride inland to experience the hills, the breeze, and the stars. By the time the cops realized we had outstanding warrants, and were affiliated with the notorious Linden Armstrong, Kayne had already so charmed them that they'd moved us to the large room of desks where we were surrounded by smiling and laughing officers who mockingly waved off the one serious cop who wanted us reported to immigration. "Oh, piss off, you fucking Joey," they said to the one officer, and I'd wondered whether his name was Joey or whether they were calling him a baby kangaroo. They served us croissants and coffee, and plied Kayne to repeat the story of Linden Armstrong, the crabs, the roast beef, and the cheese, as if it was the funniest fucking thing they'd ever heard. By the time Kayne was done with them, we were practically police-escorted to the airport. A flight to Denpesar. We still had to leave; our journey with Theo and Oscar was over. But we'd once again slipped through trouble, and I'll forever wonder why.

And now this feels like years ago, a dream, a story. From jail to freedom. The rain's stopped, but it'll eventually rain again.

For a week, we've lived in a cabin of dreams, a Thoreauvian shack perched on thirty-foot stilts at the outskirts of the cove of parties. Below the cabin of dreams are huge boulders. Varieties of surrounding palms sway. The sometimes pellucid, sometimes dense sea as driveway, beyond which Malaysia and Brunei lie. I'm exploring on our first afternoon, sauntering along the white-sand beach (I can still feels its softness between my toes, like dried silk), when I notice the cabin from afar, make straight for it, climb the stringy and winding stairs in awe, and discover a fellow traveler sipping chai on an adjacent balcony.

"This one just opened up," he says. "Guess you were supposed to take it, mate." He's a faceless narrator. I'm twelve, watching *Twilight Zone* on my mother's oak bed. My entire life as an unfolding play, part puppets, part comedy, part melodrama. I've been meditating, you see, experimenting; I shall seek experiences far and near.

The cabin of dreams costs more than we want to pay, but there are three beds to split costs. When I show it to Kayne, his face contorts until I'm rolling on the cabin's wooden floor. We're soon sipping Tiger beers on the balcony of dreams, the sky a panoply of colors and clouds, the distant music floating imperceptibly, when a girl appears below. At first she's just a silhouette under the darkening sky.

"Hello," she says.

"Hello," Kayne says.

"Come on up," I say.

We're all-inviting; we're travelers, between worlds, writing new self-chapters.

Below the cabin of dreams, below the long stilts, between two huge boulders, is a beach of seashells, the beach now glimmering under moonlight, the shimmering water lapping the jewel-like pebbles, the sand, the shells, and now this girl's feet. She's picking up shells, and sometimes pebbles, holding them to the moonlight, and as she does, her sweet brown curls and sweet, big-eyed face are illumined. She reminds me of Krissy Porterman with darker hair. She's climbing the stringy stairs, moving toward the full moon, her face lit bright, and now I'm reminded of the beautiful girl from the movie *Cocktail* and from the movie *Karate Kid*. I can't remember her name, but this girl could be her, so angelic is her face. She's wearing a thin, blue and yellow sarong tied around her waist, and a thin, white shirt that's tied above her taut abdomen.

"Wow," she says. "Oh, my gosh, this place is unbelievable!"

"Where are you staying?" Kayne asks.

"Just came from Ko Samui," she says. "Left my bag at the bar to explore and watch the sunset."

"That's just what Skinny here did this morning," Kayne says, "and this is what he found."

Her name's Jen. Her hands are soft, her skin smooth and tan. She has big brown eyes. I'm shaking her hand and smiling. I've nothing to say; I'm just trying to smile, but it's an awkward smile, for I'm dumbstruck by her beauty, the infatuation already snapping up my mind. My stomach muscles are tightening. I keep smiling this awkward smile until I have to look away, and now I'm looking beyond the balcony railing, watching the distant smoke floating across a wide shaft of moonlight, remembering to breathe. Upon exhaling, a natural smile's emerging, and I'm remembering myself. Perhaps this meditation is creating change after all?

I'm offering her a cold beer, gesturing toward the prime seat on the balcony. "Please." We're all sitting down.

She's traveling alone, just left a girlfriend in Vietnam.

She's from California, from Irvine, lived in Woodbridge, went to Woodbridge High School. She knows our friend, Trent Johnson, used to date his best friend.

She's sitting with her back straight, soaking up the scenery, sipping her beer and smiling She's folding one leg over the other, a smooth, tanned leg sliding through one of the sarong slits. My groin's stirring. I'm cemented in unfolding moments. Kayne's doing all the talking.

And of course she'll stay with us. We have an extra bed, and knew someone would come our way. Of course! We're now family, always will be. Meeting fellow clansmen so far from home imprints spirit on all hearts.

She's off to get her bag. She'll be back in minutes. She's going to bring beers. Are we going to the party tonight?

But I'm on a spiritual journey, a personal quest. This, however, is no time to get all internal. Can't it wait till the meditation retreat, till after these epic parties of parties? What the hell's wrong with me?

I'm sitting alone, aloft, laughing at myself, at the world. The dancing and vibrating revelers are flashing shadows. The jungle's thick green is glowing against tinted shades of black—charcoal, onyx, slate—the moonlight pulsing through all striations, all veins, cobwebs, latent and sprouting seeds.

This entire month I've been reading this book on meditation, on vipassana, on strategically watching the workings of my mind, on the sixteen steps to do so, and I've been religious in my daily meditations. And I'm addicted. Just like I'm addicted to traveling, to reading, to writing, to figuring myself out. Just like I'm addicted to habits, to morning coffee, to beers at sunset. Some habits are good, some bad. They come and go. Addictions must be managed; good addictions, I'm beginning to see, must take precedence. A recipe for success. A structure. A management plan. This is what I shall do. And this is how I'll do it. But even with the meditation, there are two competing voices within, and I've been writing them down.

Oh, how you rationalize!

Well ... we have brains for a reason!

Growth begins with vision and intention, with plans. One can chart one's path, follow it like a map, and strategically overcome oneself. Individual lives can be managed; all can be managed. The religions command: *Thou shall not this and thou shall not that.* Cross God and go to hell. And to hell indeed does one submit when chasing desires through vast mental skies. My aversion to such commands lies bare; I cannot submit without due process. In a way, I envy those who can; those Great Plains call me like birds singing soul songs. This meditation is process, psychological unfoldings, an evolving plan, an edifice, a structure. The book, Bhuddhadasa Bhikkhu's *Mindfulness with Breathing*, a book appropriated during traveling whims, during another synchronistic meeting, lies at my feet, the words lit dimly by a small headlamp. The book says we are breath-body and flesh-body, that breath-body nourishes and conditions flesh-body, that we just have to realize this; we just have to vigilantly watch, dare I say *control*, and settle our bodies, our thoughts, and feelings, like oceans still between winds and waves. The book says we shouldn't listen to others, shouldn't believe anything; rather, we shall experience all for ourselves, observe the product of our own efforts. This suits me. This is religion—Buddhism—but it isn't; it's science, psychology, self-study; it's mysticism. The book is matter of fact. Breath-body nourishes flesh-body. Once flesh-body settles, our minds gain clarity, and we can turn to the secrets of feelings (vedanā). To watch ourselves, ceaselessly, is to get over ourselves, to return to our natural state, to reconnect with the whole.

But how can I get over myself when internal voices are always arguing?

You're just Neitzsche's Afterworldsman, you little pawn.

So? So what? So I seek something beyond myself? And you? Ego's the endgame? This little world's all we have?

Yes, it's all we have; it's what we are. So stop fighting, embrace it, stand up and roar! Become! Stop your petty puppet chatter!

You've no vision, no perspective. If all's mystery, then mystery it is. To transcend is not to settle; puppet strings can be cut.

And then what?

I don't know. Mystery, utter wonder, God, redemption, metaphysics.

And what of earth? Of the here and now? These children before you are just running away.

We're all running away!

Finally! A statement of truth!

*So I want to run with purpose. What's it to you? There's
good running and bad running.*

*Running's running. You and your metaphysical treadmills!
One after another!*

And what's it to you?

*What's it to me? I live here, on earth! Here! In the real
world! I live here!*

*Just leave me alone, I'm trying to read my book. This med-
itation's an answer. Perhaps we just have different purposes?*

No. You live here too.

Okay. Thanks.

Beyond the shades of jungle darkness lie the bamboo stage
and the bamboo dance floor, the flourescent lights, the fused
techno and disco, rap and R&B, pulsing through all abstractions, fueling these fiery and smoking souls. All's just beyond
reach, beyond earshot, beyond sensitivities. I'm alone in my
sobriety, an outcast. No one, however, knows; no one looks
twice at the man enthroned under the jackfruit tree, this alien
creature with hanging yellow fruit sacks. All this meditation,
this free time, this synchronistic traveling, has left me feeling
high, light as a feather—perhaps not as high as these LSD,
Ecstasy, and mushroom revelers, but high in a way that I'm
tentative to interrupt. There's a lightness within, and I'm feeling distant, outside myself, watching thoughts come and go
like the birds and insects flittering above. I've just consumed
this tree's yellow flesh. I am this tree, you see, poised for
self-renewal, self-exploration, self-rejuvenation; all vagaries
of self, its many salient features, splayed like those scattered

Thai seashells on the beach of dreams. There's choice, yes, and there's also no choice. I am this and I am that; I am everything. The ghostly revelers are dancing, spinning and shaking, as are my concepts, as infinite as molecules. And I'm a child in this game, a chicklet, a tiny and whimpering creature, an embryo, a simmering mass of potential.

That book again, *Mindfulness with Breathing.* "Feelings condition the mind and force us to act...Wars, famines, corruption, pollution, all theses crises and problems originate from our failure to master the feelings from the start. If we master the feelings, then we can master the world..."

My own little Enlightenment.

This isn't about God; it's about ourselves; it's about self-accountability. If one conquers oneself, one's thoughts and feelings, one merges with God. Thoughts are veils; there's no disunion.

Whitman's words are swirling like fireflies through the smoky haze above the dance floor. Like swirling song notes, lyrics from the mouthless night. "In the faces of men and women I see God, and in my own face in the glass; I find letters from God dropped in the street, and every one is signed by God's name, And I leave them where they are..."

Mr. Herrigan, my sixth-grade teacher, is standing right over there, beside the twisting roots of a mangrove tree, watching the show, smiling and dancing in rhythm. Now he's laughing, whispering one of his favorite Darwin quotes: "A dog might as well speculate on the mind of Newton."

That book again: "Everything originates in the feelings...
To master the vedana is to master the origin, the source,
the birthplace of all things...The mind is the director and
leader of life..."

Mr. Cipoletta's smiling from the moon, sitting in a dark
crater, his arms outstretched, his head cocked and turned.
"Even beautiful Aristotle was wrong sometimes," he whispers,
the muted words spinning across the night sky, a sprinkle
of stardust, the crushed osseous matter of each and every
thinker who ever thought. I'm wondering why he's sitting
on the moon.

The book: "Our entire species is forced by the vedana to
do their bidding. When sukha-vedana (pleasant feelings) are
present, we try to increase these feelings. Pleasant feelings
always pull the mind in a certain direction and condition
certain activities. Dukkha-vedana (unpleasant, disagreeable
feelings) affects the mind and influence life in the opposite
direction; again, the results are habitual responses. The mind
struggles with these feelings, turning them into problems
that cause dukkha."

The drug-induced revelers are glowing, spinning smiles
spacebound.

The book: "Vedanā, or feelings, have great power over our
actions. In fact, the whole world is under the command of
these vedanā. For example, tanha (craving) can control the
mind. Craving itself is first conditioned by feeling. Thus the
vedanā have the strongest and most powerful influence over
our entire mind. Thus, it is especially important to understand
the secrets of vedanā...We are slaves to vedanā—sukha-vedanā
in particular—all the time."

God's unraveling himself, winking from far and near. There's no avoiding Him. There's only running; there's no hiding. He's every breath, every glinting eyeball. He's right here—right there—but we're blind, distant, disconnected; our unevolved minds can't stop dividing.

I'm expecting the voices to stop. But they're not. If anything, they're lounder.

I thought you were a damn Buddhist now?

I'm just a human trying to understand.

But you believe in God?

Yes.

What God?

Just God.

You see, that's what I'm talking about.

Why are you so upset?

Any God's no God.

And every God's every other God.

And where has that gotten you?

Fuck your platitudes! I'm trying to face myself! To take responsibility!

And where's that gotten you?

To war. With myself. But only myself. Not the whole fucking world at least!

I see.

Can't we transcend? Can't we embrace? Can't we see our commonality? What the fuck's wrong with us? God didn't give us this mighty brain to be so fucking stupid, to be so fucking mindless, so destructive!

But that's Nature. Birth demands death. And life demands destruction. Bloodlines must fertilize; soils must be tilled, energies recycled. All is perfection.

Don't preach, you stupid fuck! You're just another preacher! Fucking hypocrite! You and your little ideals, your stories. And what the hell does that mean anyway? That we're just mindless insects? That it doesn't matter what we do? That all is perfection? All is not fucking perfection! Confusion reigns! The morons are reigning! And what can I do about it?

We are and we aren't; we're better than insects and we're no better than insects. All's inexorably one, and there's no running; we are truly and literally the world; transform yourself and you transform the world.

And the morons will still reign!

Perhaps...

How can I accept the fucking unacceptable? What shall I do? Just lie down so the morons can piss all over my face?

The morons will do what they do; consequences will follow; there's no running from God.

But they still reign!

So be it. Tides come in and tides go out. Stars become and stars explode.

What the fuck is that supposed to mean?

Your anger doesn't help.

It's all I have!

It's just more anger.

I must transcend! I am metamorphosis!

No need to transcend anything; you already are.

This anger—I must transcend it!

You can't transcend what isn't a part of you. It's like transcending the wind. Just let it blow; it'll eventually still.

You're so full of shit.

Yes, I am.

Why are people incapable of comprehensive thought? Why can't we see the world's lenses for the mental ecosystems they are? Why are we so fucking stupid? How can I exist in such a stupid fucking world?

What choice do you have?

So I should do nothing?

You talk about my ideals, my stories. My ideals are sound. Think it through. It's your ideals that are laughable. The world's what it is. Do you think your ideals change anything?

Your fatalism is what's laughable. I have to do something.

It's not fatalism. It's ever evolving. And you're in charge. It's undefinable.

Well ain't that convenient...undefinable...

You can't change what is.

Well, what is has to change.

Good luck with that.

For four nights Jen's sleeping half-naked in a bed six feet away. I'm wrestling desirous thoughts like someone trying to catch a soaring eagle with outstretched hands. The meditation book says this is good, a positive challenge. Just watch the eagle soar. Smile and wave and appreciate. It's good for you.

But the eagle's big, strong, and determined.

One morning she's sunbathing topless on the beach of dreams.

My mind's doing strange things, as if desire was quantifiable energy, and this container called "Jim" is all filled up, overflowing, and wreaking havoc in unexpected, unpredicted, and unknown ways. Perhaps this energy has reached a breaking point? What would Freud say?

After four nights, Jen's off to Ko Phi Phi to go scuba diving.

Of course we'll all get together back in Irvine.

We're watching her walk down the silk beach.

"Can't believe you didn't tap that," says Kayne with one of his twisted smiles.

"Fuck off," I say.

I'm unfolding tattered pages, the rules and schedule for the meditation retreat. Until today, I'd forgotten they existed. The visiting Dutchman in Uganda had first given me the book on meditation and then waxed on about the retreat, about the schedule, about meditation, about his own self-relishings. And I was still under Sabrina's spell. We drank banana-fermented beer from gourds and talked in the round hut that served as a beer hall. Its pillars are eucalyptus, the roof baby pine branches, and thin, dried palm leaves. The sun had set. It smelled of sweet smoke. Women cooking cassava and peanut sauce, singing. Some goats were bleating. An oil lamp was hissing. The other men, the Ugandans, barely visible in the dim light, were sitting opposite corner, listening to local news on a small radio.

The Dutchman's enthusiasm is evangelical, but his smile and presence are holding my attention. This book on meditation's clearly sacred to him, and I'm reluctant to accept. His insistence, however, is sincere, and I'm soon relenting. He's then handing me this piece of paper, which, until this afternoon, has been lodged deep within my battered backpack. Today, I'm watching a bird pull strips of white tendon-like meat from the belly of a live crab when I remember it. To actually find it is exonerating; the memory was real.

I'm standing on a dirt road, soaked in sweat. Said good-bye to Kayne back in Ko Pha Ngan (we'll reunite in Bangkok), ferried to the mainland, to Surat Thani, bused out, and just walked miles through the thick humidity of green jungle. There's a strip of grass in the middle of the narrow road, and soft grass covering much of the surrounding earth. There are scattered palm trees; long, wide, and striated leaves lie still, as do the long, thin leaves, adding to the dense silence. A sweat droplet's falling onto the paper in my hands, the directions and the rules. I've arrived just in time. It specifically says to arrive before dark, and I'm rushing the last mile as the sun's slipping behind the trees. It's now dusk; the sky's shades of dark orange and gray.

The monks are chanting in a large, open hall, a calming hum that echoes through the jungle. There are other foreigners in the back, and still others entering the hall from the rear. I need to check into my room in the long, rectangular building that lies beyond, but the scene—the changing sky, the chanting monks, the humming insects and birds—is intoxicating.

The dirt path with the strip of grass in the middle winds wide around the outdoor meditation hall through palms now shrouded in darkness. The chanting from the hall is persistent, but gentle; it paradoxically adds to the silence of the jungle, just as the insects and birdsongs do.

The living quarters remind me of an elementary school, the rooms surrounding a large, central courtyard with grass and a few large trees. I could imagine it full of kids, running and screaming, but it's now empty and silent, the doorways lit dimly by lightbulbs hanging from wires coated in white plastic. It's a standard brick and concrete building with a high and slanted metal roof.

The room's eight feet wide and ten feet long. Other than some plastic hangers on a wire, two thin bamboo mats, and a hard, brick-sized wooden pillow, it's all brick and concrete.

I'm throwing on a fresh shirt and the meditation pants I bought in Ko Samui, the ones Kayne couldn't stop shaking his head over. I'm once again late for the first day of school.

Rules: Complete silence, except for two personal interviews. We're to stay within monastery boundaries, follow the schedule strictly, and keep the Eight Precepts: no killing (not even an ant); no stealing; no sexual activity (including sexual thoughts); no intoxicates; no eating after noon; no dancing, singing, or self-beautification; no personal reading materials; and no sitting on luxurious beds or seats.

I'm wondering if no intoxicates includes caffeine. Perhaps they'll provide tea. And no reading? The meditation book at least? What'll I do with no reading? Four a.m. wake-up, four to eight hours of daily meditation and yoga, and no talking. And no sexual thoughts? Not a one? Might as well ban breathing! For ten days! What the hell?

The meditation hall's about seventy-five feet long and fifty feet wide. The floor's sand. The ceiling consists of long, narrow strips of brown wood, perhaps bamboo, and there's a large hole, like a vent, in the middle that rises into empty space and another ceiling above, presumably to absorb heat. The entire structure's supported by cement pillars placed eight feet apart, aligned in perfect symmetry. There are no walls, and the surrounding sounds of nocturnal jungle are louder now that the chanting's stopped. I'm taking the only seat left in the far back corner, unfolding the small blanket, and pushing aside the small wooden meditation seat, opting instead for the cushion. There are about thirty Westerners, each wearing their own unbeautified clothes, and another twenty monks, all head-shaven and adorned in bright orange robes, most of whom probably live at the monastery. I've heard that many Thai students enter monasteries at some point, a kind of obligatory retreat for young Buddhist men, and I'm making a mental note to learn more, knowing I'd have hated such obligations, such intrusions on free will. I'm wondering where the Westerners are from, am taking them in one by one. All are sitting upright, attentive, ready for this journey. Something's brought us all here; something's driving each of us. I should be attentively listening to the thin and charming old monk sitting cross-legged on a small stage, humorously describing the daily schedule, sharing stories of people who'd had difficulties in the past. He has a wonderful air, as if he embodies both the humor necessary to explore oneself, and the necessary seriousness. He's older, but his smile's youthful and joyous. This isn't to be taken lightly, and yet it is. With this said, the rules are strict. This is the schedule. This is what we do. Structure is important. Focus is important. Effort and intention are important. I should be listening. But instead I'm weaving stories.

Perhaps I can stop myself? I shall focus on myself alone, on distinguishing what I can actually know, on watching my own thoughts, on delineating that gap between thoughts and feelings, on contemplating this impermanent reality the book speaks of—the voidness, the emptiness. I shall seek God without seeking.

But thoughts are whirling. What a unique opportunity, a sociological experiment! I'll observe and predict without speaking a word. At retreat's end, I'll speak with each subject, gather results, measure the accuracy of my observations. I'll limit the sample to a few people to ensure manageability. It's meant to be.

I'm choosing three people, allowing my eyes to fall where they may.

The man directly in front of me has thick, brown dreadlocks and smells of hemp. He's from Hamburg, a pipe maker. He sits around his small apartment in the red-light district and blows glass pipes, listening to Johnny Cash, reggae, and jazz fusion. He writes slam poetry about cities' underbellies, about social hierarchies welded in pens like zoo animals. He loves the smell of city slime in the morning. Every day at nine a.m., after his morning meditation, he eats a bear-claw donut. He plays the flute and the didgeridoo. He's originally from a small town; his family raised pigs for slaughter, and now he's a vegetarian. He's estranged from his father, who refers to him as "that damn hippy," but speaks weekly to his mother of whom he's fond. He's not a Marxist. He hates Marx, but he's not sure exactly why. I shall call him Wolfgang, for I've always loved that name.

I'm feeling the incompleteness of Wolfgang's essence. There's so much more. Sometimes stories are real. Sometimes I'm clairvoyant. Perhaps this was a bad idea after all? Perhaps I'm throwing fuel on fire that I should be watching burn out.

The charming old monk's talking about the inevitablity of physical discomforts, how we should expect them and welcome them. "Just watch them," he says. He's talking about the inevitability of thoughts bouncing through our heads like bees around hives, how these thoughts are forever distracting us from ourselves, how they trigger feelings that glaze us in emotions. He says it's all really wonderful. Even from the back, I can see the depth of his deep wrinkles, the glow in his amused eyes. "It reminds us we're alive," he says. "And where are we in all of it? Where am I? What is that? Who is that? Life is dukkha—unsatisfactoriness, suffering, pain—but it needn't be. We can see it all for what it is. Effort and contemplation can liberate us. We will, step by step, learn how, with every breath in and every breath out. We're all in this together."

The charming old monk says he wasn't always a monk, says he'd fallen in love as a young man, tells us the story as if each chapter were a few precious words. "Young love. So beautiful. She was so beautiful. And I so lost. So confused. Yet so alive! Emotions. So wonderful. Ships passing on moonless nights."

He's laughing. The other monks are laughing. Then they're not. All isn't seriousness. But all is. His depth makes us all deeper.

"So glad you're here," he says. "I've been a monk for forty years, but that first love still picnics on my shoulder. She's right there. Do you see her? Isn't she beautiful?"

There's more laughter; the charming old monk's bestowing his poetry, his humor, and, dare I say, his enlightenment. His humility's palpable, his life a beautiful game.

I'm starving, thinking about the bag of peanuts hidden in my pack, thinking about the pledge not to eat after noon. Surely that begins tomorrow. Everything else begins now: the focus, the structure, the suppression of desires.

Four seats up from Wolfgang is a thin, middle-aged woman. Like a delicate wafer. But she's disciplined and purposeful, her back taut and upright; she's absorbing every syllable that the self-deprecating monk utters. I shall call her Penelope. Her dark, shoulder-length hair with natural gray streaks reminds me of Pat Benatar's. She's from Stamford, Connecticut, born and raised. She teaches music, plays piano, has written fourteen symphonies that no one but her neighbors have ever heard. She has an ant farm, a hamster, a pet bat, a small, freshwater fish tank, and a cockatoo who serves as her main conversationalist. All creatures, all cages, are lined up perfectly along her living room wall, on a shelf custom-built by a neighborhood man for whom she's projected all her carnal desires, yet never consummated. Two years ago, when she became aware of sexual desires protruding like snakes from her ears, she bought a purple vibrator, used it once, repackaged it as if new, and hid it in the back of a drawer of family keepsakes, as if to spite her religious mother who'd driven off her free-spirited father when she was four. When she orgasmed on that one glorious evening, she'd spoken her mother's name as if it were profanity. She wants to find the father who was driven off by her vengeful and dogmatic mother, but she's afraid of suppressed feelings unlocking themselves like colorless butterflies just out of the chrysalis. She's feeling as if she's in her own chrysalis, ripe for metamorphosis. Sometimes, at night, she reads comic books by candlelight, repeating her cockatoo's gibberish with loving tones.

The first forty-five minute meditation is about to begin. The charming old monk's smile is now an equanimous gaze, silently welcoming all into his beautiful peace. But I'm still absorbing the scene. The monks have all sat down. Candles are flickering. Crickets are singing. Someone's ringing a series of gentle and vibrating bells.

It's then that I see her. I'm twelve, dumbstruck, staring blankly at Krissy Porterman. She's four pillars away, but I can feel her breathing, the rise and fall of her sinewy back muscles, the oxygen pulsing under perfectly unbeautified breasts. Her entire being's singing silent and unconscious promises. I shall call her Juliette. So charming. So quaint. So demure. Even as

I'm seeing her, and even as I'm trying to turn away, to steer myself elsewhere, to emphasize the imprudence of using her as sample number three, her story's weaving itself, and I'm carried off, shackled and helpless. And even after I've closed my eyes, that internal gaze is laughing, staring at itself with raised and amused eyebrows, pondering the lawlessness of unfolding processes.

There's no hiding the beauty. Her pressed white clothes are loose, but not loose enough. The black fishnet shawl's meant to conceal and warm as coolness descends. Instead, it accentuates rising and falling breasts. Concealment's futile. The tanned and softly muscled legs, the taut abdomen. Her long, straight brown hair's tied up in a high top bun, clasped with a bamboo fork.

Bells are ringing and vibrating.

Come back to the breath, says the book, says the charming old monk. Come back.

Juliette's from Belgium, outside Brugge, far enough to feel like she lives with sheep, but close enough for daily outings to the coffee shop with the brilliant Renaissance flair and the wall of Dutch masters' portraits. Her mother's a bookbinder, her father a lawyer at the Hague. She still lives at home, part farm, part cottage, part estate, a monument to culture, a fusion of country and cosmopolitan. As we sit, her father's preparing a case against Ugandans responsible for killings under Idi Amin. She feels guilt over her cultural superiority, her education, her beauty, her charmed existence. She recently decided to become a therapist, to study psychology, in part to assuage her guilt, her superiority. She'll want me to visit her in Brussels. Other than two African safaris with her parents, Thailand's her first trip abroad. She'll appreciate my wanderlust, my experience. Of course I'll be humble. I know her face will be perfect.

I'm glancing at Wolfgang, at Penelope, at the charming old monk.

I'm closing my eyes, envisioning my breath as cold, mountain air streaming deep into my abdomen. There's a vast silver lake, a mirror reflecting jagged peaks. The Alps. I'm sitting on smooth, quarter-sized rocks, the lake an extension of myself. Behind's a wood cabin. It smells of the smoke entrailing from the wood-burning stove. Inside's a brown leather chair, a wall of books, some journals on an antique table. Inside's my past and future self.

CHAPTER NINETEEN

Irvine 1982

"For men believe in the truth of
that which is strongly believed."

—Friedrich Nietzsche

MOM SAYS THAT Benjamin Franklin Middle School's one of the best in California, and I'm damn lucky it is 'cause otherwise I'd have been shipped off to some private school where I'd have to wear ironed pants and maybe even a tie. She's been threatening me with private school ever since Mrs. Culligan called home with news of my first failed English test. She could understand math or even science, but English is unforgivable. "If you can fart, you can pass English," she says, telling me once again how I'd scored high on some stupid standardized tests. But as usual, Mom just doesn't understand the circumstances.

Mrs. Culligan's an old lady with balding, black, curly hair and a thin, withering body. She wears black glasses with thick lenses that make her eyes appear too big for her face. At first I couldn't help but laugh when she looked at me. But then I felt kinda bad, and I guess I got used to those eyes, they looked at me so much. Mom says she'd bumped into Mrs. Culligan at the supermarket and that's why I'm getting all the extra attention. She says Mrs. Culligan's tenured and slightly burned out, but she's a good woman, says she lost her husband, and that everyone deserves a break. I'm curious, but I don't ask.

Ed Turner isn't much taller than I, but he must weigh three times as much, and all muscle too. His arms bulge from T-shirts in ways I didn't know possible, and I'm wondering if his arms are just different, him being a black guy and all. But black guy or not, those arms are cool, and I'd like to have those arms for myself. His feet are huge too, and I guess he can't find the right size, for they're always bulging out of his sandals like something out of *The Incredible Hulk*.

I've heard about Ed Turner 'cause he's been at school a week, and whether he knows it or not, he's now the top dog, the tough guy of the school. Not only is he big, but, of course, he's black, and this itself is almost enough, for we kids in Irvine know little about black people except what we hear on the news, and that is mostly of gangs and crooks and prisons full of blacks who just can't fit into society. Bad seeds, they say. I wonder, at times, if I myself am a bad seed. I've even heard of black people going to prison for smoking weed. I don't think this could happen here in Irvine, but I'm amazed it happens at all. I'm wondering if bad seeds know they're bad seeds, or if they're just pissed like me.

Ed Turner doesn't seem to be a bad seed. He sits quietly on his first day until Mrs. Culligan makes a fuss. "Class, we have a new student," she says. "Would you like to introduce yourself?"

Ed Turner's standing tall, truly a man among boys. "Name's Ed Turner, ma'am."

"And where are you from Ed?"

"I be from Georgia. Then me father get sent to El Toro. He a Marine ma'am."

"Well, it's nice to meet you Ed. But in this class we speak proper English. I *am* from Georgia. Then *my* father *was* sent to El Toro. He *is* a Marine. Can anyone tell me what the word *transferred* means?" She's writing it on the board. "Thank you, Ed."

I want to ask Ed Turner about El Toro, whether he went to the school where my mom teaches, but I'm not sure how to approach it. Finally, I write him a note. He's reading and chuckling, his big shoulders bouncing around. He's writing, handing it back. It says: *Your mama was my teacher.* He's grinning ear to ear and looking me over, as if searching for some resemblance. And he must notice some, for he keeps grinning and shaking his head.

"Jim, Ed, you have something to share?" Mrs. Culligan asks.

"No, ma'am," Ed says.

"No, thank you," I say.

"Okay then." And back to some boring adverbs or something.

Throughout class Ed Turner never stops glancing my way, smiling, and shaking his head. He's an attentive student who even asks the occasional question that is sometimes answered, sometimes not, with Mrs. Culligan turning his English proper all the time.

After class comes lunch. Ed Turner's following me across the yard to the snack bar where I always get a bean and cheese burrito. He's still smiling and shaking his head. Several times he laughs, touches me with those big hands, and puts his arm around my shoulder. I can feel people looking at us, but there's nothing I can do. He follows me into the snack bar, but buys nothing, just looks around. It makes me feel kinda bad, and I consider buying him a burrito as well. But then I wouldn't have enough for my after-school candy, so I'm trying to just forget about it.

I'm sitting on the ground, against the grainy, cement wall where there's a chance no one will notice us, and as expected, Ed Turner's plopping beside me, still grinning ear to ear.

"That a big piece a food for you be so skinny," he says.

He's reaching into a pocket, retrieving a round tin, unscrewing the lid.

"Want some?" he asks, leaning over. "Chewing tobacco."

"No, thanks," I say. "I'm starving. Want some burrito?"

"Naw," he says. "The chew kills the hunger."

"You don't eat lunch?"

"Sometimes," he says. "Usually just a chew."

"You sure are big for never eatin' lunch," I say.

"I work with Mr. Hansen, packin' meat after school. He a good man who gives me meat to bring home to Mama. He knows I got brothers and sisters."

"How many?"

"Eight. Five boys and three girls. I'm the oldest. Sometimes I work pickin' strawberries, but only in season. How 'bout you? You probably no need to work, no?

"Oh, no, I need to work," I say. "I deliver newspapers and wash cars sometimes. But that's not as cool as packin' meat."

"Yeah, I guess so."

"Where's your house?"

"On the base."

"And you come all this way for school?"

"I come where they send me."

The bell's ringing.

"Well I'm glad they did," I say, so beginning my friendship with Ed Turner.

At dinner I'm determined to get some answers. Mom's cooked broccoli and baked potatoes, but she forgot the cheese. I'm using lots of barbecue sauce, leaving none for Skip.

"Mom, Ed Turner's in my English class," I say. "He sits right next to me."

"Really? So he knows I'm your Mom?"

"Yeah, he seems to have liked you."

"He's a smart one," she says, "nice kid."

"His arms are huge," I say. "He says he works packin' meat after school. Aren't there laws against that?"

Mom's slowly bobbing her head back and forth in the way she does when I ask something she can't explain. "Yeah," she says, "some laws are funny that way. In Ed's case, he has a big family, and his parents need him to work and help out with money."

"Mrs. Culligan's always correcting the way he talks," I say. "Why can't he just talk like that?"

"She's trying to help him," Mom says. "Ed's smart, and I always told him so. But I also told him that that way of talking could eventually get in the way of his success."

"I understand him," I say, "everybody understands him. What's the big deal?"

"It's just the way it is," Mom says. "Say Ed goes for a job, the kind an educated person would get, say in a bank. Most people won't even give him a chance if he talks like that. They might think he's a lot of bad things he's not."

"Well that's their problem," I say.

"Yeah," Skip says. "Who cares how he talks?"

"Yeah, well, maybe it shouldn't be that way," Mom says, turning away, "but that's just the way it is."

I now walk to school, a glorious luxury. Kayne's at my side and, thanks to the minibike, I actually know a bunch of people. Comfort, however, seems fertile soil for chaos, and we're not three days in when the reality of junior high— self-consciousness, power structures, and the attitude of appearance-is-everything—comes crashing down in the form of Tommy Dickson.

Snack break. Middle of the quad. I'm caught alone.

"Hey, look," Tommy Dickson says, his two stupid-looking friends behind him, "it's the pussy little surfer boy with the girlie white hair." He's inching closer, all puffed up. "I'm surprised he's not wearing a dress. I hear some boys are actually girls. Maybe that's what you are? You're just a little bitch, aren't you?"

He smells of unwashed clothes, and I'm mumbling, "Wouldn't you like to know," but I'm also thinking about utter alienation and ridicule and that the truth and its repercussions still exist, and are even probable given the ridiculousness of my story. My arms, after all, are the size of number two pencils.

Next day. Snack break. Middle of the quad. People are turning and whispering.

"Ahh, pussy boy," Tommy Dickson says. "So when do I get to kick your ass?"

A crowd's forming.

"Moron-boy," Kayne says, waiting for the crowd to silent. "He's not allowed to fight. You'll get him arrested."

"That's such bullshit," Tommy Dickson says.

Kayne's staring. "It's true … Moron-boy … but I'd be glad to give you a go. I won't get arrested."

Tommy Dickson's looking around. He can't back down to such a public challenge.

"How about six o'clock," Kayne says, "at the racquetball courts. Then we won't get interrupted."

Tommy Dickson's spitting at my feet. "You got it, fuck-wad," he says.

A crowd's waiting. The sun's still floating across a lavender sky. From opposite corners Kayne and Tommy appear, the crowd parting. Tommy's shaking his head and arms. Kayne's staring blankly. Tommy's swaggering like a boxer, yelling, "Come on, you fat fuck. Let's go!" And he's yelling, "Let's go! Let's go!" But Kayne's just standing still, his eyes wide and steady, looking as if steam's filling his big, round face. And Tommy's still swaggering and yelling: "Come on, come on! Whaddaya, retarded?"

Kayne starts bending his knees, pounding his chest, and roaring like a wild gorilla. Then, with a ferocity rarely seen in middle school, he's charging, barreling Tommy Dickson across the court and into the concrete wall, crushing the air out of him. And now he's backing up and charging again, and Tommy Dickson's a cornered and cowering animal, in shock, beaten, and I'm actually feeling sorry for him. Kayne's roaring. The crowd's erupting. We're engulfed by fans.

It's the next day that it starts. Kayne and I are hanging out in front of the school, watching the girls get off the bus, when Ed Turner approaches.

"Well, you be lookin' like you havin' a good old time," he says. "Wish I be feeling like smiling, but that bus ride make me head hurt with all that singing. No offense to y'all, but them white kids can't sing a lick."

"I know what you mean, Ed," I say, "that singin' always bugged me too."

"You be hearing the singin'?"

"Where you learn to talk like that?" Kayne asks.

"Georgia, I guess," Ed Turner says. "Just how I talk."

"Coolest damn way of talking I've ever heard," Kayne says. "Think I'll talk like that too."

Ed's looking Kayne over, as if determining his sincerity. "But you already speaking the good kinda English," he says. "No need to mess it all up."

Other kids are nodding in agreement.

"Let's meet for lunch," Kayne says.

Ed Turner shrugs. "Okay."

Kids are calling it "Ed Language," and it's taken over the school. It probably would've just disappeared after a couple of days, but Principal Baxter's made a big fuss, says teachers will be giving detention to anyone heard speaking it, so now everyone's speaking it, and it's become a game not to get caught. I'm wondering where this leaves Ed, and Ed must also be wondering, for all through English he just chews his tobacco and never says a word. He doesn't seem angry, just a bit despondent, and after a few days I decide to join him in chewing tobacco; I have to smell it anyway, and it makes me feel like I'm supporting Ed in this small way. Unlike Ed, however, I'm spitting on the floor around my desk, as if spitting on the school itself. Ed's hesitant, but he gets such a kick out of watching me spit through my teeth that he's soon doing the same. Everyone but Mrs. Culligan notices; she's clueless, even when dark rings start rising from the floor like a trail of black ants.

Two days later Mom gets an official letter from Principal Baxter. It's all about this new form of improper English that too many students have been speaking, and how parents must talk with their children about why speaking in such a way is detrimental to their education and future success. He wants to ensure the parents that this way of speaking will not be tolerated at Benjamin Franklin Junior High.

Mom's asking what happened. I tell her, again, about Ed and how Ms. Culligan's turning his English proper all the time, and I tell her about Kayne meeting Ed, and how we can't help that kids are sheep. She's listening and frowning.

"Listen Jim," she says, "if other adults around town hear you talking that way they're gonna ask, 'What are they teaching over there at Franklin?' The school might lose some of its funding from wealthy donors who help make it a good school. It's just the way it is. I can appreciate your empathy for Ed, but some things can't be changed. Someday you'll realize how lucky you were to grow up here in Irvine. Most of the world's not so lucky."

"It's just stupid fun," I say. "Irvine's always got something against fun. We're not going to talk like that forever."

"Well, you just stop talking like that," Mom says. "That's all there is to it. And tell Kayne too. Understand?"

"Whatever."

The janitor cleans Mrs. Culligan's room on Fridays, so when Monday comes I've a feeling that he'll be waiting with his screwdrivers, ready to lodge one into my ear. And sure enough, there he is, standing in the sunlight, arms crossed, his thick, red mustache twitching.

Ed and I are left alone in the silence of Principal Baxter's office. Through the big windows I can see the secretary pointing and frowning and saying who knows what, and I'm feeling a stubborn sense of rebellion toward these walls and these frowns and the framed diplomas and awards peering down from the wall behind the desk. There's a picture of Baxter's family, all of them smiling perfectly, as if an indecent thought never crossed their minds, and I'm thinking about telling him, the second he walks in, that I've seen his perfect little Jonathan drunk and passed out and lying in his own pool of vomit, and that this picture's a fraud, just like this school, its proper English, and the bullshit classes clothed and disguised as an education. But then I think of future wrath and how Mom knows all these people, and it doesn't seem too smart to tell him what's really on my mind.

Ed breaks the silence. "You need say nothin'. This my fault. You too much to lose. I take the blame. You say nothin', you hear?"

"No way, Ed," I say. "We're in this together. No way I'm gonna let you take the blame. I'm the one who's really responsible."

"They expect from me, but you? No expect."

"No way."

Baxter's walking in, sitting, and leaning back in his chair. "Gentlemen. We have a problem here, don't we?"

"Yes, sir," Ed says, "and it's all my fault sir 'cause I chew the tobacco to kill the hunger and don't want to say nothin' so I chew in class, and I shouldn't have spit on the floor but I did."

"This isn't Ed's fault," I interrupt. "I was the first one to spit on the floor because I felt bad that Ed couldn't even talk in class. He used to ask good questions. He's clearly a smart and good kid, and now he can't talk at all, so I figured I wouldn't either, even though I never say much anyway."

"This true, sir," Ed says, "but I at fault 'cause it was me who bring the tobacco and talk like that in the first place, and when Jim here take the chew it's really only 'cause of me."

Baxter's rocking slowly in his chair, rubbing his chin. "Okay," he says. "So you were both involved, but it was you, Ed, who brought the chewing tobacco and who first started chewing it in class."

"Yes, sir."

"But I was the first one to spit on the floor," I say. "Ed wouldn't have done that if it hadn't been for me."

Baxter's dialing the phone, asking the secretary if our parents had been contacted. Neither of them arrive, so we spend the rest of the day in the office doing work our teachers send down.

We both get suspended for five days. And we have to attend some stupid workshop on tobacco abuse with a bunch of losers. Ed gets transferred to another school. They say he should've been closer to home anyway. I never see him again.

CHAPTER TWENTY

Traveling 2014

"A man who dares to waste one hour of
time has not discovered the value of life."
—Charles Darwin

CLOAK #3—STRUCTURE/PURPOSE/10,000 HOURS— LIKE a machine-workers jumpsuit, intended for any and all dirty work. And yet comfortable and warm enough to wear during morning studies and reflections. Mine is dark grey with reinforced knees and elbows, lined with sturdy, light-grey fleece, complete with additional and unorthodox zippered pockets for pens, books, notebooks, notes, etc. Intended for everything from the inventor's lab to strolls in the forest to long bouts of writing. And the buttons—I couldn't help myself—molded from melted metal, straight from Thomas Edison's Menlo Park Lab.

How are you honing your craft? How are you earning Gladwell's 10,000 hours? Three hours a day for ten years. Three daily hours of pure focus—no distractions—to earn competence. One hour a day for thirty years. And competence, per Aristotle, our Western guru, is happiness. Routine. Focus. Daily discipline and effort leads to competence, which leads to excellence, which then builds one of happiness' pillars. We are Edison burning wood varieties while bats flap and birds chirp morning simplicity. What are your strengths? Your purpose is carved in timeless and eternal space. Life's no game of cards, no rolling of dice. Once discovered—revealed—creation of your castle begins. No one just lucks into creation and success; they're there ready and waiting; they've earned it. Whitman's windswept leaves guided by science and structure. Nothing just becomes. Nothing good comes easy. Knowing's earned, and not knowing's earned more.

Lucas sits twenty feet away. The "Budget" cabana has four rooms, but we are its only residents, and there are two empty rooms between us. It's our fourth morning together, and we're relaxed from another full day's surf and a thorough sleep. The air's warm, thick and moist. It smells of wet jungle. Rained waterfalls last night. I've just finished writing, the morning routine complete, and we're both now watching a four-foot long gray-and-green lizard (actually a monitor) picking white meat off rainbow fish skeletons. This remarkable creature's framed by four brown monkeys hunched on buttocks, they too immersed in the feast. Paro, a local with long and curly black hair, says this is a daily routine. Fishermen, after slicing up the morning's bounty, throw fish skeletons here, about thirty feet from the edge of our thatch-covered deck, this new sacred morning spot to read and write. Paro's saying there are several monitors in the area, but there's one special one as long as this building. The locals believe this huge, special one's a now-extinct ancestor, a dinosaur, that it's good luck to see it, and that they rarely do. Several other locals have been watching the scene in silence. The monitor just walked away, and the monkeys have disappeared, the sound of creaking bamboo as they move through trees.

Last night, sitting at one of the long banquet tables with some Aussies and Kiwis and the Hawaii crew, someone asked if I was married, to which I replied, "Divorced, for the second time. And this time," I continued, "I knew it was wrong. You should see the wedding pictures; I literally look like I'm in pain."

The entire table was half delirious from surfing all day, and everyone thought this was the funniest fucking thing they'd ever heard. They all just kept shaking their heads and laughing and telling me how fucking funny I was.

"So why'd you do it?" Lucas asks. "If you felt it wasn't right, why'd you go through with it? And now, because of your son, you say it was the right decision. And if that's the case, what's the point of Cloak Number One? If we can't trust our instincts, what can we trust?"

I'm nodding, for Lucas has just explained part of my dilemma, part of the disgust with my cloaks—in this case,

Cloak #1. I'd built my life, in part, on this structure, this belief, and it's now in question. It was a road map, an answer. I can methodically meditate, transcend my thoughts, study, travel, exercise, love, and stay on purpose, focusing on that which feeds the soul, that which builds and creates, and I can thus connect to destiny, to God, to True Self, to this flow, this universal essence where life unfolds synchronistically, beautifully, effortlessly. A plan. A structure. A foundation. And sometimes it did; sometimes it does. After years of traveling on whims, I felt able to delineate instinct and thought, able to feel and sense the right path. Fundamental decisions—going to college, studying history, becoming a teacher—were all made from this sacred place, and all unfolded like rolls of silk. Friends and books and places to live—all fell into place. A tapestry of synchronicity. A seemless union with Nature, with the flow of streams, with the Universe, with God. Cloak #1 was sound. Whenever a major decision loomed, I'd meditate, go into the woods, float in the ocean, find a way to connect with Cloak #1, to that thoughtless space within. An answer train. My thoughts would still rage—they've always raged—but eventually they'd settle, and an answer would arise. A feeling. A knowingness. I was so convinced, so confident. Then I married my first wife, and thus began my unraveling. But that's another story.

"Perspective isn't necessarily linear," I say. "Sometimes it comes on the back end, and now I see it was all for James. Cloak Number One's sound. And yet there's more going on beneath the surface. Psyches are more complex; the world's more complex. All may never be conceptualized. All may never be understood. Sometimes things just happen, and sometimes we just do things for unexplainable reasons. *Thusness,* the wise men say. We have to surrender. I can have a plan and yet be comfortable with no plan at all. Equations are functional within one dimension and not within another. Not that I'm entirely comfortable with the concept, for even as I'm thinking it, I'm wrestling with that unsettled space within, that space that wants structure and answers, that wants control. Perhaps I'll forever lie under this microscope of consciousness? But how can one ever truly understand oneself when the scientist behind the microscope—me, I, ego—is clearly biased and confused? One must examine oneself. But the act itself creates separation. I guess it's all just part of the process, I don't know."

There's a monkey picking bugs from another monkey's head, and Lucas and I are watching silently. I'm thinking about how much better Lucas is than I, that he's too smart to become disillusioned, that he'll figure out his own wounds before they become, and I'm thinking about the wondrousness of life's complexity when faced with clarity, or at least educated honesty. Right now I'm feeling content with imperfection, with my own already committed history, with my utterly imperfect and wounded self. But will this last? Most likely not. But can I remember? Yes, I think I can. Maybe this is what it means to love yourself? Give yourself a break. What's done is done. Everything I've done is for James, and self-disgust isn't conducive. But "thinking" is also not enough. There must be action, steps taken to reprogram long-conditioned impulses and reactions. What are these wounds of which Lucas speaks?

Of course I've read it all before, thought about it before. But now I'm feeling naked, exposed, cracked open. Something's shifting within, just not sure what. So I go to stories once again, to inner content. Perhaps it'll let in some light. Keep doing, and see what happens.

CHAPTER TWENTY-ONE

Australia 1992/1993

"Father, forgive them, for they
know not what they do."

—Luke 23:34 (KJV)

THE WORK, WE'VE been told by many a traveler, will fall into our laps in "Surfer's Paradise," a city on the Gold Coast, just outside of Brisbane. We're dropping our bags at the hostel, and running toward the ocean, our long-lost friend. Down Cavill Avenue, the central artery of town, a red-bricked road lined with palm trees and colorful plants. Tourists are roaming. The air's salty and warm; it smells like fast food, seaweed, perfume, and tanning oil. The white-sand beach is covered by colorful towels and umbrellas advertising XXXX Beer and Coppertone, and the surf's aqua-blue and green, packed with people wading and swimming, cooling off.

We're renting surfboards. Kayne's longboarding, along with another guy who says he doesn't see many other long-boarders in these beach breaks, says he likes Kayne's style. And when Kayne says, "Yeah, I'm a manatee," the guy laughs so hard he almost shits himself. He's sticking a veiny hand out, looking at me all serious. "Linden Armstrong, at your service," he says. And when I laugh, he smiles and laughs too. "A shit layer," he says. "I like that."

Back on the beach, we're enjoying our post-surf exhaustion and the afternoon air, which is beginning to cool, and Linden Armstrong's buying beers. He's asking lots of questions about our interests, the jobs we've been working, and why we're in Australia, and four beers later the beach is clearing, a swath of pastel colors across the sky. Linden Armstrong owns a restaurant, just opened a nightclub called "The Play Room." Kayne's telling him about our stolen money, how we've been slaves, and I'm thinking Linden Armstrong might be a cop, so I'm asking about work permits.

"No worries, mate," he says, "two intelligent, trustworthy guys like yourselves—I need that. And you'd probably like to make more money doing less work? Yes—of course you would. Not to mention the babes; Aussie girls love Americans, you being so polite and all. Shit, mate, they'll be fallin' at your feet at my club. Wait till you see the place!"

He's thumbing through a notebook, clicking a pen, slashing and circling.

"Your lucky day, guys," he says. "My restaurant needs two night kitchen hands. Four hours, six to ten. I'll pay you double if you help me with my flyers on the beach, and maybe run an errand or two here and there. Wouldn't take more than an hour a day, whenever you want. I know you wanna surf, so do I mate, no worries."

Linden Armstrong's looking like a tanned surfer who just got out of the army, chiseled and serious, his hair cropped, his leg muscles flexing. He's holding a spray bottle, a big blue one, and some yellow flyers that say *The Play Room: The Place To Find Some Play.* "Just pass 'em out on the beach," he says, "emphasize how fun it's gonna be, and offer them some tanning oil. Sometimes they even want it rubbed in."

Kayne and I are looking around, the beach still full of girls.

"Whaddaya think?"

We're shrugging, helpless. As if in a trance. Choice doesn't exist.

Months pass. Seems Linden Armstrong's another traveling angel. We're making enough money to save doing half the work we were, and now we've moved out of the hostel's dorm and into a little flat, along with two Japanese guys who are blissfully quiet. No more listening to farting and coughing, sniffling, creaking beds, or endless shufflings throughout the night. An actual home. Mornings I'm relaxing with the birds and my books, now a daily routine. Every tree's full of birds, and as the sun rises, the most beautiful of symphonies is performed daily. Sometimes I crack a window, light a vanilla candle, and sit in the living room, on the one couch. Other mornings, I'll drag the couch outside and sit on the porch. After writing, Kayne and I surf, eat breakfast, sometimes take a nap, then hit the beach to pass out Linden's flyers. Two hundred every day. Half a bottle of tanning oil.

At the restaurant we're the slicers and choppers and dicers. Tomatoes, cheese, onions, avocadoes, potatoes, bell peppers, coconut slivers, kiwi, mango, bananas, grapes, and melons. There's always something to slice, and we're the ones to do it. And Linden's true to his word, out the door by ten, and usually on to "The Play Room," where he isn't kidding about the girls liking us Americans, so polite and all. He's always coming over to see how we're doing, usually when Kayne's surrounded and telling stories. He's always bringing us free drinks and saying how hard we work and what good blokes we are, stuff like that. He reminds me of a politician. People are always watching him, pointing and whispering. He's the owner, and it's an amazing place, so I guess it makes him amazing too. The packed dance floor. The sparkling chandeliers. The red velvet booths. There are purple satin drapes along one wall, and paintings and sculptures throughout. And the beautiful people, all done up. But something's off; I can feel it like humidity.

What the hell's wrong with me? All's perfection, and I still can't relax. The surf's been six to eight feet for two some months. Burleigh Heads and Kirra. Kind of waves I used to draw on Pee-Chee folders during class. And we're still saving money. So why that feeling? Why can't I relax? Am I making it up? How can I understand and trust the irrational world of emotions?

The night manager at the restaurant's a huge Maori guy with bushy black hair and forearms the size of my legs. His name's Sam. He has a tear tattooed under each eye, one, we are told, for each person he's killed. He's never before called a meeting; he's hardly even said a word until tonight.

"We may have a thief among us," he says in a soft and feminine voice. If he weren't so damn scary, I might've laughed aloud. "Over the last month our crab inventory has practically disappeared. Entire slabs of roast beef as well. Not sure how, but someone must be taking it off the premises. We're talking twenty-three hundred dollars of inventory. Really hope it's no one in this room. Think about any unusual activity you've seen."

He's looking around, those big, dark eyes peering into each one of us. His voice might be ridiculous, but those eyes are mafia.

I'm looking at Kayne, who's looking at me, and I'm remembering all his long breaks and the exhaustion that follows. Sometimes he falls asleep on the roof and can't be budged. And no one seems to care. Linden loves him, so no one says a thing. But someone must've noticed.

We're walking in silence.

At home, Kayne's grilling steaks.

"So tell me what happened," I say. "How?"

"What you talking about?

"Just fucking tell me, Kayne!"

"Okay, okay, Skinny. Just settle down. Jeez."

"Don't tell me to settle down! If we're gonna get out of this, I need to know everything."

"Okay, okay. I had that big apron, you know, with the big pocket. I'd eat in the freezer until it was full of shells, then I'd go out back and empty the shells into a box I'd hidden. When I took the trash out at the end of the night I'd dump the box at the end of the block, in that little supermarket dumpster."

"And what were you doing on the roof, on those long breaks?"

"Just sleeping," Kayne says. "It's just crab and roast beef. They've got a freezer full of the stuff."

"No, Kayne, it's twenty-three hundred dollars. You dove head fucking first into their inventory!"

"Okay, okay …"

The next afternoon another meeting's called. Sam's little voice and ruthless eyes waste little time. "We've discovered that at least some of the crab might've been eaten on the premises. The janitor found shells in the third shitter."

Heads are turning, looking at Kayne. Everyone's noticed his long bathroom breaks, and always in the third shitter. And Kayne's blowing it; his big, round face is red and about to explode.

Linden appears, looking serious, almost sad, says he's just talked to Larry, the supermarket manager, told him the situation, and Larry's been noticing shells in their dumpster for weeks. Linden's looking at Kayne, whose face is still red. As if to abolish any doubt, his belly's protruding from the bright aqua T-shirt.

We're in Linden's cramped office. There's a desk, cluttered with folders and loose papers. Ironically, there's a picture of a giant crab on the wall, one of those restaurant-advertisement-type posters. Sam's opening the door, but there isn't enough room.

"I'll take care of it," Linden says, the door creaking shut. "Have I not been good to the two of you? Have I not helped you out? I talked to you on the beach that one day, and I thought, 'Here are two nice, trustworthy guys,' and I thought, 'I'd like to help them out. Americans were so good to me when I was in their country.' And what do I get for it? You steal from me! You fucking steal from me!"

"Linden," I say, almost whispering, "you're right, this really sucks, you've been great to us and this is bullshit. Kayne just doesn't think sometimes. He means no disrespect, I assure you."

Kayne's nodding, staring at the floor.

Linden's leaning over, looking up at Kayne's downturned eyes. "And what do you have to say?"

"Jim's right, I just get hungry. I wasn't thinking."

"Just go home," Linden says, shaking his head and waving us away, "just get outta here. I'll call you tomorrow. You're gonna do some extra things for me."

"Okay," I say. "We're really sorry, Linden."

"Just get outta here."

Linden calls first thing next morning.

"Got a package for you to pick up," he says. "You're gonna start working off what you owe."

I want to ask questions, what exactly he wants, how long it'll take, stuff like that. But I'm also relieved, figure it can wait, shouldn't push it. And anyway, he's already giving me directions to the post office, says to call him after we've picked up the package, that it's addressed to me, then the line's dead.

I'm staring at the red phone, wondering how the package could already've been addressed to me. Linden must've planned on us picking it up. But how?

The post office just opened. The lady at the counter has disheveled, curly red hair that barely conceals her scalp.

"Picking up a package for Jim Murphy," I say.

The lady's frowning. She's disappearing behind two swinging steel doors.

Two minutes. Five minutes.

I'm looking at Kayne and he's looking at me.

The lady's peeking through the steel door's round windows. We're locking eyes. She's flinching. She's poking her head out. "They're looking for your package," she says.

"Something's wrong," I say to Kayne. "Something's wrong. Let's go."

We're walking hurriedly down the sidewalk. I'm looking back. The woman's outside, waving and pointing.

Sirens.

We're ducking into an alley, opening a cracked door, and walking through an empty restaurant kitchen. We're running.

Calling Mom again. Not sure exactly why. I'm still determined to understand the precariousness of most peoples' lives, to transcend middle-class privilege, so I'm committed to concealing our crisis. And besides, if I told her the truth, she'd just worry herself sick, and I can't have that.

The phone's ringing.

My stepfather.

"Hey, Roger," I say. "Jim here. I've only got a few minutes. Mom there?"

"Hey, Shithead," Roger says. "Heard you got a job. About time. So whaddaya want now?"

He's yelling. "Your no-good son's on the phone!"

Mom's voice. "Hi, Honey. So glad you called. You okay?"

"Yeah, we're okay."

"How's everything?" she asks. "Having fun?"

"All good, Mom," I say. "Just wanted to check in, let you know we were okay. Only have a couple of minutes."

"Well, good timing," Mom says. "Was hoping you'd call. Your dad's ex-girlfriend called last week. She's been looking for you, and I of course had no way to get ahold of you. Her and her new husband are sailing in Venezuela. I think they're going around the world. I'm not sure exactly what their plan is, but they said they thought of you. They need help on their voyage. I told them you were in Australia, and they said they'd pay for your flight over, that they'd pay for everything, all food—everything—if you'd just help them sail around the world. She said they'd get you back to Australia if that's what you wanted. Let me find the number here. So glad you called. They've been trying to track you down."

"Back to Australia?" I say, "They're sailing to Australia?"

Mom's still searching for the number. After a moment, she says, "Yes, Honey, they are. I guess they're going to eventually leave the boat somewhere in New Zealand."

"They know I'm with Kayne?"

"They know," Mom says, "said it's fine. They could use the two of you. I told them it was unlikely you'd want to go back across the world, but she was persistent, said she had a strong feeling about the whole thing, that she'd long ago talked to you about such a journey. I always thought she was a weird one. Promised her I'd try though. So glad you called."

She's giving me the name and number in Venezuela, some harbor with a romantic Spanish name.

"She said to leave her a number if they weren't there when you called, that she'd call you back."

We're saying our good-byes, and I'm already thinking about synchronicity, about my impulse to call, about the craziness of up and leaving, and the reality of possibly coming back. I've heard we could hop a boat to Indonesia, fly out from there. And to see Ana Paoula again, in a slinky bikini no less. I'm wondering what her new husband's like. I'm staring at the phone. I'm picking it up, slowly tapping the numbers, one by one. It's ringing.

CHAPTER TWENTY-TWO

Traveling 1994

"Show me the way to the ocean,
break these small containers."

—Rumi

O N THE SIXTH morning, as flickering candles give way to dawn's grey light, as eyes open to Penelope and Wolfgang's empty meditation pillows, I'm struck by the finality of their disappearance. Their complete absence makes their previous presence and my stories feel like a dream. And despite my increased equanimity—five days of silence, six hours of meditation daily, and eating like a bird—I'm still weaving stories as seamless as the crickets' song.

Penelope has gone to meet her only true friend, Emily, in Rome. Emily had previously begged her to join, but Penelope was committed to Thailand, had committed the moment she first experienced the peace of meditational depth. Emily, however, had so waxed on about Italian food and wine, and olive-skinned men with huge, doe-brown eyes, about roaming the bustling streets of Rome on foot and by Vespa, about her goal of writing at least one poem and drinking one glass of chianti in every piazza in Rome, that Penelope can still picture and hear the sincerity etched into her face and voice. After four days of replaying Emily's pleas within the confines of her skull, Penelope succumbed, justified by assuming the voices in her head were intuition, were speaking of some larger purpose, and that she'd simply been wrong in following her stubborn desires to delve further into meditational depths. She could always meditate. There's that wellness center down on the lake. She'll do a three-day retreat when the leaves turn every magnificent shade of fall. Those ceaseless voices, these visions of Emily pleading, clearly have a higher meaning. Perhaps she'll meet the man of her dreams in Rome? Perhaps she'll meet the composer who'll finally recognize the brilliance of her symphonies? Penelope had packed her things and walked the jungle trail under the last slivers of moonlight. She'll be in Bangkok in twelve hours, probably enjoy a dinner and some live music. She'll be in Rome by tomorrow evening. She can't wait to see the surprise on Emily's face.

Wolfgang wasn't distracted by such alluring options, although it was thoughts of a girl that justified his leaving. In his case, the dense pain simply proved too much. He'd followed the charming old monk's advice, tried to wait it out, but he too had finally left in the thick of evening five. Not eating after noon just didn't work for him. He was lethargic and weak, lightheaded, and constantly sweating. And his large, Germanic body just wasn't made for all this sitting. His back was killing him, and the yoga only made it worse. And that girl! She was all his thoughts saw.

She used to be a prostitute. He'd seen her walking home in early mornings, sometimes from his window, other times as he walked for coffee and a bear claw. Then one day he saw her in a bookstore, chatted briefly about Camus' *The Stranger*, about its perspective. If he hadn't known she was a prostitute, he never would've guessed, for she revealed no signs of overt sexuality; she was, in fact, almost conservative with her modest sweaters, loose, wool pants, and colorful scarves. The scarves and her fondness for berets and fedoras were the only clues of her liberal nature.

So Wolfgang had simply decided to go home. He was feeling too dense to enjoy his time alone in Thailand, or anywhere for that matter. So he just went home, decided this girl's presence in his thoughts was the purpose of this whole experience, that it's okay to live his routine life in Hamburg, that it makes life bearable, even happy in a simplistic and angst-free way. He'll soon be back in the comfort of his Hamburg apartment, blowing his glass pipes. The hiss of the torch. The liquid glass morphing. He'll soon be wandering dark streets again in a haze. The comfort of a bear claw, the smell of his clothes piled in the corner. I'm wondering if he'll ever get over his father's distance, his father's judgment. I'm wondering what he sees when he looks in the mirror. I'm wondering how long it'll take for him to approach the girl again, and how he'll get over her profession. I'm smiling, feeling compassion, wishing

Wolfgang could've just given himself a break. At what point does the pain become unbearable?

Even as I'm watching stories unravel, I realize they're creation, as ephemeral as the clouds. Of course there are slivers of curiosity, an optimism that such creativity is psychic, soft whispers from God, tiny seeds of truth. But this unusual state of clarity, this strong sense of dual-wholeness, has made it clear: my stories are just stories, and thoughts are just yarn. Ever since the end of day three, when thoughts became still water, I've felt an uncanny ability to observe all thoughts from a short distance, and more interestingly, distinguish through feeling, through intuition, through a deep sense of knowing, which thoughts to follow and which to let float on by. And now, after a full ten days of silence, I'm prepared to leave it all behind, to let the clouds do their thing. I'm off to Bangkok to meet up with Kayne and another friend of a friend. I'm gathering belongings, taking one last look around the tiny concrete room, walking the dirt path to the meeting hall. Although resigned, curiosity reigns, and if Juliette's still here, I'll ask.

Another aspect of this calm state of dual-wholeness is that the voices in my head have stopped—not entirely, but they are whispers, as if just awakened, tentative to disrupt the morning calm. And when I do hear them, it's not always clear who's idealist and who's realist, who's detachment and who's attachment. They've so merged that commentary's rendered mute. Or temporarily silenced, I'm not sure. It's as if the voices are still there, but their messages trail off before I can make sense of them, like someone talking through loud sounds or into a wind that's whisking all meaning away.

So when, upon walking the windy dirt path one last time, I begin to hear their commentary, I take special note, wonder if my calm mind and assumed clarity are already waning. I've already decided that I'll allow Juliette to make the decision for me. If she's still here, then that's sign number one. If she glances my way, notices me, then I'll ask her. Otherwise, my curiosity and stories would just decay in the jungle, like everything else.

You have to talk to her, ask her, see if you're right.

No, I don't. They're just stories. It's all story.

The Universe speaks through your thoughts; it knows things. You just have to listen.

I'm tired of listening to my thoughts; they forever deceive!

Your filter's too dirty! The windows to your soul are filthy. I can barely see you!

Yes, filthy with your bullshit. Leave me alone. I'm done with you.

Juliette's speaking to the charming old monk. Both are smiling and calm, at ease. There are several Westerners scattered among orange-robed monks. The sun's just risen above the tallest trees, the last remnants of morning mist absorbed. Most everyone's drinking tea, including Juliette, and most appear to be reveling in the fact they can talk, yet enjoying the comfort of not feeling the need. I'm reminding myself that she's from Belgium, about to go off to University in Brussels. She's bowing to the charming old monk, her hands in prayer. She's walking over for more tea, and I'm moving toward her. She's pouring, turning, and nodding. Up close, she has distinct cheekbones. She's a large woman, with broad shoulders. I'm remembering how her flowing brown hair looks from behind.

"Ten days ago," I say, "I decided to test my stories about three people. Two have left, but you're still here."

She's smiling. "And what's my story?"

The voice is deep and guttural. She has, I now see, an Adam's apple, and her hands are thicker than expected. I'm remembering what guys on Ko Samui were saying about Adam's apples.

"You're a man?" I say. It just comes out.

"I'm in transition," she says. "But yes, I was born a man."

"Well," I'm saying, shaking my head, "That wasn't part of my story."

"And what was my story?"

I tell her.

"Well," she says, "My name's Samantha, not Juliette, used to be Sam. I am going to college, but in America, Cal Berkeley. Grew up in Mendocino, little town called Blue Lake, just outside Eureka. My father's been a logger his whole life."

"Yes," I say, nodding, "of course."

"That's funny," she says.

"It is, isn't it?"

"And how about you?"

I tell her.

"I thought you were from California," she says. "You look like a California surfer."

"Yes," I say, "guess I do."

"Crazy, isn't it," she says, "all our stories?"

"Yes," I say, "seems a theme these days."

"Nice to meet you, Jim."

"Nice to meet you, Samantha."

I'm thanking the charming old monk for his wisdom and humor, saying many a silent good-bye, and walking the long, quiet walk back through the jungle to civilization.

The bus is late. Just prior to departure, it rains. Large droplets tapping corrugated metal. Sporadic sheaths of rain and wind. A warm coffee. The rain stops. Then the clouds lift and the ground steams. It cools. I speak to no one, am complete and whole, get on the bus. High on fresh caffeine, I'm reveling in the street scenes beyond the dirty bus windows. The sounds of passengers speaking Thai, the loud, rumbling engine rising and falling, the motorbikes and trucks and splashing puddles. I'm feeling, dare I say, content in my loneliness, whole. I fall asleep, awake in Bangkok, fresh and alert. The streets are bustling. Everything's moving so fast. The screaming traffic. The whistling train above. The sea of faces. The dirty and beaten cement. That dual wholeness is still intact. I, Big Self, am still watching little self do its thing, delineating, deconstructing, creating and celebrating its existence. And it's clear: there'll be no peace, no surrendering to God, no pure and unpolluted connection, as long little self, this "I," this ego, exists. But how can it not? How can it be destroyed? As long as I "think," as long as I'm watching the world, doesn't the ego exist? To destroy it would be to destroy myself. "Just watch the show," the charming old monk would say. "Just watch it." But what exactly is this little self? What created it? Why is it the way it is, so neurotic? And can it be changed? Or eliminated altogether? The wise men say it can be, but I can't imagine.

Meeting Kayne and his friend at some fancy hotel, the Mercure Fortune, where his friend has a room. They'll be there later tonight. Kayne says I should take a swim, a sauna, and a jacuzzi, says they have a special night planned for us, which of course means trouble.

Just watch it …

A one-room salon under the train tracks, beside the buzzing traffic. Flouresecent lights, the smell of boiled rice and coconut moisturizer. I'm blinking, and half my head's shaved. A surrendering laugh. The young girl, the apprentice, is nervous. I'm smiling and nodding. She's shaving the rest.

The pool's like floating in silk. The towels are thick and fluffy.

Kayne and his friend, Joey, are all smiles. They've just arrived from Joey's palace, as Kayne calls it, in the South, in Pattaya. Kayne's laughing and giving me shit about my hair, doesn't believe it was an accident, thinks I've been brain-washed by the "orangemen."

"Ten fucking days of silence," Joey says. "I can't stay silent for ten minutes."

I tell them I'm going to Nepal to hike the Himalayas. Kayne doesn't want to hike, but he does want to hang out in Kathmandu. If I'll wait four days, go ride elephants up north with him, he'll go to Kathmandu with me. He knows I love elephants.

Evenings in Bangkok are lightshows and Asian city songs.

The elephant's thick head hairs tickle the skin.

Lungs thick with forty days of thin Himalayan air.

A mind settling into infinite spaciousness. Yet stuck in physicality. Little self's strong as ever, although quieter, even silenced at times.

Beautiful loneliness.

A decision, as if external, from depths, from beyond: I will become a teacher. Learn. Travel. Teach. This is my purpose.

A call home. Mom. Mr. Cipoletta's died. There's a memorial next week. A decision made for me: going home.

CHAPTER TWENTY-THREE

San Francisco 1983

"School is not easy and is not for the most part very much fun, but then, if you are very lucky, you may find a teacher. Three real teachers in a lifetime is the very best of luck...My three had these things in common—They all loved what they were doing. They did not tell—they catalyzed a burning desire to know. Under their influence, the horizons sprung wide and fear went away and the unknown became knowable. But most important of all, the truth, that dangerous stuff, became beautiful and very precious."

—John Steinbeck

T WAS THE summer of 83' when I first met Ana Paoula, my dad's super-hot girlfriend.

Mom loses it one day, says she's sick of my shit, and that Dad can deal with me, that he can see for himself. So off to San Francisco I go, unsure of what to expect. Dad sounds pretty mad on the phone, but he isn't the mad type; I'll smooth him over in no time. Fortunately, it all happens fast, a matter of days, and Dad isn't quite prepared. He's working long hours for some bank, and they're putting him up at a nearby hotel, the Franciscan or something. I'm to get off the plane and take a taxi straight to the hotel. "I'll deal with you there," he says.

When I arrive I'm quickly whisked away by a tall doorman in a stupid-looking red robe with big, black buttons and gold tassels. He's sporting a conspiratorial grin—I'm sure Dad's told him I'm in trouble—and he walks like he's got a stick up his ass. He says, "You're not to leave the room." I reply, "Yes, my lord."

The room's large and ritzy. The walls and ceiling are shades of thick, dark wood. Same with the night tables and the dining room set. The chairs are red velvet. The bed's a dark-green velvet. I'm opening the heavy, yellow drapes, and looking out on the city—the Transamerica Building, the glistening waters and sailboats of San Francisco Bay, the Bay Bridge, the billboards, the bustling streets, the vintage green-and-red streetcars on Market Street. There are two golden fans. I'm turning them on, walking into the bathroom. Before this, I hadn't expected a woman, but the many toiletries and brushes reveal a feminine presence. I'm holding a brush, pulling a strand of black hair as long as my arm. I'm showering, wearing the thick, white robe with the big "F" on the front, plopping onto one of the red velvet chairs, clicking the remote—the Giant's game—and browsing the oversized, leatherbound menu. Unlike the idiot doorman, the lady on the phone's very nice. Waffles with strawberries, fruit, and fresh orange juice. She calls me "sir." I like being called "sir."

The red velvet chair's a throne. The silver-laden meal arrives, is rolled in and served. I'm halfway through the green sports page, pondering a nap, when there's a click, the big wooden door opens, and there she is.

"Ahh, you must be Jim," she says, swaying on over and kissing me on the cheek, something that takes me by surprise. "I've heard so much about you." She's slender with silky black hair and olive skin. I'm watching the door, expecting Dad.

"Your father's working for a while," she says. "You in trouble, yes?"

"Guess so," I say, shrugging.

"Yeah, I know how that is. Don't worry, we're gonna have fun."

I want to ask questions, but I can only stare. She smells like vanilla. She's wearing black tights, thick, white aerobic socks, white Reeboks, and a loose fitting black tank top.

"My name's Ana Pauola," she says. "I'm your father's girlfriend."

"Oh."

"You tired, yes? Airplanes make me tired."

"Yeah, I'm a little tired."

"Well, just relax. I'm gonna take a little shower. Your dad'll be here soon."

I'm watching the bathroom door close, and listening to the humming and trickling shower and the click of the big glass door. When Dad arrives I'm dipping the last of the strawberries into the silver bowl of whipped cream.

"Hey," I say, waving and reaching for the orange juice. "How 'bout this place?"

His lips are moving. I think they're saying, "Shit."

Dad's new Camaro has all the electric stuff, a T-top, even a spoiler. When he first got it I tried to persuade him to get the *Smokey and the Bandit* eagle put on the hood, but that's yet to happen. The car's cool, but it would be even cooler with the eagle.

We're driving. I'm playing with the windows and the stereo, and rummaging through the glove compartment, anything to endure the awkward pauses and stupid questions. He's doing his best to be angry, to maintain an air of authority. But I can tell he found it amusing to find me enjoying the Franciscan so much. And besides, he hasn't seen me in a while, and I think he's glad to have me around. I figure he's still carrying that stigma of divorce, that feeling of parental guilt that gives us kids more control, a platform to justifiably argue and generally be a pain in the ass. In other words, Dad's guilt renders him unable to truly punish me. Of course, he doesn't know I know this, nor does he know it himself probably, but it's true.

He's asking the usual stupid questions about school and sports.

"And is there a lucky girl?"

"No, Dad," I say, trying to maintain an ounce of stoicism.

"I bet you're breaking hearts."

"You're killin' me, Dad."

He's recently moved, and it's the first time I've seen the new house. It's a nice neighborhood. Clean streets and well-groomed gardens. Driveways with fancy cars. Lots of bricks and pilllars and big front doors. His big front door has golden nobs and a stained-glass window that reflects swirling colors around the entryway. Inside, the carpets are white, the walls plastered with artwork.

"Does Ana Pauola live here?" I ask.

"Oh no, no," Dad says, as if my fragile psyche couldn't take such a blow.

"Why not?"

"It's just better that way."

But as we're topping the flight of redwood stairs, I'm noticing several bouquets of flowers, a brush on the marble counter, and a woman's dress strewn over the leather couch. There's even a bikini on the floor, on one of the oriental rugs.

Mom's doing the same thing, trying to hide everything. Every night she's sneaking over to the neighbor's house, this strong-looking guy with a dark beard. His name's Roger. He acts real nice, but I can tell he's an asshole and that he's just being nice 'cause of Mom. For a while now he's been stopping by the house, usually with some ruse about needing milk or butter or something. He's always patting me on the back and calling me "Chief" or "Big Guy." Sometimes he'll shake my hand all strong, the deep wrinkles in his neck and face will pulse, and he'll stare at me like he's teaching me something. Mom says he fought in Vietnam, that he's a tough, but good, man. Vietnam or not, he seems like an asshole to me. And do they really think we don't know they're shacking up? I'd rather they just talk to us about it. Of course, I wouldn't respond, wouldn't give up power. But at least they wouldn't be treating us like complete morons. What's it with parents anyway? Do they really think we kids don't see what's going on? Or is it just standard procedure for everyone to just play along?

My bedroom's boring. A bed, a walnut dresser, a few old photographs on the walls. I'm grabbing my skateboard, heading out.

"Not so fast," Dad says. "There's someone I want you to meet."

The loud, ominous doorbell's ringing.

"Go ahead," he says, "get it."

The guy looks like a preppy Santa Claus. He's wearing green knickers, a yellow sweater vest, and a thick tweed jacket. And his long, thick beard's white as snow. An unlit pipe dangles from his mouth. One thick hand's now taking the pipe, the other's reaching out. "Well, hello lad," he says. "Name's Mr. Cipoletta, means 'Little Onion' in Italian."

"Hey, I'm Jim, just means Jim, I guess," I say, shaking his hand.

"Yes, Jim, guess it does." He's smiling and walking past.

From the top of the stairs, Dad says, "Thanks for coming." They're shaking hands and looking at me.

"Mr. Cipoletta here is going to be your tutor, our own little summer school. He was a history professor at Stanford, but he's also gonna help you with all your studies."

"Little Onion" is nodding and sucking on the unlit pipe.

"It's about time you started working to your potential, Jim," Dad says.

"How long's it gonna take?" I ask. "It is summer you know."

"It'll take as long as Mr. Cipoletta says it'll take. Every day, same time, just like summer school. When he says you're done, that your homework is complete and your lessons finished, then, and only then, can you go out. Understand?"

"But—"

"But nothin'."

I'm grunting, wondering what happened to all that parental guilt.

The "Little Onion" and I sit down at the big, marble dining table. Dad's made a big deal about insisting he smoke the smelly pipe in the house, and I just shrug when he asks if I'd mind. He's lighting it, savoring the pungent smoke. He's curling his mouth to blow smoke upward, toward the high ceiling and the redwood beams from which a large chandelier hangs. Outside the fog's rolling down the street, children are screaming, and the sound of electric buses—a snapping, clicking, and braking sound—is constant. I want to get away, to explore, to get on my skateboard and find a bus that'll take me to some unknown place where I can look at weird people who'll make me feel normal. I want to smoke one of the many joints I've brought and wander around the park. I want to go buy candy or even a good book. Anything but sit here with a guy wearing knickers and a sweater vest.

"So," he says, stuffing his pipe again. "What shall we talk about today? Your dad tells me you like history."

"Not really," I say, "I just find all the bullshit amusing."

"And what do you mean by that?" he asks. "What's the bullshit?"

"Well, first of all, we're supposed to remember all these names and dates, and even when I do I never feel like I've learned anything. So what's the point? And second, these history books are a joke. Everything's so damn biased and we're supposed to just sit and suck it up like little robots. Whenever I do bother to ask a question, it's always the same thing—'Well Jim, that's a good question, a good point'—then we move on with the brainwashing, so I hardly even bother anymore. I had one good teacher a couple years back, a teacher who listened and didn't seem full of shit, but other than that, it's the usual bullshit. A few weeks ago we were talking about the American settlers moving west and the clashes with the Indians. I say to the teacher and the class, 'Does no one else see that we came in, took over this land, and just killed all these Indians, completely screwed them over, all that disease and stuff? Even killed all the poor buffaloes.' And the response is the same old shit. We end up talking about our 'manifest destiny' and some asshole, Machiavelli, spoutin' off about what's best for the all-important State, then go right back to reading the same stupid book that mentions the Indians as if they were just a speedbump that our big truck had to absorb. All that 'manifest destiny' crap, as if we had no choice but to betray and kill anyone that got in our way, as if this so called 'destiny' makes it all okay. I don't buy it. I think it's all just a big story—fiction—the history we want it to be, not what it really is. The reality was ugly. Selfishness, greed, destruction. And it's all like that, all just different peoples' versions of what happened to support their own ways of thinking, their own stories. So what's the point?"

For a minute the "Little Onion" just sits smoking his pipe, expressionless, as if waiting for more. "That's good," he finally says.

"Good?"

"Yes. Excellent, in fact. You're a critical thinker. And you're exactly right. The victor usually writes the history; the victor controls the flow of information." He's smiling.

"There was a German philosopher named Friedrich Nietzsche who I think you would have liked. He called the student phase of one's life the period of the camel, for a camel gets down on his knees and asks to have a load put on him. Nietzsche also resented the way people just tend to believe whatever they're told. He called it the 'herd mentality,' said people were like sheep the way they just blindly follow one another."

"Yeah, well, ain't that the truth. Smart guy, that Nitzey."

"Neat-chee."

"Neat-chee. Yeah, well, whatever. Never really seen a camel before. They get down on their knees?"

"Sometimes."

"Cool."

"So what would you have done?" he asks. "If you were a settler, that is?"

"How should I know?"

"Would you have killed the Indians?"

"No. I would've left them alone. It's their land."

"Do you want to travel?"

"Whaddaya mean?"

"Do you want to see the world? Would you enjoy the adventure of going somewhere you've never been, somewhere that's different?"

"Sure, I wanna go everywhere."

"Then you probably would've wanted to go West, would've wanted to explore that new territory, to experience that adventure, yes?"

"Yeah, I guess so. Doesn't mean I'd have killed the Indians though. I'd at least have shown them a little respect. I mean, it was their land. They'd been there a long damn time. And they knew what they were doing; they knew how to protect the land. All we do is destroy it."

"Right," he says, "that's good, you would've had respect for them, that's good. But what if, when you'd met them, you realized that they saw you as the enemy? Other white men had already killed their people, and therefore they weren't going to trust you, no matter what. They wanted to kill you. What would you have done then?"

"I don't know," I say, "guess I would've tried to talk with them."

"You couldn't, you don't speak their language."

"I'd get a translator."

"Even if you had one, it doesn't matter. They don't trust you."

"I'd look at them. They'd see they could trust me."

"Maybe, but they'd already seen many of their people killed by whites and the diseases brought by them. There's a long history of distrust, and they're only seeing more whites coming. You're white. They don't trust you, so they're hostile. They're going to kill you. What are you going to do?"

"I would've apologized, told them those other whites were assholes."

"Doesn't matter. You're white. They'd already met good whites, might even realize you're good. But the assholes had caused much harm. Their loved ones had been killed. There are always a few assholes to screw things up. And it goes both ways. There are good Indians and asshole Indians. And in this case there are Indians who want to kill you. So what would you have done?"

"I don't know," I say.

The "Little Onion" is puffing his pipe. "Life isn't fair, son," he says, nodding, "and history is never simple. It involves real people, and people are complex. We're all a bit crazy in a way."

"You're crazy?"

"Sure, I feel crazy sometimes."

"I think I'm crazy."

"Why?"

"'Cause I think everybody's full of shit. Like we're all living in this little world of illusion. It's all bullshit, everybody just putting on a big show."

"You see, I think there's a trace of wisdom in that."

"My mom calls it inexperience, says I need to learn more, that until I've properly educated myself, all my banter is rationalization for screwing around, whatever that means. That's what she says though."

"Well, it took me thirty years to figure out how right my mother usually was. You gotta laugh, kid. Stay critical, but don't let those opinions harden. A hardened mind is a hardened mind, no matter what you're thinking." He's smiling, and I get the impression that his entire brain is smiling because the wrinkles appear to surround his head.

Mr. Cipoletta comes, as promised, every day. We sit at the table. He stuffs his pipe, lights it, and blows smoke toward the chandelier where it swirls and floats and disappears. Then he asks me what I think about a given issue. Affirmative action, capital punishment, environmental legislation, abortion, gun control, foreign policy, immigration, taxes, the economy. We talk for a while, then he has me write it all down, brainstorming as he calls it, has me choose a thesis and challenges me to support that thesis in writing. Then we talk. And I have to admit, I don't really mind 'cause he lets me write whatever I want, never says I'm wrong, just tells me to support it, even helps me find information to do it. Then we break it down, point by point. We do talk about names and dates, but he doesn't make a big deal about them, just says they're important to remember for understanding the whole picture, like small pieces of a puzzle. "If you're missing a piece," he says, "you can still make out the whole picture, but having all the pieces makes the picture clearer." When we start with math, we spend an entire day talking about Greek philosophy, how Plato believed in some transcendental realm, and how they believed that math was one way to connect with this realm. He talks about Newton and his ordered Universe, how he was trying to explain how it all worked, like a machine, a clock, and he talks about Einstein and the accuracy of missiles and the possibility of time travel. Put like this, those equations actually seem cool; they mean something. He's going on about quantum physics and the structure of atoms and the mystery of it all.

"There are surely laws, structures," he says, "but there's also a lot more going on that we don't know about, that don't always follow the rules. Who knows what you might see in your lifetime? People living in space? Time travel? Flying cars? It's all possible, we're right there."

He reminds me of Mr. Herrigan. He's telling me to call him "Cip." I'm telling him he can call me "Viking." He's laughing. "Tomorrow," he says, "we're talking about Vikings."

Ana Paoula now visits daily, although she still doesn't stay the night. Dad's attempt, I assume, to maintain his son's fragile innocence. She usually shows up about five o'clock, and always with an armful of groceries. We chop vegetable or prepare some kind of sauce, then she plops onto the couch beside me to watch a Brazilian soap opera. I can't understand a lick of Portuguese, but the show's full of hot women, and I get to listen to Ana Paoula's sweet accent. She's always leaning in close, those green eyes sparkling, that silky hair resting on her olive shoulders. "Okay, they're married, but he fancies her, and that guy knows it, and he wants to blackmail him 'cause he's rich." And I'm always nodding and saying, "Right, got it," all the while sniffing her coconut lotion, trying to control the blood rushing to my groin. Sometimes she'll lay her hand on my arm or even my leg or chest. She has little inhibition, tells me I have beautiful eyes, speaks so close I often think she's gonna kiss me.

It's all rather confusing. She's my dad's girlfriend, and this automatically makes her an adult, part of them. But she doesn't seem like an adult. She's more like a kid, wants to talk and laugh about dumb stuff, like how funny someone on the street looks or who's sleeping with whom on *Gilligan's Island*. She's convinced that the professor's sleeping with all the women, maybe even Gilligan, she says, giggling.

One day she's staring at me, smiling. That afternoon, after Cip's visit, I'd gone on one of my random bus trips. Smoked a joint and got on the first bus that came, making sure the bus came back the same way. Sat in the back, watched all the loonies come and go. Despite the Visine, my eyes must've still been red, for Ana Paoula whispers, "You have some of that funny green stuff?"

"It's brown," I say, "but yeah, I have some."

"We mustn't let your father know."

"No problem there," I say.

"I have some onions," she says, "We can chop them, say we were chopping onions. Your Dad won't be home for a while."

"That's a great idea. I have some Visine too."

On the patio I'm lighting the joint, handing it over. She's puffing and puffing, the smoke lingering, and I'm fanning it away with my hand. "What a great idea," she says, smiling and handing the smoking joint back.

The weed's making me giddy, and I'm having to restrain the urge to talk, not wanting to blabber about who knows what. I have so many questions, but I don't want to say too much. She's still an adult, my dad's girlfriend, so better to keep calm and cool.

One more long drag. The fog's now floating in thick whisps; it's beginning to drizzle, and it's getting darker, and her beautiful bare arms have goosebumps.

"Let's get you inside," I say. "I'll make a fire. I wanna hear your story, why you're here and what you're doing."

"I'll start chopping onions," she says, "make us some guacamole."

When she's finished, we're back on the couch. She's close, and I can see her breasts dangling in the loose dress. I'm feeling like I could kiss her and that she'd kiss me back. "Okay," I say, "so what's your story, what brought you here?"

She's smiling and scooping guacamole with brown tortilla chips. She's going on about an uncle who lives in San Francisco, about her strict father who'd finally allowed her to visit, about how she'd dreamed her whole life of living in San Francisco. Her family wants her to marry some older guy, a family friend. She's talking about meeting my dad, how he'd asked her lots of nice questions about herself. She says he's a good, caring man, says I'm a lot like him. She wants to work in a flower shop, and she eventually wants to open her own. I'm still holding my tongue. There's something she's not telling me. I can see it in her eyes.

We're watching *The Brady Bunch*, falling asleep. We're awakened by the closing front door and footsteps on the stairs. The room's now dark, an orange glow, the fire crackling. My head's on Ana Paoula's shoulder, a hand on her thigh. I'm moving away, feigning sleep. Just as Dad's cresting the stairs.

CHAPTER TWENTY-FOUR

Traveling 2014

"The path to sainthood goes through
adulthood. There are no quick and
easy shortcuts. Ego boundaries
must be hardened before they can
be softened. One must find one's
self before one can lose it."

—M. Scott Peck

CLOAK #4—UNCONDITIONAL LOVE AND COMPASSION. More like a silk scarf than a proper cloak, large enough (like a cape) to provide shelter from the sun, but most often folded, thus providing warmth, like a light shawl, a serape. Mine is ocean-blue that gets darker when layered and draped, a shield from weather, a beacon of warmth and beauty.

Love completely. Understand—all are suffering. Never forget.
Don't hate. Not even the mindless fanatics. They might as
well be flies, flittering in the world's shit. So lost. So blind.
Your pain is everyone's pain, and everyone's pain is yours.
Transcend your righteousness, your pride, and love them all.
In the end, the Big End, you're right. Then laugh at your need
for righteousness. Unburden yourself and bow; may all be at
ease. Everyone is simply where they are. Love is salvation.
Listen. Just listen. Thought is particular; love is thorough and
all-consuming; it understands all wholes within The Whole.
So go there, set up camp. And when you stray, come back.
Always come back.

Day Seven. Tomorrow we leave. An unexpected journey. More
synchronicity. If I'm not careful, I'll never get back home. But
this isn't true. If you'd told me last week that we'd be shooting across the world to yet another place of dreams, I'd have
claimed insanity had prevailed. The logistics, the money, the
physical demands—so many rational impediments. But now
that surrender's complete, everything's wonder and excitement. This is, after all, what I'm here for. Freedom. Wonder.
Adventure. Life's walls lifted. Routine cracked open. Why
are we always shuttering ourselves in?

   Another sunset. The beach. The sky's purple and pink and
orange—again. Wonders. How we've come to leave, how it all
came together—the reason I'm here. Spontaneity. Untethered
spirit. Adventure. The soul spreading its cobwebbed wings.
Is it real? This feeling of freedom? Of space? Or is it just the

luxury of time? The usual questions. But I don't care. I'll get home to James. Work will continue. Life will unravel. One of the Brazilians' girlfriends is blowing quarter-sized bubbles and twirling to soft jazz. My fear is like those bubbles. Temporary. Transluscent. Just floating by.

Tomorrow we leave.

Unbelievable. And to another place of dreams. I've so many years of skepticism, of "reality," of thinking that I have to remind myself of miracles—which demand faith, an absence of excessive thought. So I was intrigued as I watched myself watching it all happen. Perhaps the hours of perfect waves, these aqua massages, have quelled the questioner. Whatever the case, I've been watching miracles unfold.

It's the end of day three. Another all-day extravaganza of waves. We're sitting with others—the Hawaii crew and the hilarious Aussies—at one of the long banquet tables, devouring spaghetti, meatballs, and lavishly buttered bread. One of the Aussies makes an offhand comment about the plight of Tibetans under Chinese rule. He's been grumbling guttural, Bintang-fueled slurs about various worldly slights, and the table of seven, mainly his friends, are ignoring him as friends can do, even telling him to fuck off with a smile. I hear him though, note his reference to Tibetans, and am momentarily catapulted back to meeting them deep in the heart of the Himalayas, a time—perhaps the first real time— that I myself was flowing for extended periods. So I'm sitting remembering this, thinking how that period feels like a dream but was not a dream, and thinking how so much of life feels like a dream, such "flowing" periods even more so. But I'm also, like the others, listening to another of the Aussies talking about an ex-girlfriend who was always trying to stick foreign objects up his ass. What pulls me away from this hilarity is Lucas turning to the piss-filled Aussie and saying, "Yeah, that's fucked, what the Chinese are doing." I'd yet to hear Lucas once swear, let alone go straight to the speed of "fuck." I swore plenty, especially around this crass and funny group of Aussies, but Lucas possessed a purity, a natural depth. So I'm turning to Lucas and asking, actually stating, that he, like I had twenty years before, must've experienced the Tibetans on his trip to Nepal and during his trekking through villages high in the Annapurna Range. It is, of course, another example of synchronicity, of the underlying overlap of our lives, and we're both now smiling in acknowledgement. Then I ask, "Have you heard of Ladakh? In Northern India?"

His head's tilting, his eyes alight.

"I researched it a few years ago," I add, "mapped out the whole thing. Another summer adventure. Then James was conceived, and plans changed."

Nothing more is said, and for a moment the surrounding laughter's like distant birdsong. But I've the distinct feeling something has happened, has coalesced.

A fourth night of glorious sleep. I'm awakened by waning moonlight seeping through the slatted walls of our jungle cabin. At first, I'm thinking I'd left my headlight on, so fast had I fallen asleep, but this moonlight's milky and is filtered into distinct and symmetric lines across the floor. I'm standing up and walking outside, and there's Lucas, sitting and staring into the jungle as the same moonlight streaks through foliage, spreading light and shadows like shards of broken glass on the jungle floor and the dirt before us. Lucas looks up, unsurprised, and again says he has an idea, that he'll tell me later. So I just nod, still half-asleep, and sit cross-legged to meditate as dawn changes everything.

All day, while bobbing in the warm aqua waters and strolling the sandy jungle paths that parallel the ocean's edge, my curiosity's lingering. I figure he wants to further explore Indonesia, perhaps catch a ferry to Sumatra in search of orangutangs, for me to re-visit Nias, or for us to hit the Mentawais and one of the new surf camps with teak tree-houses and still remote and pristine white beaches. Upon reflection, the fact that he wanted us to go to Northern India, to Ladakh, was obvious. That it had come up so spontaneously and that we'd both longed to visit practically made it inevitable. The twinkle in Lucas's eye and my own sense of something coalescing were real. I should've known, should've at least considered it. But at the time, the concept and the reality of organizing such a complicated trip kept all such thoughts suppressed. Such a miracle just didn't add up. And like I said, I'd researched it myself, five years ago. Planned it all out—even purchased a new high-altitude stove, upgraded my sleeping bag and tent, and began gathering the nitty-gritty, so I knew the detailed planning for such a trip. And Lucas knows too, hence his hesitation. He'd wanted to research before bringing the idea to life, as if wanting to avoid having to kill it.

The wonders of the internet.

On this day, even from a remote Javanese island, Lucas is calculating all expenses, researching flight availability, even inquiring into equipment and porters. Just before the afternoon surf, he says, "If we want, tomorrow we can be on a plane to Ladakh. It's logistically possible. Just like the old days, just like your stories, off on a whim."

Tomorrow we leave.

Miracles.

Sometimes we just have to listen and get out of our own way.

Lucas says he's considering marrying his girlfriend, that he's soul-searching, says she's tall and slender with thin, dark-brown hair and blue eyes. She paints, reads voraciously, loves antique stores, animals, classical music, and good Scotch. She's studying zoology, wants to be a vet. He's showing me a picture, and I'm practically falling in love myself. He says she's perfect, but he's still young, wants to travel, wander, explore himself more before marrying.

I'm nodding, telling him I felt the same way. But I'm lost, always have been, was either longing for a dream or avoiding, and he shouldn't listen to me, should trust himself. Nothing's ever perfect. All I've ever done is confuse myself, and I'm afraid I'll just confuse him.

"So you actually went to Venezuela after that first trip to Australia?" he asks.

"You'll see."

Sarah, one of the Hawaii crew's girlfriend, is ambling toward us. She's handing over my manuscript, says she liked it, says I should publish it, as if she knows I'm a closet perfectionist. She can't believe we're going to Ladakh. She's always wanted to go. She'll be calling us for advice in the future, says she has something to tell me—if I want to hear it, that is.

"Please," I say, "speak freely. I've got nothing to hide."

"You sure?" she says, looking at Lucas beside me. "It's personal."

I'm nodding.

"I'm a therapist at home," she says, "been working with people for twenty-five years. I have a 'diagnosis' for you—again, *if* you want to hear it."

"Please ..."

"Your stories," she says, "tell a story of someone with what we'd call 'love addiction.' Some call it anxious-attachment. It's caused by abandonment, and it's as common as these palm trees."

"Love addiction?" I say. "Aren't we all love addicts? Don't we all want love?"

"Of course," she says. "But we're not all love addicts. There's nothing wrong with you. In fact, over the years I've been amazed at just how common it is."

"So what does that mean?"

"I have a book for you," she says, "actually have it with me. It's something for you to think about by yourself, then perhaps work on with a therapist when you get home. It's really very common. Again, there's nothing wrong with you. Don't get stuck on the label. It's simply a starting point to understand how we sometimes can love and expect too much from others, and how we often unconsciously behave out of fear because of our pasts."

"But I wasn't abandoned," I say.

"Sure you were," she says. "If these stories are true, your dad left you at an early age. It doesn't always involve neglect or abuse. Your dad seems like a great guy, but these kinds of things affect us. Surely other things happened too."

"But I talked to him all the time," I say.

"I understand," she says, "but it's not that simple. You'll have to figure it out yourself of course, but that's what I see. Like I say, it's very common. From my experience, a majority of people experience some form of abandonment. We've all got something."

She's walking away. Lucas is behind her.

Tomorrow we leave.

Miracles.

I'm whispering. "What a bunch of shit."

Another "just like that." A speedboat to Kuta. A shuttle to Denpesar. The magic of flight. Time travel over old dreams, journeys once taken by land. A layover in Bangkok. Another in New Delhi. And now, hovering above Leh, the mighty Himalayas below. If we must think, why not live in dreams? And why not follow them?

For three days, we sit in this same spot, at the edge of a concrete patio, in front of this wondrous monastery built into the mountain. The cliff before us falls precipitously, and the brown, raw mountains rise high and low. Below, in a gorge that inspires spaciousness, a river flows, its color dependent upon cloud shapes and time of day. Yesterday, it was cobalt blue, the day before aqua, the day before that a shiny silver, like a mass of flowing liquid metal. Today, right now, the sun's deflected by thin clouds, and the water's dark green.

Usually we sit in silence, still absorbed in the long, morning meditation and the magical chanting of monks reverberating through ancient chambers. There are choruses of gongs and symphonies of singing bowls. We sit and watch the changing of the clouds and the light, the colors of the river, and the colors of the mountains, which take on all shades of brown and sometimes grey. Yesterday, the silence was allowed to linger, and the morning unfolded like a blooming flower. On a walk we saw four ibex clinging to a cliff. We're told an elusive snow leopard lives nearby. Occasionally, small yak trains pass. We're surrounded by magic, and we know it. Just the fact that we're here, together, is magic. From silence, life unfolds in bright colors, and we've both been reveling in the experience.

Today, however, Lucas is brimming with curiosity, full of questions, and we're speaking in whispers, just like the seven Tibetan schoolchildren behind us. The wind-battered walls of the monastery rise high and flush with the mountain, and an ancient cypress tree stands watch above. It's cool and the wind chills, but occasional sunbeams warm us; the dotted white flowers in the lime green fields below appear to stand tall with every burst of sunlight.

Just like Hanah, Lucas has continued to read my stories as they unfold—as I revisit and rewrite them—and he's just caught up with all of the completed pages. Usually as calm as the wise, old monks, this morning Lucas is squirming with excitement, even playful in his enthusiasm. That he's now part of the story seems appropriate, for we both realize that our personal stories are unfolding together as we sit, as we travel, as we seek something that we're trying not to seek. That I'm sitting here, back in the Himalayas, twenty-some years later, feeling similar—calm, clear, chalk with perspective, a sense of purpose and control—creates that distinct feeling of timelessness, as if the real me, the person beyond all my created identies, hasn't actually changed at all. And Lucas and I, focusing on that timeless space, and focusing on creating purpose and growth, have known one another forever. And this consistent and prolonged meditation has rekindled a sense of gentleness, dare I say, happiness within myself. The more I look within, the more I vigilantly meditate, the more I focus solely and purely on the empty space of empty space, the more all cognitive thought-trains dissolve into what might be called "possibility," or perhaps "potential". All this has been leading me somewhere after all. But unconscious messages have been holding me back. *You're not enough...you need to do this...you should be doing more.* And as years pass, if we're not careful, we become these messages, spirit gets trapped, and too much gets avoided. But we're not those messages. Something has coalesced. If life's a forest, it's no longer just its contents; it's an ecosystem, a whole. Lucas is me twenty years ago, and I am him in a malleable future. We are both mirrors, showing parts of the other in ourselves. Twenty years from now, he will still, in part, be me. Twenty years ago, I was, in part, him. When we die we'll unite in universal dust and in the sounds made by all particles colliding. We are evolving together in a creative wheel that'll spin forever. That we both so heartily seek and embrace awareness is invisible fuel, the power that keeps the wheel spinning fast enough to transcend time. We're both capable of transformation. I can transform the past, he the future, and vice versa. Awareness and perspective create infinite possibilities. All is essentially creation.

"Mr. Herrigan's great," Lucas says. "His whole thing on the gap between thought and emotion seems to be the point of all this meditation. That's how it feels for me. The meditation just slows it all down. Makes it easier to see straight."

"Seems so," I say, "but I've never quite figured out how to stay in that gap. My good intentions, my purpose, my cloaks, are all wrapped in thought. And anything wrapped in thought is separate from pure creation. And then there's the unconscious stuff. So much to get confused by. All this love addiction stuff, this book Royce's girlfriend gave me, is blowing my mind."

"Yeah?" Lucas says. "What's that all about?"

"I'm still absorbing it," I say. "But my stories seem to say it all. Let's just say I do a lot of fantasizing, of falling in love with a fantasy and not the reality. The fact that I had so much pain over Sabrina, a woman I really didn't even know, a woman I'd created an elaborate fantasy around just because she fit my physical ideal, says it all. Even now I feel pain and loss over her. Crazy, but true. And much of it, according to the book, comes from insecurity, from low self-esteem. All these years I've been too hard on myself, ceaselessly trying to love and understand others without really loving and understanding myself."

"I see," he says, nodding almost imperceptibly.

"But I don't think you have that problem," I say.

"Your cloaks are sound," Lucas says. "There's nothing wrong with silence, God, and voidness, with boundless curiosity, purpose, discipline, and learning, with emphasizing love, compassion, forgiveness, and tolerance. There's nothing wrong with any of that. I mean, those things really are the heart of most all religions. Underneath it all, that was my father's whole message. And you've reminded me. I want to create a life of purpose. Thank you for reminding me."

There are vultures soaring near a distant raw peak and others down near the now-aqua river and near the stretch of lime-green grass dotted with white flowers. For several minutes we watch. The wind's whipping up in brief, sweeping moments, changing all colors. The lime-green grass sometimes yellows, and it sometimes darkens under shade. Other times it's shimmering as the winds blow through. The beige mountain becomes brown. The river turns dark green or blue.

"How did we end up here?" I ask. "I mean, look where we are. A few days ago, we were in Grajagan, we thought this up, and here we are. And yet it feels so right, just like I was traveling twenty-some years ago. But it's crazy, downright crazy."

"It is," Lucas says. "And when I first started thinking about it, that was the overwhelming sentiment. The money, the logistics, it would've been much easier to just go to Borneo or Papua New Guinea. But there was also this overwhelming feeling that you and I were meant to come here. The way it

came up, the way it all came together. And now I don't question it. It was worth the money and the travel. And it seems
to be why you came on this trip. To rediscover spontaneity
and psychological space, freedom, the creativity that comes
from adventure. Sometimes we all need to run away. Your
stories say it all. You never forgot."

"No," I say, watching the vultures soar. "Guess I didn't."

The book says a love addict falls in love with a fantasy, that
he or she, in their elaborate projecting, overlooks the reality
before them. They've long digested the movies and songs of
yearning heartbreak and joy, read the symphonic poetry and
novels celebrating a love that's all-consuming and irrational,
that overwhelms with visions of mighty vistas and heavenly
seas of passion, and they are believers: true love exists; your
soul mate's out there; your second half will complete you. So
off they go. Searching, seeking, dreaming, longing, weaving,
and projecting until reality's no longer real.

Could this be me?

*No, it's not you, you self-help moron! Everybody fantasizes
about love and romance.*

*Not like me they don't. I do overlook reality. I see beauty,
my physical ideal, and I become as obsessed as a heroin addict.
My stories take on lives of their own.*

*Who doesn't? Love is that powerful. And attraction and
chemistry are real. It's beyond reason, even beyond sanity. So
what? It's emotion, and emotion isn't always sane. It sweeps us
away. So celebrate, you damn fool! I thought you were gonna
stop thinking and just live for once. Ever heard of passion?*

It's not that simple. Love should be sane and reasonable— based on reality.

Nothing's perfect, dumbass. Haven't you realized that? I thought you were experienced in the ways of the world. I thought you were ready to go beyond your little ideals.

So why haven't my relationships worked out? My first wife and I were mad compatible, yet we grew apart. My second wife and I had little in common. But she was hot and fit my fantasy, so we got married. Married! My rationales make circus monkeys look wise!

You took risks. And life didn't play along. Join the club. It's called growth. And growth requires pain. Go read some more books! Cry me a fucking river!

The book says that love addicts likely experienced abandonment as a child, that they blamed themselves for their parents' problems, and that they are often full of unconscious guilt and shame, which manifests as low self-esteem and a desire to please others.

Sound familiar? Dad leaving affected me more than I realized. I hardly remember anything from that time. Mom says I was inconsolable when he'd visit and leave. And I am a people pleaser; I bend over backward to please!

So whaddaya going to do, New Age Sensitive Boy, go to a therapist? Cry your heart out? Oh, my inner child's wounded! Poor fucking me! I need to be reparented! I thought you were a man of action, an individualist? You're always quoting Nietzsche. What kind of man are you?

I reckon you're the one who needs some reparenting, who might benefit from some damn psychotherapy! We're all wounded. Might as well embrace it.

Yes, wounded we are. Poor fucking me!
Fuck off!
And he still has some balls! Hundred points for New Age Boy!

The book says that love addicts attract love avoidants, people who were likely smothered growing up, and who have an unconscious fear of intimacy that manifests as emotional unavailability and often a lack of communication skills. Love avoidants, as a way to avoid intimacy, usually busy themselves in distractions outside the relationship, and they usually distract themselves (as do love addicts) with various addictions.

Again, sound familiar? Even with Hanah, even with that relatively healthy relationship, there was always this sense that I was only scratching the emotional surface, that she had subtle emotional walls. Eventually, all she seemed to do was work and go out with friends. And addictions! My life's defined by them. Sure, some are good, testaments to my manic nature, my lock-on focus. But all, good and bad, are distractions.

Blah, blah, blah! They're called women! They're as complex as the universe! Whaddaya expect? And who doesn't damn distract themselves? Look around. That's all everyone's doing! Try lightening up, focusing on being a man, and going with the flow. Go ahead, go to your therapist, New Age Boy!

I think I will. There's something to this. I'm not sure what exactly, but there is. I can't believe the amount of literature there is on this! I can't believe I hadn't read about this before.

It's just another convenient answer. Can't you see that? Thought you were done with the books.

There's more going on than we think. And I still learn from books.

The book says that both love addicts and love avoidants have powerful defense mechanisms that keep them in denial. The older they get, the more elaborate and entrenched these defense mechanisms become. They deny their denial.

I'm tired of being in denial. All this meditation has cracked me open. I'm ready to change.

You go change, butterfly! Go meditate, do some yoga, go sip tea with other wounded chicklets.

I think I will. And you go right on with your denial. Don't grow. Don't evolve. Just keep pluggin' along, tough guy!

Fuck off!

No, you fuck off!

CHAPTER TWENTY-FIVE

Venezuela/The Sea 1993/94

"We live in the flicker—may it last as
long as the old earth keeps rolling!
But darkness was here yesterday."

—Joseph Conrad, *Heart of Darkness*

THE CAPITAN, ANA Paoula's sixty-year-old husband, has large maps laid across the table, maps of sea-currents and reefs. His voice is gravel. He's a round man in every way. And a hairy man. He has black eyes that're always staring hard. Other than the roundness, he reminds me a bit of my stepfather, Roger.

"We will stop briefly in Colombia, through the Panama Canal, and off," he says with exaggerated flair.

We're explorers. The Arctic, space, the ocean.

"First," he says, "the Galapagos, a few weeks to the Marquesas, give or take." He's pointing and slashing across the abstract world below us. "Tahiti, The Cook Islands, Samoa, then onto New Zealand, then Australia. This is the route. These are the currents. You ready for this Kayne?"

"I'm ready!" Kayne says, "I'm ready!"

"Many have died at sea, Kayne. Disease and pirates. Hurricanes, wild cannibals, reefs, sea monsters. Used to be no maps, no GPS, just the stars and their own wits and eyes. But the strong and the prepared have survived. Are you ready, Kayne?"

"I'm ready!"

I'm wondering what all this is about. And who am I? Am I also an explorer? I want to be an explorer. I'm standing up, walking the few steps over. I'm looking over Kayne's shoulder. But I'm ignored. Invisible. Maybe the Capitan knows who I am.

"I've heard about pirates," I say.

The Capitan's turning. "What about them?"

"I hear there are pirates that steal peoples' organs, particularly in the Caribbean."

The Capitan's mouth is moving side to side, almost smiling. "Yes," he says. "Vessels disappear. Rich people need organs. Hunted down like prey. Violated. Carved up like pigs in a slaughterhouse."

"They actually use animal organs in people, don't they?" I ask.

"No animal parts going into me," he replies. "But don't you worry." He's unlocking a compartment on the floor. He's pulling out guns. A shotgun. A .44 Magnum. A Glock. An AR-15. "Ever fire a gun?"

We're nodding. "No."

He's handing them over, one at a time.

Each is heavy; each is death.

"Later, we'll shoot," he says, "Everyone should know how to shoot a gun."

He's placing each back in its proper place. He's showing Kayne around. "This is the Global Positioning System. This is the radar. At least two people should always know how these things work."

I'm thinking about the Capitan's childhood, about his life, and about Ana Paoula's life with him. It makes me appreciate my father. I bet Ana Paoula misses him.

The Capitan's standing bowlegged behind the large, chrome wheel, cigar smoke billowing, his kingdom below. Bystanders wave from docked boats. The joys of relaxation. They won't be leaving this evening. Take care, for the sea's humbling. Be well. We're all at its mercy.

I'm standing watch at bow, the blue silk below, the unknown ahead. This time the ocean. Ana Paoula's sipping white wine from a plastic glass. Kayne's sitting on the wood deck, eating a bowl of cherries. The wind's picking up, sounds of water slapping the hull. The Capitan's ordering Kayne and me to unravel and wind up the sail. That sound—the whipping and flapping of thick canvas. We're steering toward nowhere, a coordinate. The sun's falling, the sky morphing. Undulations. The sea.

The sea has wreaked its havoc, tearing and pulling and spitting, building and destroying, smiling and laughing at us. Moments of peace and solitude and tranquil breezes. Caribbean coves and coral shallows. Whitewashed beaches. Dilapidated shacks. Leather-faced men who smell of fish. Harbors and the Panama Canal—that bridging of East and West. That short cut. The Galapagos. Suitcased-sized lizards, swimming. Birds with big blue feet. Then, suddenly, thoughts of how simple and quick a remedy death would be. No more swaying. No more movement. No sounds. Please, no more.

The automatic pilot breaks in the Marquesas, and despite the Capitan's hardiest attempts, he's yet to fix it. He's yelling and screaming, but it fails to listen. We take three-hour shifts, Kayne, the Capitan, and me, all night, every night. Yesterday, the winds were thirty knots from the northwest, the swells eight to ten feet from the south. The hull's bending and creaking, like an old house in a storm. Waves are splashing across the deck. The silvery light of the moon, the dolphins, the vastness and wonder of it all. It might go on forever. I'm screaming, silently. Mighty, wondrous screams. The Capitan appears, yelling and screaming, his kingdom, his baby, suffering. He takes the helm, realizes it's no use, then disappears below, muttering Portuguese profanities.

The Fijian Islands have coral reefs like underwater daggers. Every cove's a threat. The Capitan speaks of early explorers and cannibals as if they were yesterday. It's dusk. We're sharing whiskey and wine.

"A ship on a reef is a helpless animal," he's saying. "And the cannibals know it. So they wait. They've seen such ships before, their magic, their shooting sticks and shiny swords. They know the creatures will eventually come in. It's a classic siege." He's whispering, but now the whisper's volume is rising in proportion to the widening of his eyes. "Imagine the fear. You know they're waiting. You've no choice. If the stories are true, they'll roast you alive. Or eat your brain as you sit and watch them. I'm just glad we have guns."

It's easy to see how the reefs and these stories kept explorers away all those years. The Capitan is ridiculous, but his stories are entertaining. It's almost silent. The jagged mountains and palm trees lie still. I should know better, but I can't get the stories out of my mind.

Finally, a day off the boat. Alone. The *Warm Lover* is anchored in a Yasawa cove. The green mountains rise steep and jagged. They remind me of Kauai. There are roosters crowing and children screaming and playing before going off to school. A canoeful of young women invite us to the village for the evening kava, a ceremony that beholds the ancient gods in spirit, but more commonly is the equivalent of having a beer at the local pub.

Land. Solid. Layers and layers, all the way to the core. I'm following a line of uniformed schoolchildren up a narrow trail and along an escarpment that renders views of most of the island, helping a man plant cassava, then walking down and strolling through tide pools with hearty women who're laughing and chatting and collecting octopus from coral crevices. We're eating—rice, octopus, fish, fresh bread, peanut sauce—and playing with five children on the bamboo-matted floor. I'm swimming back. On the *Warm Lover*, I rinse with fresh water warmed by the sun. The sweet smoke from the island is black and swirling and floating into the orange and purple-gray sky. Someone's pounding kava root, a rhythmic clanging of metal. I'm disappointed to miss the kava, but looking forward to the quiet of a windless dusk alone.

In the berth, I'm pulling on fresh shorts, pouring a beer. Light footsteps. A barely perceptible sway. I'm turning. Ana Paoula's in the doorway, naked.

I'm turning away. "I thought you were ashore."

"I swam the other reefs, while the tide was high," she says. "Just magical."

"It is, isn't it?"

She's wrapping herself in a sarong, making mint tea, slicing cheese and a green apple. We're sitting atop as dusk transforms—eating and drinking and listening to the distant beating of kava, where Kayne and the Capitan are sitting cross-legged, drinking from coconuts. Despite all our time together on the *Warm Lover*, it's the first time we've really been alone.

"I see what my dad saw in you," I say. "You put up with a lot and you don't complain. You're pretty amazing."

She's smiling. "That's what women do."

"So why did you get married and settle in Brazil, after all that?" I ask. "I thought you wanted to be a florist."

"Why did I marry Xavier, and not your dad?" she says, touching my arm. "Is that what you mean? I guess I owe you an explanation."

"You don't owe me anything," I say. "It's him you owe an explanation. He was pretty beat up when you left."

"You're right, Jim," she says. "I do owe him an explanation. We just didn't really talk like that. But I think I owe you one too."

The mountains are now dark silhouettes against a deep orange and gray sky. Black smoke's still billowing between two dimly lit huts. It smells of burning garbage.

"Xavier has known me since I was a child, he's a close family friend," Ana Paoula says. "Our families did business together, and our marriage was arranged when I was sixteen. I, of course, resisted the arrangement, wanted to experience life on my own terms, but this proved impossible in Brazil. I moved away from Sao Paulo, first to San Salvador, then Recife, but nowhere did I feel independent. I could never prove it, but I swear I was being watched, and several boyfriends left me with no explanation. So I left. Went to California. Your dad was so genuine, so sweet and understanding. And it's true, I wanted to shed my past, to be someone different, to give myself to your father. But deep down I knew it wasn't going to happen. And your dad knew it too. I needed to live in Brazil. My family is imperfect, but they're my family."

"But what about love?" I ask.

"Love comes in many forms."

"And is this love?"

"It's a form, yes. Soon I'll have children. They'll be safe and secure. Brazil is rising, I want to be part of it."

We're silent. A seagull lands on the railing. Ana Paoula's touching my arm again. "You've become a good man," she says. "Your father would be proud. And you should know—I loved your father. It wasn't his fault that I up and left."

"So why didn't you tell him that?"

"Some things are better left unsaid."

I'm nodding, looking at the sunset and scanning the horizon. The mountains are now dark against a cobalt sky. I'm thinking of my father, his quiet reserve, the way he rarely shows emotion, remembering his defeated body language when Ana Paoula left. I'm thinking about how painful it must be to move away from one's family.

We talk of other things, useless things, like we used to on Dad's couch. In another life I might've loved her myself.

Back in Australia. Kayne's wanted by the police. Most likely we both are. We were lucky to have gotten out in the first place. And now we're back. We should leave. We should've told Ana Paoula and the Capitan, convinced them to go to Indonesia. Or we should've stayed in New Zealand. But we didn't. Despite all logic, it felt right to come back. We've convinced ourselves that when things feel right, when spontaneity reigns, everything will work itself out. And right away, verification: at Sydney Harbor's main pub, we bump into Rudy Waller.

Rudy was a bartender at "The Play Room."

"Well, I'll be," he says, scratching his chin, staring at ghosts. "I'll be damned." He's a good looking guy with long, wavy brown hair, strong, stubbled cheekbones, and green eyes. "You been in Australia all this time?" He's noticing

Ana Paoula and the Capitan walking in, watching her as the Capitan heads to the bar and she walks toward us.

Kayne's off to the restroom.

I'm shaking my head, unsure of how much to reveal. His eyes widen as Ana Paoula cozies up next to me.

I'm introducing them. "We've all just sailed here from Venezuela. That's her husband at the bar, the captain of the boat."

Rudy's staring. He can't take his eyes off Ana Paoula. "Fuckin'-a, mate," he says, finally. "That's crazy, fuckin' crazy. Venezuela? How the hell did that happen?"

"It's a long story," I say. "I know, it's crazy. We had to leave though, you know, so we did, we up and left."

"Yeah you did. People were sayin' the law got you. Or something worse. Everyone was a bit worried, mate."

"I know, I'm sorry," I say. "Didn't have much of a choice. We had to keep it secret. It was all pretty weird."

"Don't worry," I say to Ana Paoula, "we're innocent, just a big misunderstanding. We're gonna be fine."

"You sure?" she says. "You could stay with us, you know, stay on the boat until we go back to New Zealand in a couple of weeks. We're going to stay at a hotel here in Sydney. Xavier may not admit it, but he likes having you guys around, and we could still use the help. He was even talking about finding someone here for the trip back to Auckland."

The Capitan's back. I'm still wondering how much he knows. I introduce him to Rudy.

"We're good," I say to Ana Paoula, wanting to end the conversation. "We have friends here. Gonna work a bit and figure out our next move. We'll be all right."

"So you're headed back to Surfer's?" Rudy asks.

"Thinking that," I say, "work for a bit, lay low for a while."

Rudy's looking at me and he's looking at Kayne, who's slugging a beer. "You don't know what happened, do you?" He's looking around, at all of us. "Oh, mate! Major drug ring Linden had going. And not no marijuana, mate—acid, coke, the big stuff. The restaurant and nightclub was all a front."

Rudy's looking at us, and he's looking at Ana Pauola and the Capitan. "We used to work for this guy," he says, "had no idea what he was up to."

"Someone must've known," I say.

"I don't know, mate." Rudy says. "No one I knew. Reckon Linden had people doing things they didn't even know they were doing. Just like you. The police interrogated everyone. None of the staff was involved. Don't know how he did it, mate. Some say it's mafia. I don't know. But he's a goner. May never get out of prison. Fair dinkum, mate. Went down right after you left. And what happened anyway? I heard about Kayne and the crab and roast beef and all that. Fuckin' hilarious. But why'd you split so quick? What happened?"

"I'll tell ya later," I say.

"No, please," the Capitan says. "This we gotta hear."

Everyone's looking at Kayne.

I tell them about the package and the police. "And that's when we called home and got Ana Paoula's message about Venezuela. Hopped on the next flight out. Guess the police hadn't started searching for us yet. But now we can't be sure."

"But what's this about Kayne and crabs?" the Capitan asks.

"Oh, nothin," I say. "It's stupid."

"Please?" the Capitan says. "I love stupid."

I'm looking at Kayne. He's smiling, and now he's telling them in the way only Kayne can.

"How much crab you talking about?" Ana Pauola asks.

"Not just crab," Rudy says. "Roast beef too."

"A coupla thousand dollars worth," I say.

The Capitan's grinning ear to ear. "I'm gonna get us all a beer for that one."

Ana Paoula's laughing and hugging Kayne.

I'm watching some greyhounds racing on the tellie and people at the bar placing bets. Pool balls are clacking. Another group, huddled around a long table, is watching an Aussie-rules football game. I'm walking around the bar, looking at pictures, mainly patrons of the bar and boats and fishermen with their big catches. When I return, the Capitan and Ana Paoula are preparing to leave. They're staying at a five-star hotel, have reservations at a famous restaurant. We're saying good-bye. Kayne's shaking the Capitan's hand and laughing. Ana Paoula's hugging me tight. We'll visit them in Brazil. The Capitan's reaching out for Ana Paoula's hand. They're heading for the door.

By the end of the night I'm telling Rudy the whole story, about the post office and the deluge of cops, even about my theory that Linden had been using us all along, that he'd set Kayne up, baited him with the food in the fridge. But Rudy's all-assuring. Linden'll no longer be a problem. The case against us probably doesn't exist. And cops in Surfer's are mellow anyway. He's going on and on about how the surf's been six foot for a month straight. Burleigh Head's and Kirra are firing daily perfection. Rabbit Bartholemew's the Baryshnikov of surfing. We're gonna hit it every day.

"We can leave tomorrow," Rudy says. "In the old Opal. Take a few days, Crescent Head, Angourie, you name it. Even got boards for ya. And I know the manager at the Beach Club. Heard they need people at Charlie's as well. All good, mate, all good."

We're going back to the place we'd desperately left not so long ago.

CHAPTER TWENTY-SIX

Home/California 1994

"Now and then I go about pitying
myself and all the while my soul is being
blown by great winds across the sky."

—Ojibway (Native American tribe) saying

HOME. A FAMILIAR yet foreign place. Irvine. I'm expecting it to be different, for people to seek me out, wondering where I've been. But it isn't. They don't. Everyone's still just moving around, living.

Driving north for Cip's funeral. The sprawl of suburbia. The rush of L.A. freeways. The dry hills. Palm trees. Coastline—beaches. I'm all the time stopping to stand on cliffs and watch the ocean swirl. To hear birds and feel the breeze. To walk on mountains, sit under towering trees, listen to winds whistling through valleys. Above one Big Sur valley, a cabin's empty. I sleep under the stars before fog rolls upward, swirling around the moon. In the morning, the fog's thick in the valley and the birds sing slow. I sit and read and wait as sun burns through fog and birdsong broadens and fills.

Mr. Cipoletta once compared death to clouds, quoted Thich Nat Han, and said everything simply changes form. Imprints. The way he'd prepared me for school, for a future I didn't even see coming, his methods for success. Set me up with binders for every class, with different colored flashcards. Showed me how take detailed notes, how to condense those notes onto flashcards daily, to study them in every free moment. How to read, annotate, collect all relevant information, to ask questions plump with meaning and paradox. Diligence, organization, and focus. He didn't push me; he knew I'd do it, knew I was ready. I did it for him. I did it for Mr. Herrigan. I even did it for Mom and Dad. And now, with college ahead, I guess I'm seeing I did it for myself.

The Central Valley. Steinbeck country. Farmland. Lettuce and broccoli, cabbage and celery, garlic and cherries. Nurseries. Flower farms. Flat and wide and expansive. Distant hills. Soft and rolling. Pastel shades, shimmering and shifting. The golden hills of Silicon Valley, the shadows in clefts where hills meet. I'm remembering Oscar and Jim's ocean of ideas, their arguments, their open dialogue. These are the minds that change worlds. People are claiming that Silicon Valley's the heart of this computer revolution. They're probably here already.

The hills thicken through Woodside, swathed in trees, then more suburbs as the city gets closer. The radio's reporting civil war in Rwanda. There's widespread bloodshed, rumors of genocide, but few details. I'm remembering my Ugandan friends and their predictions. This isn't just another report, another story. The reports imply illogical chaos, as if no one's really to blame. Just another civil war in Africa. But I know better, and I'm left feeling uninformed. How can I exist in such a deceptive world? Makes me feel helpless. Must I just harden my heart?

Dad still lives in the same house. It looks different though, changed as things do after long-enough periods of time. There's a new potted lime tree in front, new blue, silk curtains in the windows, a new brass doorbell, and a new rust-iron fence surrounding a fresh bed of flowers. It's a beautiful street, lined with large trees, each house unique with its own garden and entryway. The driveways all have nice cars. So lucky. We have so much. Guilt. I'm walking up the marble stairs, ringing the doorbell.

Dad's just standing there. I'm crying. Not sure why.

"I'm so sorry, Jim," he says. "No one's here. Come on in. I have a fire going."

We're hugging, walking up the long wooden stairway. It's warm.

On the kitchen counter, where Ana Paoula and I used to chop onions, is a stack of notebooks. Dad's moving them to the coffee table. "Mr. Cipoletta's son brought these over for you," he says, walking back into the kitchen. He's grinding coffee beans, preparing a French press.

The fire's crackling, glowing shadows on the walls and ceiling. There are several new paintings. American landscapes. There are ten notebooks, each about an inch thick. I'm examining them, one by one, flipping through pages, reading, stacking them neatly on the floor. Stickers and drawings adorn the covers and some of the pages. A mandala, a cross, a snowcapped mountain. A mosque, some Chinese writing, some Arabic. An elephant, a rhino, a monkey, a cow on a windy cobblestone road, a medieval catapult, a castle, a donkey loaded with sacks of oranges. A blank slab of marble, a bamboo hut on stilts, an elm tree with a large nest of birds. A lifetime of learning, of quotes and passages, all in his own writing. A testament to travels.

Dad's handing me coffee. Music—jazz. He's sitting and I'm nodding and he's flipping through notebooks. He's asking questions. I'm telling him about the failed jeans venture in Hungary. The woman I glimpsed and chased around the world. My fantasies. My yearning. The limestone cities, the cistern and mosques of Turkey. Losing our money, again, in Greece. The synchronicities. The adventures. Stories distilled. Egypt and the slave work in Israel, the colors and chaos of Uganda, the crab-eating episode in Australia, the sapphire run with the bikers. The police. I've been writing it all down. Stories. Going to make it a novel some day. We're sitting on the couch, the fire crackling and shifting. I'm talking about Hanah, how I think I love her, how I'm considering going to Bolivia to find her, to tell her, how I might be crazy after all.

"You're not crazy," he says.

"I'm going down to find her," I say. "I love her."

"Yes," he says. "I can see that. Don't wait to tell her. And how's Ana Paoula?"

"She's good," I say. "She wanted me to tell you you're a good man. And she wanted me to tell you that she'll always love you."

He's staring at the fire.

"Did you hear me?"

I'm thinking how we're all in pain, at every age, at most every turn. They say pain teaches—if we embrace it. Running or numbing just stirs it up. Enter it, the wise men say.

"I agree," I say. "You're a good man."

"Thank you," he says, standing and walking back into the kitchen. He was never comfortable with expressing feelings. "Mr. Cipoletta's son asked for you to say something at his memorial," he says, reaching for dishes. "Just you, his son, and a professor friend. The son said Mr. Cipoletta had a lot of respect for you, that he really liked you."

"Respect," I say. "I'm just a spoiled brat, a whiner."

"Yeah, well, some things are worth whining about," he says. "Guess it's all in how you do it."

I'm walking to the window. The sun's falling beyond buildings and trees. I told Hanah a lot about my father. I'm wondering what she's doing. In my mind she's still sitting on the porch in Australia. The sun's setting through palm leaves, the birds are singing, and she's smiling, sipping a cold VB, ready for a story.

Dad's already cleaned my one suit. We're driving across the Golden Gate Bridge, through the rainbow-painted tunnel, exiting, and winding down the narrow Sausalito streets. The erratically parked cars. Houses on stilts hugging hillsides. The shimmering bay, the boats, the speckled lights of the surrounding shoreline. A large garden, a terraced plateau surrounded by a small wooden fence with rusted nails and bolts—the site of the memorial—overlooks the bay. Cars fill the narrow driveway and line the street, the large crowd drinking wine and enjoying the last rays of light. I'm standing by the fence, alone. The memorial, I've been told, is meant to be less a mourning and more a celebration of a life lived well. But I don't feel like celebrating, so I'm staring at the island of Alcatraz and the sailboats until the people settle into their seats.

Cip's professor-friend is speaking. I'm hearing my name, then walking to the podium. There's a dog in the back, sitting upright in the middle aisle, a cocker spaniel. He's staring at me, and I'm staring back, and I like this 'cause it's keeping my mind off all the staring eyes, helping me stay focused.

"Mr. Cipoletta was my tutor," I say, "since I was thirteen years old. It's a common story in a way. I wasn't doing well in school, not really trying, or interested, and Mom and Dad were fed up. You know how it goes. All I did was argue. Not sure why, but that's what I did. So I'm shipped off to San Francisco. Figured Dad would be all permissive 'cause of the divorce, figured I'd be screwing around all summer. So when Dad introduces me to Mr. Cipoletta and tells me he'll be tutoring me two-some hours everyday, I'm pissed. I'm tired of everyone telling me what to think, how things are, treating me like a moron. I'm pissed, and I'm wondering why everyone else isn't. War, violence, religious dogma, government corruption, superficiality everywhere I look, selfishness—I'm just fed up, numbing myself, trying to find a way to exist in such a hypocrytical world. And I'm only thirteen, too young to feel so much corruption. But that's how kids often feel, I reckon. The world's confusing. And because most of us are confused, even most adults, the kids aren't taught otherwise, aren't taught how to process all the polarities, aren't taught how to really think. Most of us, it seems, are living in confusion, and we don't even know it.

"So then I meet Mr. Cipoletta, and he's different, you know. No condescending looks. No efforts to fix me. He just listens. He listens, says I'm smart, and that I'm right to be questioning things, to be seeing two (or more) sides to everything, says this is the real definition of intelligence. He even says I have a right to be pissed off, that he wishes more people were. He's buying me book after book, showing me how to read smart, how to annotate. We have a process you see, a process he teaches me. I ask questions and he asks questions, and we deconstruct ideas until there were fewer questions, and it becomes clear which questions may not get answered.

"Mr. Cipoletta made me comfortable with not always having answers, with the relativity of most ideas. He verified my thoughts, taught me to support them, to see all sides of everything, to keep what he called a 'nimble' mind, a mind able to assert itself without becoming stiff or dogmatic. He taught me to think, inspired me to travel, inspired me to live a life of purpose, and I will forever be grateful."

The dog's now lying on its belly, its legs stretched long and flat, its tongue out, panting, still staring at me.

"And, you know, he was always thanking me for thinking and caring, for wanting to learn. He was always telling me how much he enjoyed our conversations. And he was serious. But we both knew who got the better of the deal. Mr. Cipoletta was a true teacher. I'm not entirely sure yet, but I think I'm going to become a teacher because of him. He showed me the power of education, of teaching others to educate themselves."

I'm staring beyond the dog and the people, beyond the trees and the water, beyond Alcatraz. I'm staring at the distant clouds, gray and finely feathered. And now I'm looking at the moon, full and bright, right there.

"What I'm left with is a vision of how I want to be, how I want to be more like you, Mr. Cipoletta. Less judgmental. More compassionate. More understanding. To always seek perspective. I'll never forget you for this. I will always remember. I promise."

Tears are streaming down my face. I'm walking off the stage, standing to the side, shaking the hand of the next speaker, Mr. Cipoletta's son, Nathaniel. He has Mr. Cipoletta's pudginess, his round face, his nose, his soft eyes. He'll also soon have gray hair that'll then turn white. During his speech, he also speaks of his father's influence, his inspiration, his constant support. It makes me think of my own parents' support, and when the speech is over I find myself standing before them. Me, Skip, Mom, and Dad. "Thanks," I say. "Thanks for everything." There's a moonbeam on shimmering waters. Mr. Cipoletta would've enjoyed the view.

CHAPTER TWENTY-SEVEN

Irvine 1990

"The real voyage of discovery consists
not in seeking new landscapes,
but in having new eyes."

—Marcel Proust

MOM'S CRACKING THE door, peering into my room, says Dad wants to talk to me, that he's expecting my call, that I'm to call right away. Of course, I don't want to call, am tired of hearing all the disappointment, the prolonged silences, the suppressed lectures that long ago wore themselves out. My first semester of junior college shot to hell. Classes were dull as shit. I slept or just left and went surfing. Even Mr. Cipoletta and his structure couldn't shake my listlessness.

"Did you hear what I said?"

"I heard," I say. "Does it have to be right this second?"

"Yes, it does."

"Shit."

"Don't you talk to me like that. I'm still your mother, you know, and you still live in this house."

"Believe me, I know."

I'm pushing Radar the cat to the floor, walking to the phone, pressing numbers.

"Hello."

"Hey Dad, Mom said you wanted me to call."

"Yeah, Jim, I did. I've been talking with Mr. Cipoletta, and we have an idea for you."

"Yeah?"

"We know you're not much into school right now. Of course we wish it were otherwise, but to be quite honest we've both been there before, so we can't really say much. We think this might be a good time for you to take a trip."

"A trip?" I say. "What kind of trip?"

"Go travel. Go wherever you want. They have these 'round-the-world tickets that are pretty reasonable, and you can choose your flights anywhere in the world. I'll help you get enough money together for the flight, but you'll have to work to save your own money, and you'll have to work as you're traveling as well. Mr. Cipoletta did it as a young man, so did I, and we both agree it would be the best thing for you right now. We're thinking you and Kayne could go together. My only stipulation is that you don't call us for money. If you need money, you figure out how to get it. That's how the real world works."

"Anywhere we want?"

"Anywhere you want, buddy. It's a big, wonderful world out there. Best way to learn about it is to go see it for yourself. Whaddaya think?"

"Sounds great!" I say. "Gonna call Kayne right now!"

Kayne can't believe we hadn't thought of it sooner. We just hadn't realized we could get reasonably priced 'round-the-world airline tickets, and that we could work as we went. Figured it was just too expensive. And Kayne's parents also agreed to help him buy the airline tickets. This is really going to happen!

We go straight to the library, check out an armload of travel books, and spend the afternoon on his living room floor, perusing the books, a big world map beneath us. The world's a big flower, blossoming before our eyes. No, it's not just a flower—it's a jungle, a universe! We're just a couple of kids from Irvine. And look at all these places!

"Kayne, this is gonna be great!"

"Yeah, Skinny, it's gonna be great."

The world's ours to paint our hearts upon.

Acknowledgments

Another cloak—there are actually many—is gratitude, the concept of never forgetting how relatively lucky we are, and actively and consciously acknowledging this thankfulness on an ongoing basis, ideally every day. My regular list is long, includes such things as *Thanks for the Warriors' great run* and *Thanks for so many great burrito spots*. But I've pared it down to specifically acknowledge those who made this particular book better.

The following people were instrumental in improving this book: Harper (Don't Be Too Damn Didactic) Lindstrom, Ron (The Galloping and Inspiring Wordsmith) Palmer, Don (What the Hell is Going On Here?) Lawler, Marie (Get to the F-In Point) Salerno, and Frank (We Gotta Go Deep, Really Deep) Ehrenfried. In addition, thanks to Candace Johnson, the editor who did her job damn well, and Kimberly Martin, Stephanie Anderson, and Jason Orr, the consultants whose advice, knowledge, and skill proved invaluable. All displayed excellence worth celebrating.

Thanks to my family for always supporting my need to stare at the stars. I love you.

Thanks to all the teachers who made learning fun and interesting, who inspired us kids to think and wonder and explore, and to improve ourselves and our skills. Specifically, thanks to the late Dr. Tom Garrison and to Dave Grant. You were the real deal, and you changed lives, mine in particular.

Thanks to Julianne for challenging me to grow and be a better person. I love you.

And thanks to all the writers and thinkers whose excellence and determination provide infinite inspiration. I salute you.

I am grateful.

www.ingramcontent.com/pod-product-compliance
Lightning Source LLC
Chambersburg PA
CBHW031035120726
47905CB00007B/2193